BOOK 2
IN THE THRONES OF (

THE
SEED BEARER'S
BRIDE

A NOVEL OF FALLEN ANGELS, NEPHILIM,
AND THE WOMAN WHO DEFIED THEIR POWER

JEAN HOEFLING

Other works by Jean Hoefling

Fiction

Gold in Havilah: A Novel of Cain's Wife

Ashes Like Bread: A Story of Lamech and His Two Wives (2019 Readers' Favorite Bronze Medal for Christian Fantasy)

"Killing Eden: The Spiritual Death of Adam and Eve" (short story)

Non-fiction

Journey to God: How I Made a Pilgrimage to the Heart of Orthodoxy (Without Going Very Far) and Found Peace, Love, and Stillness

For Jaden

What hath night to do with sleep?

–John Milton, *Paradise Lost*

TABLE OF CONTENTS

THE TROUBLE WITH ANGELS

W e humans are hard-wired for mystery and transcendence. We crave a higher reality that stands out vividly against the sometimes mundane details of our material world. And one of the best sources for that kind of transcendent mystery is the Bible. A great example is Genesis 6:1-4, about an intriguing event that forms the premise for *The Seed Bearer's Bride*:

> And it came to pass, when men began to multiply on the face of the earth and daughters were born unto them, that the sons of God saw the daughters of men, that they were fair, and they took them wives of all which they chose… There were giants in the earth in those days…when the sons of God came in unto the daughters of men, and they bare children to them, the same became mighty men which were of old, men of renown.

Looking at the text as it's translated to English, it's natural to assume the "sons of God" refers to human men. Who else would be marrying those good-looking daughters of men and having kids with them? But the Hebrew meaning of the term, *bene haelohim* (בני האלוהים), refers to a being directly created by God, in this case angels (see Job 1:6, 2:1, 38:7 and Luke 20:36). In traditional Jewish and Christian theology, with the exception of Adam (the first human

1

man), human beings are not directly created by God, but are Adam's DNA progeny. We have navels to prove it.

On the other hand, "daughters of men," *benoth adam (* בנות של גברים), translates to *daughters of Adam*, which became "mighty men, Nephilim, giants. *Nephilim* הנפילים) means *fallen ones* or *mighty ones*. Humans mating with humans doesn't produce giants, but supernatural beings mating with humans might. And *voilà*, a great foundation for a fantasy novel.

It's a challenge to our sense of the incredulous to think of angels interacting sexually with humans. In Christian theology, the role of angels is to praise and serve God in various ways, not procreate. Angels are called the "bodiless powers," and bodies are needed for mating as we know it. Yet if we accept that the Bible is full of concepts and events we adhere to without fully understanding (such as the concept of the Trinity or the resurrection of the dead), then procreation between humans and angels, though forbidden, might be possible.

Angels are all over the Bible and are biblically described as men (Joshua 5: 13-15; Mark 16:1-5; Genesis 18 and many others). These celestial ones apparently have the ability to take on some version of material bodies in order to interact with people. In Genesis 32, the patriarch Jacob wrestled all night with an angel, who injured Jacob's hip socket. In Genesis 19:16, an angel took Lot by the hand and in Genesis 18:8, three "men" whom Abraham recognized as God ate food Abraham and Sarai prepared and allowed their feet to be washed.

The First Book of Enoch is a non-canonical work that was revered by Jews and then Christians for several centuries before and after Christ. Part of the work is a narrative of two hundred Watchers (a classification of angels, meaning "wakeful one," and mentioned in Daniel 4:13), who "kept not their first estate, but left their own habitation" (Jude 1:6) in order to cohabit with women, producing enormous, hybrid offspring that dominated the earth. The narrative of *The First Book of Enoch* coincides with the Genesis 6 account.

We also have the clear endorsement of the early Church Fathers on this subject. Irenaeus, Ambrose, Clement of Rome, and Justin Martyr, among others, concurred on this phenomenon of the antediluvian world expressed in Genesis 6:1. Tertullian referred to the Nephilim giants as a "demon-brood" whose "great business is the ruin of mankind." Irenaeus wrote this in his *Discourse in the Demonstration of Apostolic Preaching*: "And for a very long while wickedness extended and spread and reached and laid hold upon the whole race of mankind, until a very small seed of righteousness remained among them and illicit unions took place upon the earth, since angels were united with the daughters of the race of mankind; and they bore to them sons, who for their exceeding greatness were called giants."

The renowned first century Jewish historian Flavius Josephus also wrote of the Nephilim in his *Antiquities of the Jews*.

But what would be the motivation for this massive cosmic disobedience, this enmeshing between angelic beings and flesh-and-blood bodies? Sexual attraction is obvious from the text, but more sinister is the possibility that in their fallen state, these celestial beings wanted to disrupt the human gene pool in order to prevent the coming of the savior figure promised to Eve in Genesis 3:15, whom I call "Anointed One" in *The Seed Bearer's Bride*. In Hebrew, the meaning of the word *Messiah* is "anointed one."

For those who want even more fodder for speculation, compare the Greek word *oiketerion* ("habitation") in Jude 6 with the same word translated as "house" in 2 Corinthians 5:1. Both times the word indicates a change or transfer in bodily form, in the first case for angels and the second for human beings during the resurrection of their bodies at Christ's Second Coming.

It's not like the idea of giants is anything new. The lore of ancient cultures is full of these intriguing characters. Think of the Titans of ancient Greek mythology; the cannibalistic race of the cyclops found in Homer's *Odyssey*; Gog, Magog, and the giants of the island of Albion (ancient England and Wales), who were said to be "ill favored" and possessed by evil spirits. For what it's worth, enormous effigies of Gog and Magog are still wheeled through the streets of London every November in the Lord Mayor's Show. Giants are alive and well in the legends and art of ancient Sumer, Crete, India, Africa, Scandinavia, ancient America, and everywhere in between. Myths aren't created in a vacuum. Their roots usually have a foundation in reality.

As to the angels in my book, some of their identities and functions will be familiar, such as guardian angels. Other castes and hierarchies that I discovered in my research were new to me, like the "harps" and "glories," which can be found in *On the Heavenly Hierarchy* by Dionysius the Areopagite, a fifth century philosopher and Athenian bishop. Besides my use of *The First Book of Enoch* and other pseudepigraphal sources, and allowing for some poetic license, I've tried to communicate my basic presuppositions about the nature, function, and history of angels, taken from the Bible and established Christian tradition. One interesting Christian belief found in 1 Peter 1:12 is that there are mysteries about Christ "into which angels long to look." They aren't omniscient; like us, they are always learning.

Along with angels and giants, the constellations also play a role in *The Seed Bearer's Bride*. Let me stress that what I learned in my research regarding the most ancient beliefs about the role of stars has nothing to do with modern astrology as we know it. For an excellent introduction to these very old, non-occultic beliefs about the constellations, I recommend *The Witness of the Stars* by E.W. Bullinger. I've used the Hebrew names from Bullinger's book for the constellations I animate in my story. In several chapters I personify some of the more familiar constellations as a way to raise the story's stakes and advance my characters' beliefs about the savior, Anointed One. The ancient Egyptian Denderah Zodiac, as well as Hebrew, Assyrian, and other old beliefs about the prophetic purpose of the stars are remarkably similar to each other. They are a "book without words" written in the sky, and the focus is a messianic figure.

The Bible offers other insights into the purpose of those tiny lights in the sky. Genesis 1:14 states that they are "for signs and for seasons." Revelation 12:1-4 gives a fascinating description of a "great sign [that] appeared in heaven, a woman "clothed with the sun, and the moon under her feet, and upon her head a crown of twelve stars," possibly a reference to the Virgin Mary or the alignment of the stars and planets at the time of Christ's birth, which produced the famous light of extraordinary brilliance that brought the Zoroastrian magi of Persia to the Christ child in Bethlehem. The ancient Hebrew name for that constellation is Bethuleh, which means "a virgin."

Whatever you believe, buckle up for some entertaining fiction set in the antediluvian world and teeming with characters who love, hate, dream, scheme, and vacillate between doubt and faith as they try to figure out life, just like the rest of us.

I hope you enjoy The Seed Bearer's Bride.

www.jeanhoefling.com

PROLOGUE

And on the new moon of the fourth month,
Adam and his wife went forth from the Garden
of Eden, and they dwelt in the land of Elda.*
BOOK OF JUBILEES 3:32, 33

The nubile girl stood at the edge of the rock outcrop high above the lake called Elda and gripped the rough stone with her toes. There, west of Eden, a glossy gibbous moon floated low in the sky as the girl tensed her body for another dive. Her wet hair clung to the contours of her back and legs over the knee-length undergarment, for she had left her outer gown on the shore. She felt the anticipation of knifing her slim body into the depths once again. The lake was sacred to the girl's people, the Sethites, for in these waters the forebear Eve had tried to wash away her sin on the day she ate of forbidden food and God sent her out of paradise. Even now, centuries later, the waters reflected the dome of the starry firmament like no other lake on the holy mountain, accentuating the myriad constellations that told the story of the coming savior, Anointed One, who would one day lead all who willed back to Eden. Legend proclaimed that after Adam's eyes became weaker at his fall, angels had moved the stars closer to earth so that the lessons about redemption might be easier to see.

"Baraqua, come down," an older girl on the shoreline called. Water seeped up the hem of her blue gown. "A girl who has shed the first blood of her womanhood should not be out alone after the sun has turned its back on the earth. Do you want our mother's punishment?"

"I'm not alone, Bathshae; you're here," Baraqua said. Cleverness came easily to her since her first blood and she had sat at dawnlight one morning among the older women, who painted bright henna flowers on the backs of her hands and sang blessings over her for a fruitful womb. As to their tired mother's chastisement, it would not be severe. Baraqua was the youngest of seven daughters and Gayile, wife of a respected scribe, was weary of discipline. Picking through a basket of dried beans to find the occasional stone would be the worst that would happen if she stayed away from the camp another hour.

"You mock me," Bathshae said with a tentative scowl. She left the water and stood impatiently on the shore of the lake, her eyes fixed on her younger sister.

"I would never mock you," Baraqua said. "You are life to me— air, food." No one was dearer than this sister born a year before herself. But the night was too perfect to think of leaving. No threat of her mother's tedious punishments would keep her from such a moon, such clarity in the stars, those enigmatic lights that crowded the heavens and spilled over the smooth and rippled surface of the lake. She breathed in the sweet night air, putting off her dive a moment more. Nowhere on the holy mountain that rose at the center of the earth was the air so alive with the ancient spirit of Eden. The young men sang of Elda around the council fires on feast days, claiming the lake was bottomless.

Baraqua shivered in her rebellion, glad to make her constantly fretting mother even more anxious. "You return to camp, but I will remain here until the constellation of Dahrach the dragon shifts eastward after midnight," she said pertly. She would no longer be managed, even by Bathshae.

Bathshae bit her lip and glanced into the thick stands of fir trees that lined the lake. "Anything could happen out here," she said.

Baraqua laughed. "It is you who worry in place of our mother, for she is already asleep. Besides, she was once young on such a night. She will forgive her youngest daughter for swimming among celestial lights and thinking of love."

"Love!" Bathshae put her hands on her hips like their mother did. "What noise do you make now?" The words made Baraqua want to laugh. Bathshae was too gentle, too meek to give any impression of authority. But she continued to argue. "There might be a band of men about, or—"

"Band of men?" Baraqua called down with a tease in her voice. "The men and boys of our clan crawled onto their sleeping mats an hour ago. The sun itself was still asleep when they left to harvest in the amaranth fields."

There was urgency in Bathshae's voice now. "The watchmen believe they have lately seen renegades from the lost tribe of Cain in these woods."

Baraqua sighed. "Their minds conceive that because nothing ever happens on this mountain; tales like that give the musicians something to sing about." It was true that the Sethites lived a sheltered life compared to surrounding peoples. They must remain steady and obedient, for through the Sethite lineage Anointed One would be born into the world. They offered to God Most High the blood of a lamb each Sabbath in worship. They tended grain fields and gardens and brought up children in the ways of Adam the forebear, who in the ancient time had walked with God in Eden as a man does with a friend.

"There will never be another night like this," Baraqua said. "I have waited all my life for something to happen to me and tonight it will."

Bathshae was noticeably impatient now. "White wolves and renegade Cainites will not care about what you've waited for."

Baraqua crossed her arms. She should be back in the crystal water, not arguing. "Nothing can harm us this near Eden," she said, glancing up the mountain.

Bathshae frowned in the direction of the ancient, unkempt garden. "You know as well as I that there hasn't been power in Eden since Adam was sent away," she said. "Serpents wrap the trees, while weeds clog the jeweled bowers where God's divine council once convened."

"Not so," Baraqua said. She felt provoked and restless, wanting to prolong the time on this night that felt alive with hope. "Once, I saw an angel in the glade where Adam claims the tree called Life grew."

"How do you know it was an angel?" Bathshae retorted, her voice rising. "Come down from that rock, for I have had enough."

"I just know," Baraqua said. The history of their people, The Chronicles of Adam, were full of accounts of celestial beings that had once populated the holy mountain as copious as leaves on a tree. They were rarely seen anymore by anyone but innocent children, though they sometimes came to elders in their dreams. And the Sethites knew that the archangel Michael served as guardian of their mountain, whether they saw him or not.

"Thoughts about a ruined paradise won't protect you from a burly Cainite," Bathshae said. "Do you wish to conceive a black-eyed monster? Those descendants of the murderer Cain eat the flesh of animals, and your child might eat you."

"You don't scare me," Baraqua said more quietly, staring into the lake. She imagined the lady Eve weeping on the shore of the lake on that day of exile, scrubbing her skin with crushed shells to try to eliminate the curse her disobedience had brought to the earth. Like Eve in her grief, Baraqua felt closed out of something she believed should have been. Her life had barely begun yet felt like a waste. An anger she did not understand surged in her. She faced Bathshae and clenched her fists. "Leave me alone," she shouted, immediately shocked at her own harshness. For her soul was knit to her sister's as though they were one person. Bathshae's face crumbled in bewilderment. She looked helpless and small on the shore. An instant passed, then two. Why don't you beg forgiveness and place your hand before your mouth in the gesture of apology? Baraqua berated herself. In the instant she resolved to do so Bathshae turned and ran up the slope. She entered the trail that led back to the Sethite camp and did not look back, but Baraqua watched her swipe tears from her face as she disappeared into the deep twilight.

She let out her breath and turned back to the water, ashamed. She was alone now, but it was not what she had expected. She tried to remember the last time she had been alone anywhere on the mountain. "Still, the moon is as bright without her," she said aloud, trying to convince herself. Bathshae's footprints were impressed deeply in the mud where she had dug them in to run. The lake seemed wider than it had a moment before, too open, too exposed. It was darker, and she could barely make out her rumpled gown lying in the grass.

A man was standing among the trees on the other side of the lake looking intently at her. Had he been there the moment before? He was taller than any Sethite, even Adam the forebear. He wore no clothing yet did not seem unclothed. Despite the distance between them she saw that his face was of an exquisite masculine beauty and that his skin shone like the moon. Something began to churn in her low belly. Not even the most splendid and intelligent of the Sethite elders and orators had the look of this man. Adam's son Seth read star prophecy with the ease of drawing breath and knew how things grew among root threads beneath the surface of the earth. Adam had once had the ability to see to the far reaches of the cosmos. Yet she knew this man saw farther and knew more. He was not human.

She straightened her undergarment. The slip had almost dried since she took her last dive. She wondered if the man was a foreign chieftain, or perhaps a sage from that place at the icy borders of the earth where sapphire pillars arched into the sky.

11

The man's gaze on her grew stronger, and he began to walk toward her on the surface of the lake. His feet did not disturb the water, nor did his body cast a reflection under the moon. In the space of a breath, he was below her among the reflected stars. She could not tell which direction was the sky and which was the water as he looked at her out of extraordinary eyes. She thought of the hidden arts Adam warned against and wondered if this man knew those arts. To know something new would brighten the dullness of living on the holy mountain.

"Were you born at the ends of the earth?" she said. She felt important and beautiful as his eyes appraised her, though he did not speak. "Tell me what lies above the glassy firmament of the sky. Tell me how high the heavens reach." Why did she assume he knew? Tell me when you will take me away from here, she wanted to say.

The man held out his arms and she took a step toward him on the rock. She would dive, barely move the water, show him that she too was gifted. She came up on her toes and felt something slice the inside of her ankle. A piece of obsidian protruding from the rock had cut the flesh around her ankle bone and blood squeezed from the neat line.

Pay no attention to flesh that bleeds, for you will soon be like me. The words seemed to come from the man, yet his mouth did not move. Her ears did not hear the words, but her heart did.

Behold, my gift to you. He gestured, and the water beneath the surface of the lake lit up as though swarms of fireflies hovered there. The light reflected off what looked like an island mound covered with dwellings and edifices made of dazzling white stone. Baraqua's heart welled with something she had never felt before. The beauty of the scene took her breath.

I will do anything—Something had changed in an instant. Her muscles tensed and she knifed the water, plunging into that liquid light. With her eyes wide, she gazed at the edifices before her that seemed to be set on land between canals, forming a pattern of ever widening circles around a central massive. The watery jewel radiated light from its center. She had never seen any created thing so perfect as that formation of buildings and light, with the smooth crystal crowning it all. Perhaps this was what was called a city. She had heard about cities built in the plain of Nod or crowning the hills of Cush, places she had never been.

When she could no longer hold her breath she swam to the surface, an ache in her heart for the man and for the city beneath the lake. He had said she would be like him. The man would free her, give her a home and an inheritance. How would it be to walk on water and to live in that city beneath the lake?

The man reached for her as she surfaced, cold hands closing around hers. "When do we leave?" she said. But a burst of light exploded at the corner of her sight. A power she could not see was pulling her from the man, creating space between them. The city beneath the water trembled before her eyes and disappeared. The man dissolved, leaving no ripple on the water. She shuddered. What had this night rendered to her after all?

A wind sprang out of the treetops, surged down to skim the lake. She swam to the shoreline, picked up her outer garment, and scratched her way up to the ancient trail Bathshae had taken, the beating of her heart like drums of warning. She crashed through thorny bushes as sharp stones bit at her bare feet and the wound in her ankle throbbed. The light of a few fires glimmered in the distance, orienting the direction of the camp. She looked back once. High above the lake, a form as ambiguous as mist danced in a sky gone starless.

PART 1

MAHAL

YEAR OF ADAM 461

CHAPTER 1

And Mahalaleel lived sixty and five years, and begat Jared—
GENESIS 5:15

Renegade stars had invaded the constellation of Dahrach the sky dragon, of that Mahal was sure. The youngest Seed Bearer of the Sethite clan stood in the dew-sopped grass that grew as high as a man's hips and ruffed the edge of the cliff meadow. The moon was full, making of the sea far below a roadway of gems that disappeared into the western horizon. This night should have been as peaceful as every other when Mahal and Dinah escaped the noise of the camp to come to this meadow and glory in its stillness. But it was not so. His wife was not with him and something in the stars of the writhing dragon was not as it should be.

"Why would God set a serpent to wrap the pole star at the apex of the sky?" Mahal muttered. The dragon Dahrach symbolized the rebellious angel Lucifer, cast out of heaven in the ancient day for attempting to usurp God's throne. He scrutinized the familiar pattern with well-trained eyes, for Mahal was a master of stars and their lore. Eighty lights normally composed Dahrach, but tonight three other entities pulsed forth a sickly green light among the stars in the serpent's head.

A vague unease settled at the back of Mahal's neck. The fifth in the line of Adam, he had been tutored at the feet of that forebear' himself, the earth's first man. He knew the position of every star that composed the portents of prophecy along the pathway of the sun, those celestial arrangements that spoke wordlessly of God's plan to deliver humanity from their banishment from the Garden of Eden.

He rubbed his eyes. He had come to the meadow to escape the harping of the midwives while his beloved Dinah labored to give birth to their first child. Was his fatigue and worry about Dinah and the unborn baby making him see things that couldn't be? The eerie invaders throbbed as though animated by a life their own. He tried to remember if Adam' son Seth, or Seth's son Enosh, had ever mentioned such odd celestial bodies. No, he was sure they hadn't. What did Dahrach know?

He scanned the meadow. Strong moonlight lit each blade of the long grass. It was the kind of moon under which he and Dinah had conceived the very child she carried within her now. That had been a night he would never forget. But now it was time to return to the birthing tent. Despite his mother-in-law's criticisms, he would insist on being there for the birth of his son, his Jaden, which meant "God has heard" in the lost language of Eden. Jaden, long-awaited; Jaden, brought into reality through much prayer and fasting, a miracle of God. For it was many years since Mahal had been joined in the nuptial union with Dinah without siring a child. Surely this son would be Anointed One, the man who would fulfill the old prophecy God had given to Adam's wife, Eve, on the long-ago day when that first woman ate of forbidden food in Eden. Jaden had been conceived beneath the very stars of promise— archers, lions, bulls, crabs, altars, chalices, and serpents—every large and small formation was a chapter in the divine hope the Sethites waited for, a lore passed down from Adam to each generation so that the promise would not be lost. Mahal longed to believe that Jaden would be the man to finally destroy the power of the serpent who had brought shadow to the earth.

It was Dinah who had encouraged Mahal to take the air in the meadow. "You are more at home there than anywhere," she had reminded him. Mahal had come to this meadow since early manhood to escape the people's gossip and lack of faith in him. And why? Because he had never prophesied as a Seed Bearer in the direct line of Adam should. He was faulty, defective to all but the most righteous men and kindest women.

But he made no move to leave. The pulsations in the head of Dahrach were stronger now, darting like mischievous children. He began to pace at the edge of the cliff, trying to push back his fatigue and apprehension. He would wait to see if the stars returned to normal. And then he must return to Dinah. He would not care what her mother Daniela said. She had never approved of Mahal anyway, and could he blame her? Her daughter had married a man both unable to seed her womb and incapable of speaking forth his virgin prophecy.

"It's not fitting for a Sethite husband to keep watch over a laboring wife," Daniela had scolded when Mahal hovered near Dinah with oil of lemon to refresh her spirits. "See to your pregnant ewes if you must meddle in birthing." It was only an excuse to temporarily rid her sight of the man who was not worthy of her daughter.

"Don't I know the customs of my own people?" Mahal had retorted. It was not often that he lost patience with his critical mother-in-law. "I had to wait too many years to call Dinah wife and will not leave her now." It was his way of reminding Daniela that she and Barkiel, Dinah's father, had forbade him to take Dinah to wife in the first flush of youth, in that crucial time when children of a man's loins are strongest born. When the prophecy never came, they had finally relented.

He looked out again over the sea below the cliffs. That western land had become water a generation before after Zyla, Mahal's prophetic sister, had predicted a local flood. The mysterious Zyla had also prophesied about Mahal's child.

19

"In his day *they* will come down," was all she had said the night he came to her to ask if she could foresee whether he and Dinah would have a child at all. There had been no joy in Zyla's eyes when she spoke the few words. All the years since he had avoided thinking about "they." Something about the word was ominous.

He thought of his Dinah, strong in integrity yet delicate in body. His wife had borne the shame of her barrenness like a jewel of adornment and her quiet acceptance was a balm to Mahal's cynicism and melancholy as the years passed. Dinah's perfection was that she bore everything with perfect grace.

"For Dinah and Jaden, I give thanks," Mahal whispered into the mist. He was used to beseeching the Creator aloud, apart from the ritual prayers at the altar of sacrifice on Sabbaths and through feast day hymns. Some thought such familiarity with God Most High irreverent. Yet hadn't God made human beings in his image and likeness, with mouths meant to speak the musings of their hearts?

"Soon I will hold you in my arms, little Jaden," he whispered again. The baby had been wrought of pure longing. His eyes would be as pure and clear as Dinah's, his countenance as bright as Adam's. Adam had always treated Mahal with respect, no matter what the others did.

The grass stirred and Mahal's head jerked toward the sound. He had expected a doe and her fawn, their eyes luminous in the darkness. But nothing stood in the grass behind him, though a few ibex nuzzled red lilies near the woods.

We will snuff the babe's life. The words came from everywhere and nowhere, from the sky and land at once. The tone was vacuous, mocking, cold behind Mahal's ear.

"Show yourself!" Mahal said loudly. He imagined he sounded confident and brusque like his grandfather Enosh, whose voice filled every space he entered. No one disobeyed Enosh's terse commands as chief of all practical works in the camp. But he was not like Enosh.

He turned in a circle, dreading to turn his back on what might be nearby. Could a Cainite be hiding in the grass, hairy as a tree ape, with breath like a rotting frog? It was rumored that a few of that tainted race had survived the flooding of the River Gihon and kept camp on silent western shores. A few Sethites dredging for sea vegetables claimed they had seen men that looked like the legendary Cainites astride scaly sea monsters, managing the beasts as though they were tamed horses, plunging with defiant laughter through waves as tall as eucalyptus trees.

He glanced back into the stars. The pulsing green lights were no longer there. He clenched his fist, wishing he had any kind of weapon.

Surrender all, for you can do nothing against us. He felt a presence, darker than a moonless night.

"Only cowards hide," Mahal shouted. That was more like something Enosh would say. The presence was as close as his own breath.

"Mahal!" The voice was Dinah's, coming from the edge of the meadow. His wife stood alone in her white birthing gown, her dark, unbound hair draping her form, her arms folded across the bulge of their unborn child. What was she doing here in the middle of her birth travail? Mahal sprinted through the wet grass and pulled his wife close. The firm child-belly was between them, the body of the new Seed Bearer they had made in love under a slanted moon. As usual, Mahal felt slightly unmanly at how safe and complete he felt when Dinah was nearby. Her bones felt as tenuous as a bird's beneath his hands as he held her, his fear mounting. Yet to his mind she was as staunch as the burliest field worker.

"Let us lie down in the hyacinth where we conceived our Jaden," Dinah said, her breath uneven from a birth pang she had to bend under.

"I must take you back to the midwives immediately, for something is not right in this meadow," he said, urgency in his gut. He put Dinah at arm's length so she would see how serious he was.

He forced down the image that reared in his mind of a creature with curling talons that reached for Dinah's belly. He imagined he heard a woman scream and watched the moon turn black and fall from the sky amidst a cascade of green, pulsing stars.

"No!" he shouted and shook off the scene. Startled, Dinah began to cry. He ran a hand over his face. What sorcery had the strange presence imposed upon his mind to cause him to think such things?

Dinah studied his face. "You're angry. What is it?" She scanned the meadow behind him.

Mahalalel drew her close again. "I'm—" He needed time to think, but there was no time. A drop of sweat trickled over his upper lip and blood pounded against his temples. Sweat and blood, the summation of a man's life spent in an unquenched thirst for respect. Except for Dinah and the unborn child, his life was an ash heap of disappointment. But this night, this hour, he would not think of that. He would fight with everything in him against the force that wanted to harm his child. He would prove himself worthy of his eldership and earn the right to receive his virgin vision.

"False stars stood in Dahrach tonight," he said bluntly. "Our meadow is now an infestation of—" He did not want to say the word, evil. Not on the night.

Dinah looked into the sky and back at Mahal. Her calm expression unnerved him. "I dreamt today of a crowned serpent that fell from the sky in search of a newborn child."

CHAPTER 2

"You dreamt this thing?" Mahal said. He gripped Dinah's shoulders so tightly that she squirmed.

"Yes," Dinah said, steady-eyed, the wind playing in her unbound hair. "But what being in all the cosmos would want to harm an innocent child?" she said.

"You know the prophecies as well as I," Mahal said. "God's great serpent-enemy is determined to prevent Eve's old prophecy about a son of her body crushing his head. 'Crusher' was the name Adam and Eve once used for the man we call Anointed One. This is why we keep to ourselves on the mountain, to prevent tainting of Sethite seed."

"Don't I know this?" Dinah said. A cry like a hurt animal escaped her and Mahal shuddered as she cradled her belly and bent over. She must be sheltered quickly. He took his wife's small hand in his and pulled her toward the trees beyond the meadow. "We will make you a birthing place in the wood." But he knew no shelter would keep away what had come to the meadow to seek his child. Was the son of Mahal not meant to live after all?

Dinah stumbled after him. "Yes, the trees. I won't return to those midwives and their slander." She grimaced as another birth pang shuddered through her, but she kept walking.

At her words Mahal felt the old twinge of unhealed wounds. "Half-elder," he had been called. "False one." Even with the passing of years, the insults cut.

"What did they say this time?" he said, trying to increase their pace. They were deep in the wood now. He was angry that foolish women had distressed his Dinah while she labored. He regretted his impulse to ask such a question, for all that mattered was Dinah and the child.

Dinah stopped abruptly. "The pains overtake me." Her face was pinched with pain, her hair a moonlit tangle around her shoulders. "I will tell you what they said because you will not rest until I do," she said. "Yet it sorrows me that you cannot turn away from the mere words of fools." She took another breath. "Dorah the midwife thought I was sleeping, but I heard her say that any son of Mahal's will only be a burden to the clan because Mahal will never be fully a prophet."

"Forgive me," Mahal said, reproving himself for his weakness. His own wife was stronger than he. She should not have to tell him what glib gossip had fallen from the mouths of those women.

Dinah leaned on him like a fawn against its mother's flank. "Quickly, for the child will soon make its way out."

Mahal picked her up and began to run. At least his bodily frame was stronger than Dinah's. Her breath warm blew against his heart.

"You, who succor souls and heal all wounds, do not depart from your lowly servant now," he pleaded with the God of his fathers as he ran. He remembered a cave deep in these woods where he had played as a boy with his brothers. He loped between the trees, guided only by a dim memory. He heard movement and turned, forcing himself to face whatever was behind him. But it was only Dorah, one of the older midwives. She was panting with the exertion of running and droplets of condensed night mist clung to her heavy eyebrows. She dipped her head briefly but did not put her fingers to her forehead in the Sethite sign of deference to a Seed Bearer. Few Sethites did in Mahal's presence.

24

"I followed her as soon as I guessed where she had gone," Dorah said. "I would never have allowed her to wander alone like this."

"You drove her away yourself with words of disrespect for her wedded husband," Mahal said as sternly as he was able. The brusqueness of most men was not in him naturally and he often excused the failings of others to his own hurt. "Be gone now, for my son will enter this world in peace, not among petty women." He licked his lips nervously and scanned the wood, trying to sense where the enemy might be. He had no time for Dorah.

Dorah dropped to her knees and raised her arms imploringly. "Forgive me, lord Mahal," she said. "My loose tongue is a fault I seek to amend. But I am haunted by the memory of your own mother's death at the birth of your sister, Adah. If I hadn't left Mual's side she would still be alive to bring comfort to your father. I cannot bear the guilt of that happening again if Dinah does not receive proper care."

"My mother was meant to leave the world that night," Mahal said, remembering the shock that had run through the camp at his mother's untimely death in childbirth. "Your slander has put my wife in danger. Return to the camp and tell Adam and Seth that I will deliver the child myself."

Dorah put her forehead to the ground and a little wail escaped her lips. "The elders will send me to the tent of chastisement for this."

"Then bear it as penitence," Mahal retorted. "And tell the elders they must burn the incense of holy galbanum this hour to make their prayers rise more quickly. My son is in grave danger. Never has so much been threatened in so little a time."

The midwife stood up and put her fist to her mouth to stifle what she might say next. Then she turned and ran into the darkness.

"He comes quickly, my beloved," Dinah whispered as a rough cry raked her throat. In his mind Mahal drew a circle of protection around the two of them. He imagined a wall of holy fire and the archangel Michael raising his sword in protection.

"You will deliver our son on a bed of lilies," he said. Foolish words at a precarious time. Anything to convince himself that all would be well. He moved on with his precious burden, fighting despair. It was too dark to see. He did not know where the bent white pine was that had grown outside the low cave. If Dinah or the child died, he would never return to the camp. He would become a renegade beside some obscure river, wearing rough cloth over his loins and heaping ashes into his hair.

We will snuff the child's life. The voice was a cold whisper behind his ear. He whirled, but there was nothing but shadows as long as the mouths of ghouls that crouch at the gates of nightmares. Every tree branch was the claw of a harpy, every twig the gnarled finger of a specter, greedy to abuse.

"Save us, God of my forebears," Mahal whispered. But why should One who created the heavens and the earth with a mere word listen to a man who, at the age of sixty-five, had still not spoken forth the required prophecy to make him whole of purpose?

"Lord Mahal." The voice was that of Akliah the eldress, leader of the women of the prayer caves. She stood at his elbow wrapped in a rough cloak, her eyes wary. Behind her were those of her inner circle; Keret the prophetess, the widow Sasha, and Hekat of the Cainites, all revered for their devotion to prayer and chastity. Keret and Sasha held pitch torches high, steady resolution in their eyes. These women had always seemed to Mahal to be impervious to fear.

"I have seen the battle for your child in a vision this night," Akliah said quietly. "The cave you seek is nearby."

Mahal wanted to weep with relief. It was said that the eldress had fought unseen wars in heavenly realms and wrestled with Lucifer's strongest minions, though Mahal had never dared to learn more. He bowed his head in thanks and followed Akliah between the trees. In twenty strides he was ducking into the cave, insignificant compared to his boyhood memory, that time long past when the path of life had seemed straighter and battles could be fought with wooden swords.

"Lay her on this sandy place," Akliah directed, gesturing toward the back of the cave. Mahal set Dinah down, shrugged off his cloak, and spread it on the softest mound of sand. From outside the cave, growls as of some wild animal began. "Do not try, for it is hopeless," something roared, garbled and gagging, otherworldly.

Akliah raised her arms toward the mouth of the cave. "I cannot send you away this time, but I command you to silence!" she shouted with surprising fierceness. Keret was feeling along the sides of Dinah's belly. "The time is now," she said and nodded to Sasha, who moved quickly to make of her body a support above Dinah's head.

"I promised a bed of lilies," Mahal whispered, taking Dinah's hand. "You deserve—"

Motion from the cave opening made him turn. Three hulking creatures as tall as cave bears beat immense wings against the moonlit forest beyond. They screamed and slammed themselves against the rock but did not speak. Mahal forced his eyes away and into Dinah's. "Nothing will harm the child," he said, forcing strength to his voice. He trusted Akliah.

"To battle!" Akliah cried. She and Hekat the Cainite ran to the mouth of the cave where Akliah thrust her staff into the earth and Hekat raised her arms. The two began to pray in Edenese, the language of the Garden. The softness of the inflections was a strange contrast to Akliah's aggressive war prayers. The creatures trembled under the words, for though powerful in appearance, they seemed no match for the praying women. Akliah looked back to see what was happening and the dark creatures seized the moment to pounce upon both women and wrestle them to the ground.

"And you have no weapon to defend them," Mahal muttered to himself in reproach. Yet in manly instinct he ran to Akliah as the talons of one of the creatures encircled her throat.

"God will preserve me, Mahal," Akliah said with effort. "Deliver the child immediately."

Mahal ran back to Dinah. "The baby emerges," Keret said, indicating what Mahal should do as the tiny body of his son slipped into his hands.

"Jaden! God has heard!" Mahal shouted, dizzy with joy and shock. He drew the baby to him and wiped the little face with the scrap of soft linen Keret handed him. But the child's limbs did not move. Jaden did not open his eyes or make the normal sounds of a baby in the instant after birth.

"He is too cool of flesh," Mahal said to Keret. "Why doesn't he move?"

Dinah sat up and pushed damp hair from her face. She reached for the baby. "He needs the warmth of my breast."

Akliah was beside Mahal in an instant. "Take my place beside Hekat," she ordered Keret, her eyes on the baby. Keret ran to the entrance and Akliah snatched off her head covering, revealing the shorn head of her vocation. She wrapped the infant lightly in the cloth and began to stroke the pale cheeks and then the torso. "Breathe, tiny Seed Bearer," she whispered, and Mahal heard a sob catch in her voice.

"We cannot hold them back much longer, Akliah," Hekat called out.

"For the sake of all that is good and sacred, you must bear it a while longer," Akliah retorted. "You must—"

But Mahal took the child from Akliah and brought its face close to his own. Delicate blue veins ran through the child's closed eyelids. The little mouth was like his and the shape of the jaw was Adam's. He was looking at himself, his kin, and at all humanity.

The child's skin was turning blue. *Your breath. Give him your breath.* The command came from within. He closed his mouth over the child's mouth and nose and gently exhaled. He drew in more breath and exhaled again. The third time the baby stirred, opened his eyes, and gazed at Mahal for what could have been an instant or the span of eternity. Every dark doubt that had stalked him coalesced to joy. The baby gasped, his face blushed red, and his little arms began to flail as he emitted his first cry. Mahal laid him in Dinah's arms and the prayer women knelt in the sand and lifted their hands in praise to the God of Adam. "The child lives," they repeated through their tears. The new Seed Bearer had been born and would take his place among the others. Gross evil had been conquered.

Mahal stood and faced the creatures. How dare they pummel holy women or try to destroy his child. He ran to them again and the creatures sprang near him. Their eyes were the renegade stars that had lodged in the head of Dahrach. Their wings beat and their skin was unearthly.

"In the name of the One who brought worlds into existence, leave and do not torment us again," Mahal shouted, and this time his tone was as commanding as that of Enosh.

Something like surprise came to the creatures' eyes. A mere son of Adam was commanding them to go, and somehow, they must. They dissipated and a peace Mahal had never felt before filled the cave, so palpable he wondered if he could hold it between his hands. And beyond the cave was silence.

CHAPTER 3

...and she bare him a son in the third week in the sixth year and he called his name Jared, for in his days the angels of the Lord descended on the earth, those who are named the Watchers—
BOOK OF JUBILEES 4:15

The Sethite camp was a turmoil of celebration. "They come!" a young girl shouted as Mahal and Dinah entered the clearing and were guided toward the communal fire. Akliah followed with the baby, still wrapped in the head covering of her vocation. Little children were pressing flowers into Dinah's hands and men came forward to offer honor, touching fingers to their foreheads out of respect.

Mahal was astonished. "Such honor and respect for one such as I?" he said to Dinah. He had expected no such welcome.

"The people wake up to truth today," Dinah said. She looked as fresh as a woman who had just risen from a night of undisturbed sleep.

"Favored of God," the women murmured in the customary greeting for an elder's wife as they pressed Dinah's hand. People parted to let them approach the fire and they were made to sit on a bench near the elders' thrones, the custom for new parents of distinction in the clan. They were given tea infused with jasmine and bowls of spiced apricots, the traditional food after the birth of a child. The scent of burning cedar logs rose high from the communal fire and shafts of early morning light filtered through the high trees around the clearing. Children ran among the tents, the little girls carrying dolls made of carved wood and braided vines and straw hair dyed as black as Dinah's, with swaddled poppets strapped to the dolls' backs. Young boys were amassing firewood from the stores beyond the camp, their faces animated with self-importance. Beautiful in their festal garments and oiled faces, women were setting out trays of fruit and honey cakes, stopping at Dinah's side to offer advice on the care of newborns. To Mahal, everything seemed clearer and lighter than it ever had—the air more pristine, the people more intelligent, every scent and sight filling him with an unexpected joy.

"They look at us as though we are a delegation from the throne room of God," Dinah said, drawing Mahal's attention to Adam, Seth, Enosh, and Kenan, the four older elders who sat upon their carved thrones at the head of the clearing, with their wives on their own thrones beside them; Eve, Azura, and Naom, all gesturing in the Sethite way to show their pleasure at the birth of the child.

"Let them think so," Mahal said with a laugh as several of his sisters came near to pile tiny articles of clothing, goat cheese, and crocks of herbs in Dinah's lap. "I will enjoy it while I can." One of Dinah's sisters placed a corona of rare red camelia on her head, accentuating Dinah's dark beauty in the early morning light. His wife had never looked more beautiful to him than on this day. It was a day of luxury, and the feasting and dancing would continue until sunset.

White-robed Naom, wife of the elder Enosh, left her throne and came to Mahal and Dinah. Her eyes shone as she took Dinah's hands. She whispered something to her and the two women laughed. Naom held up a tambourine and faced the people. "Our righteous Seed Bearer comes with Anointed One in his arms!" she sang out.

"Anointed One! Anointed One!" chanted some of the women, who set down their platters and took up tambourines streaming with embroidered ribbons. Dorah the midwife came into the clearing with cymbals on her fingers and began to sing in a rich, throaty voice that contrasted with her plain features:

"From the maws of the underworld, Lord Mahal snatched the blessed child;

From the clutches of death he brought back the soul of Anointed One, breathing into him his own divine breath."

The people cheered and some got up to dance as Dorah sang on, while older men stamped their feet.

"Divine breath?" Mahal said, turning to Dinah. "By heaven, what did Dorah tell them?"

Dinah laughed softly and put her hand in his. The morning sun was on Mahal's back, a comfort after the cold hours in the cave. He wished he could sleep. "They finally see in you what I have always seen," Dinah said and kissed his hand.

Dorah sang on, skirting the fire, moving between shafts of slanting light and shadow as nimble as a girl.

"The double-mindedness of the people makes me uneasy," Mahal said. "Yesterday your mother sent me from the birthing tent as though I were the lowest of men. Today they say my breath is divine and I deserve a heavenly throne."

"Be happy while you can, for it will pass," Dinah said. "Human hearts are as changeable as wind." She shrugged. "Look to God alone for approval. We have each other and we have our son." She took the baby from Akliah and began to suckle the child, and Akliah went to sit on a stool set out for her near her father Adam.

Dinah was right; the praise would not last. Yet Mahal was grateful for the song's embellishments. Maybe now the people would respect the fifth Seed Bearer in Adam's line. Yet he was still the man who had never prophesied. Some would never forgive him for this inadequacy.

The elder Seed Bearers left their thrones and gathered before the bench. Otherworldly Adam stood closest to Mahal, looking at him intently with trust and friendship. Mahal had never had to wonder what Adam thought of him. The forebear's name meant "humanity." His body had been sculpted from red clay by the hand of God himself. As proof, Adam bore no birth scar on his belly as all born after him did. Taller and wiser than any man, the forebear's sagacity had been hard-won out of much suffering and relinquishment of will in the four hundred sixty years—by the reckoning of the sun—that he had lived.

"May God Most High bless this child now and always," Adam said. He took the baby from Dinah and covered the little head with his hand and sang a blessing. Before the disobedience in Eden, it was said that Adam's voice reached to heaven. Every morning in Eden, he and Eve had harmonized with the celestial choir of the seventh heaven.

Seth came near to place his hand on the child's head. The third-born son of Adam and Eve, Seth's name meant "anointed compensation." He had been born after Cain, Adam's first son, killed his righteous brother Abel and fled the mountain. Because he was a substitute for both Cain and Abel, the clan bore Seth's name. A man of astonishing capacities, Seth understood the stirrings of the four winds that made their abodes at the four corners of the earth. He was like his brother Abel had been, a righteous and holy man in the sight of God. No one had ever heard Seth slander another person.

Next, Seth's oldest son Enosh came forward to pay his respects. Enosh was not overtly penitent and refined of mind like Adam, nor studious and grave like Seth. His body was thick and strong, and the elder's strength was his inventive skill. This third in the lineage lived to design and build useful articles for everyday life. His name meant "mortal," and that meaning played out as Enosh occupied himself with wood and stone, water and soil—the transient materials of the fallen earth outside Eden. He had invented a disk with a bar that tracked the sun's movements across the sky, giving the people a way to keep the hours. His water mills beside the River Eden made it possible to grind grain to flour far more quickly than by hand.

Mahal held Enosh's eyes a moment, waiting. But Enosh was among those who had not held Mahal in honor even though he was Mahal's own grandfather. Now the man stood with his arms crossed and said nothing to either of the new parents. Seeing that Enosh would not speak or give a blessing, Mahal's father Kenan came near and put his hand on Mahal's shoulder. A scribe of great skill whose hands were deeply stained from the inks he worked with, Kenan's name meant "sorrow," a prophetic appellation to remind the people of what the sin of Adam and Eve had brought to humanity. Kenan's face was more lined than the faces of Seth and Adam, for he had never stopped grieving the untimely death of his wife Mual years before, which had happened when death of the body was even more uncommon than the present era.

"Keret and Hekat came to me well before the sun was up," Kenan said to the people standing near. "If half of what the women sing about this morning is true, my son's life-giving deed earns him full elder's status even without offering any external prophecy."

There was murmuring among the people at these words. Who had ever heard of such a thing? But Adam gestured his approval and Kenan continued. "The longer I live, the more I am convinced that to do battle in the unseen war is the highest calling of a prophet. By the authority of God Most High, this night Mahal sent away the false eyes of Dahrach; he will be called great when his story is set down in the *Chronicles of Adam*."

Mahal fought back tears at his father's praise, as healing as a balm after the long years when the two had been at odds over Mahal's failure to prophesy.

But Enosh frowned. "There is no unseen war," he said curtly, as though they were not clear defiance of every teaching of Adam. "The attackers at the cave must have been Cainites, even though it was too dark to see them."

"Do you doubt the words of the prayer women and all present in that cave?" Kenan said to Enosh. The people grew quiet at the unexpected tone of the exchange and Akliah left her stool to stand behind Mahal and Dinah.

"Your heart has grown hard toward the unseen world, elder Enosh," Akliah said, lifting her chin. "There are myriads of both holy and fallen angels about, though the shadows of this present world obscure them from our sight. It will not go well with you if you continue to doubt established realities."

Enosh looked uneasy for a moment. It was no small thing to be rebuked by Akliah, for that daughter of Adam was held in esteem as though she were an elder herself. Despair crept into Mahal's warm mood. He should have known something would happen to interrupt this moment of ease. He stood, unwilling to receive Enosh's glare from a sitting position. He knew what he had seen in that cave. And he noticed that what emanated from the elder's countenance was not the same as what shown from Adam, Seth, and Kenan's.

But Enosh turned away as though he dismissed Akliah. A few people began to whisper. Women looked down at their tambourines and the platters of honey cakes in their hands as though they did not know what to do with them. Mahal felt Dinah squirm. She was never more miserable than when people attacked him.

But Enosh was not finished. His strong nature must have the last word. "I insist it was too dark to see the enemy," he said. "Cainites breed constantly and I believe their offspring have infiltrated the southern flank of the mountain more than we want to admit. It was these who came to the cave to harm the child." He spread his muscular legs wide. Dinah's breath came unevenly now. She should be in her tent, attended to by the women. The heat of anger spread across his neck. Why would a revered elder like Enosh contradict all that the Sethites believed? Why would he spoil the only thing worthy of honor that Mahal had ever done? But Enosh had seemed restless in recent months. Mahal had overheard him arguing with Adam and Seth about expanding Sethite settlements into other lands. He seemed impatient with the clan's simple way of life while other people groups were building walled cities and living in houses of baked brick. But Adam was adamant the Sethites keep to their humble tents. "Those who lounge in brick houses soon forget their Creator," he would say when the subject arose.

Seth put a hand on Enosh's arm. "My son, scribes are even now recording what Dorah, Keret, and Hekat have told them. Their witness agrees with Akliah's and Mahal's, that the beings who sought the child's life were of a malevolent and otherworldly nature."

"What does that nearsighted midwife know?" Enosh said with a sneer. "The people will become frightened if we talk about such things. Let heaven take care of itself while we live life well on the earth."

Adam's voice was stern. "You were taught the old stories, Enosh. Heaven and earth were once melded. How can we separate them in our hearts now?"

Enosh clenched his fists. "I say they were Cainites. We must start fortifying our camp immediately in case they come for the child again." Mahal had never noticed how low the bony bridge above his grandfather's eyes hung. "Tell the people that it was Cainites who tried to strangle Akliah," he said to Mahal. "Otherwise, they will not cooperate with me in building fortifications."

Mahal kept his breath steady. Had there ever been such open rebellion in the camp, even among men of low mind who lived at the outskirts? People were walking away, too embarrassed to listen.

"We will think for ourselves on these matters, elder Enosh," a man near the back of the throng called out. "We continue in the old ways and listen to Adam."

Mahal reached for Jaden. He would not be intimidated by his powerful grandfather. "Let it be written in the *Chronicles* that this night, entities not of this world descended out of the stars of Dahrach and brought false light to the cliff meadow above the sea." He was surprised at the strength in his voice. He looked down at his son. "As surely as this child lives by a miracle of God, I tell you that no wooden fortification will keep away the beings that attacked us if they choose to return." He nodded to Adam. "The God who made heaven and earth will be our only resource in that day."

Enosh's jaw was working and sweat gleamed on his forehead. "I have lost tolerance with this nearsighted people," he said. "Adam prohibits the crafting of iron weaponry to ward off invaders. He forbids the building of real homes or the mixing of fibers in the fabric of our clothing," He threw up his hands and let them drop in his disgust. "The peoples of the earth increase in number while we Sethites remain few because we are told to fast and abstain from our wives so often. Our people have lost the respect of the Cushites and Noddites. We are trapped on this mountain, weaving a tale about a rescuer who may never come. Within a generation we will disappear from history."

"You say you want to build fortifications to protect Mahal's child, yet you doubt whether Anointed One will come at all," Kenan said.

The tension had become too great. Adam put his hand on Enosh's shoulder and spoke to the people with careful cheerfulness. "God has greatly gifted my grandson Enosh, who has made our lives richer. But today we celebrate our revered Mahal, who has given us a new Seed Bearer."

Revered. Mahal vowed he would not waste Adam's confidence.

A spasm passed over Enosh's face. "I celebrate no man who lifts himself above his betters by telling tales of sky beings."

The voice of Dorah carried over the murmuring crowd. "Mahal is no man; he is a god with the power of life in his breath."

Adam turned on the midwife and his tone was almost fierce, "I rebuke you, daughter of Non," he said. "Never claim deity for a man, even one who has sustained spiritual battle. Serve God alone."

A man's harsh laugh came from beneath a boab tree. It was Enosh's son Tarshish, who had brought shame to Enosh and Naom by dallying among Noddite women.

"Why do you laugh, Tarshish?" Adam said, "Do you think idolatry a small thing?"

Tarshish pushed away from the tree and flicked a lock of unwashed hair from his eyes. "I laugh that someone suspects Mahal of being a god," he said, his eyes on Mahal in open disdain. "He didn't even deserve Dinah, never earned her."

Dinah gasped. Mahal felt his jaw tighten but held his peace when Enosh did not rebuke his son. Tarshish walked out of the clearing and Enosh went with him.

Adam's face was troubled as he looked after the two. Then he turned to Mahal. "Tell us the name of the child."

Mahal felt Dinah slip her hand in his again. The cherished name they had guarded was theirs no longer. They must share their child fully with the people, and if he were Anointed One, with the whole earth. He opened his mouth to speak the name, but nothing left his throat. Somehow, Jaden was not the child's name. He watched beams of smoky light pierce the ground between the cedars, trying to understand. Something had changed in an instant and he could not control it. Trees, people, and light dimmed from his sight. A whirlwind was surrounding him and he went to his knees, caught within its vortex, submitting to its will. And then he knew: he was about to receive the long-awaited vision of his eldership. He clutched the baby tightly and put his forehead to the ground. He must endure whatever happened and pray that he and his boy survived.

In his day they will descend. The words of his sister Zyla's old prophecy beat in his mind. *They. Descend.* The sounds ran fluid into Edenese, coalesced, making the sound, *Jar-ed.* Appalled, Mahal missed a breath. It could not be. Through the whirlwind, he watched lights fall through an opening in the firmament, writhing worm-like as though they sought a place to burrow. The writhing lights fell down the sky with infinite speed, leaving smears of dirty light over the moon as they passed, like a careless rape of that ruler of the night. Mahal felt weighed down with foreboding; what could these lights be?

The camp with its bright fire and festive adornments reappeared and the whirlwind vanished. His head was still to the ground, the baby whimpering against his chest, and Dinah's hand was on his back. He raised his eyes, sweat dripping from his face. Dinah's eyes were as calm as though nothing had happened. He stood. He held the baby high, an unfamiliar strength surging in him. What he had seen was unearthly, devilish. He did not want to speak of it. Yet he must, for it involved his own son.

"The child's name is Jar-ed," he said, loudly enough for all in the camp to hear. He wanted to weep, for the name of his long-awaited son was that of a portent of evil.

PART 2

BARAQUA

YEAR OF ADAM 582

CHAPTER 4

*I found him whom my soul loveth; I
held him, and would not let him go—*
SONG OF SOLOMON 3:4

The face of the man and the memory of his touch wouldn't
leave her, no matter how many hours she prayed. Baraqua,
daughter of the scribe Rasujal, knelt near the entrance of the
prayer cave low on the western flank of the holy mountain. Late
afternoon sun slanted beneath the rim of the cavern to illumine the
painted murals that embellished the walls; the six days of creation
expressed there in vivid colors; the one beauty of the somber caves.
The mural closest to Baraqua was of the Creator ushering the
forebears Adam and Eve into paradise. The artist had captured a
look of bliss on their fresh, illumined faces. Beyond that mural was
a scene of Adam giving name to every animal of the earth, his entire
body free of clothing and radiating a light purer than the sun's. On
the opposite wall Eve vomited the forbidden food she had eaten at
the suggestion of a jeweled serpent that coiled in the grass beneath
her. Eve's body was matte and dark, no longer bright, for the unseen
garment of holy virtues had fallen away when she sinned.

Baraqua shifted on the packed dirt floor, her heart weary from the
endless prayers and from the persistence of her love for the man
Shai. The long, oat-colored prayer robe scratched her skin when she

moved. But when the sun sank a bit lower, she would be free to go to the fire with the other initiates for the evening meal the women partook of together each sundown. *For the purification of all my desire, Lord have mercy*, she prayed silently, trying to be patient with the sun's slow descent. The cave was one of three, separating the initiates like herself from those who had proven themselves and wore the full mantle of the prayer vocation. Young and old, they were women who had turned away from life in the Sethite camp to wage battles not fought with sword or brawn but with the power of words and thoughts toward God alone.

She studied the young women who knelt on either side of her. Their heads were bowed, hands clenched before them in ardent concentration. She wondered if any of them knew that the sinking sun made their faces radiant, almost as though they were inhabitants of Eden. How could such young girls be this devoted to a deity whose home was the heavens, too high above the earth to imagine it as real? Baraqua was only there out of desperation to be released from love. She smiled ruefully; the others pushed toward heavenly love with all their might while she only wanted to lessen the brunt of the earthly one.

She had kept her secret well, the longing for Shai the vinedresser that had occupied her for a year. She had spoken to no one of it during the six cycles of the moon she had spent in the prayer caves, though her every thought had been of the man whose scent she could still detect, whose lips she remembered on hers. All this time had passed, yet God had not taken away the ache of Shai from her heart, nor had her father come to relent of his prohibition against Shai and give leave that she might marry that one she loved. She suppressed a sigh. To the women of the caves sighing was a sign of weakness. Because she had stayed on so long she assumed Akliah the eldress would initiate her soon with the mantle of prayer, sealing her forever as a celibate woman. After all, Shai had admitted openly that her face had never come to him in a bride dream, the requirement for Sethite marriage. All was futile on that account. Yet despite the months since she had seen him, Shai ruled her heart more than ever. She sat back on her heels and brushed a small spider from a fold in the rough garment. Enough of these furtive, whispered supplications. Enough of tears and a longing that never subsided. She stood up and stretched. Those ones who prostrated at the back of the cave could think of her what they would. She had not been summoned by the eldress, yet she would go on her own and speak to her. For to return in humiliation to her mother's tent was unthinkable. Without Shai, to remain in the caves was her only recourse. Surely, once the mantle was placed on her shoulders and vows made, the strength of her love for him would lessen; she must be content with holding him in her heart forever. An image of her father coming down the mountain came to her mind. He would try to fetch her back, claiming that some scribe or maker of parchment had beheld her face in his bride dream and was claiming her for a wife. But it would be too late. The mantle would already be placed over her and her father would return to his tent in humiliation.

She sat down on one of the rock niches at the sides of the cave where women sometimes rested. At least here she would have purpose for living. Here she would belong and be respected. She wondered if the other initiates had ever loved as she did. Did any of them weep in the night for the arms of a man? Some were cousins, yet she knew nothing of their hearts. How bleak her future seemed. Yet she must endure it.

"Are you in pain, daughter of Rasujal?" The voice was Haagar's, the young girl who often prayed beside Baraqua. The little creature was still a child yet wept with arms crossing her heart for hours at a time. "Tears cleanse the heart from sin and bring the glow of holiness," the eldress Akliah often said. What sins had innocent Haagar ever committed? She would be receiving the prayer mantle on the next Sabbath, within weeks of her coming to the caves. For it was said among the people that the daughter of Samuel the clay artisan had been anointed from birth for a life of devotion to God alone.

"Yes, pain," Baraqua answered. It was the first time she had revealed anything of her heart to the other women. "Weep for me, for I have loved where I should not," she murmured in such a low tone she wondered if Haagar heard.

"Shouldn't love?" Haagar's eyes were wide. The girl was too innocent to understand the complexities of what passed between a man and a woman. All her life, Haagar would know only the bliss of God and nothing of a man's kisses or even the low fire of longing that burned like a disease once it caught hold. She turned away from Haagar's sweet face. Let the girl pray in peace. Let her lift that pure heart and beseech the quick coming of Anointed One, who might arrive more quickly because such a girl had prayed. Perhaps in the revived Eden Baraqua and Shai could live as husband and wife, a thing impossible among Sethite rules and traditions. She would never repent of what she felt for him. He had uncovered her hair and run his hands through the long strands, an act lawful only for a husband. She did not regret the memory of that or the twilight hours when he and she had met beyond the pomegranate orchard and pledged their love without a thought to what their families would think. As one linked to a scribe's family and closer to the lineage of the Seed Bearers, it was unthinkable that Baraqua marry outside that line, especially without a bride dream.

Her mind drifted to that final evening before she ran to the eldress Akliah without letting her father know. The day had been white as a pearl, the low, creamy skies intermingling with the mists that had lingered in the low branches of the angel oaks where she and Shai sat. From his pouch, Shai had taken a river pearl mottled in rose and sky blue. The pearl was cunningly suspended on a chain of some substance Baraqua had never seen. He had probably found the chain when he had travelled beyond the mountain with his father, ever in search of better vine cuttings.

"A pledge," Shai had said, and fastened the pearl at her neck. She fumbled now under the coarse prayer garment and touched the pearl still in the hollow of her throat, as smooth and luscious as love untested.

She remembered Shai's words and the sensation of his breath against her cheek that night. "You are beautiful, graceful as a doe. Your hair is like a shining cascade, running down the ruby bluffs of Eden, lustrous under the morning sun." She had taken off the head covering of her maidenhood and let her hair fall over her shoulders, and Shai had buried his face in the hair and told her he wanted to remain there forever. The scent of jasmine had been everywhere. She had imagined that they were Eve and Adam, hidden in the ancient garden, the only two people in all the world.

But Shai's face was not at the tips of her fingers now, only the knotted prayer rope tangled in her hands. "Trace your prayers and bring heaven to earth," Akliah had said the day Baraqua came to her and she pressed the prayer rope into her initiate's hands. *Heaven here?* Baraqua had wanted to cry. *Heaven is wherever the man I love is.*

She heard a few of the initiates beyond the cave entrance setting out the simple evening meal. It would be the same as always: parched grain, dried fruit, and tea. Talk would be sparse, and when twilight dissolved to night, they would go each one to her sleeping pallet while Akliah and the most robust of spirit stood half the night, entering into invisible battles and making petitions for the destiny of souls. For Baraqua, the oblivion of sleep was always welcome. Only then could she find relief from the despair that increasingly permeated her heart.

She pictured her father and mother at their own evening meal, high in the camp at the summit of the mountain. She flushed with anger; what kind of father does not notice the love light in his daughter's eyes? How could bloodlines and a bride dream be more important than happiness? A lifetime on her knees would be better than marrying someone besides Shai, no matter what dream that man might boast of.

"We will leave the mountain," Shai had promised as she fingered the pearl at her throat. "I will hew out a boat of spruce wood and hoist a sail made from my brother's castoff tent. We will follow the mood of the sea until we find that place where the pillars of the earth soar into the sky." The moment seemed a thousand years ago.

One of the other initiates entered the cave and stood before Baraqua. She smelled of wood smoke and fresh sweat from hoeing the garden. "The eldress will see you in the glade," the girl said. Trails of tears were on her cheeks and Baraqua wondered how anything was accomplished in a community where incessant weeping over one's sin was the norm.

She nodded and tossed her prayer rope onto the rock niche. The eldress had only called for her once before. Surely this time it was to gather the other women for Baraqua's vows and initiation. She had performed her duties in the caves as devoutly as the other girls during her sojourn and she was a scribe's daughter. Inclusion in the community would not be denied her.

She did not speak to the women preparing the meal as she passed. It seemed most were too engrossed in prayer or their own thoughts, even as they worked, to interact with others. She walked quickly into the path behind the cave toward a grove of delicate birch trees where the eldress Akliah often sat in prayer and contemplation. The dying sun was comforting on her back as she walked, and the scent of the flowering meadow raised her spirits. Maybe it would not be so bad to belong here. Six moons in the shadows of the cave had won her at least this. She willed Shai's face aside. The God of the forebear Adam would help her forget that she had once loved a mere man.

CHAPTER 5

A kliah, eldress of the prayer caves, was sitting on a low stool thumbing the knots on her prayer rope when Baraqua entered the clearing. Her eyes were inscrutable orbs in her motionless face as she stood to greet Baraqua. The woman's unbroken serenity was unnerving and Baraqua wondered, not for the first time, if Akliah could read minds as it was rumored. She saw no encouragement there, no sense the eldress meant to bless her as an incoming member of the community. She forced herself not to look at the intricate scar that a succubus devil had long ago etched into the breadth of Akliah's forehead. It was the ancient brand of Lilith, a lover of the murderer Cain many years before. As a young woman Akliah had been Lilith's slave in the land of Nod. Since she had escaped her slavery, Akliah had never tried to hide the mark that symbolized the foolishness of her youth. "Memory is a gift useful in our repentance," she often said. The woman was taller than Baraqua by more than a head, as were all the first children of Adam and Eve. Except for Abel's lameness, the bodies of that first family had been perfect, and the regal look of the Creator was more prominent in Seth and Akliah than in any of their other offspring.

When Akliah said nothing to her Baraqua drew in a breath and spoke. "I am ready to vow before the community this very night, holy eldress; I wish to receive the mantle of my surrender to God and to stay with you always." She made her voice strong, but what she said sounded to her like the well-rehearsed lie that it was. She hoped Akliah did not detect this.

The edges of Akliah's mouth turned up with what might be amusement, then spoke. "The youngest daughter of Rasujal fills the air with impulsive words, but her heart is far from the caves."

Baraqua felt her face flush. "Forgive me. In my haste to take the mantle—" How could this woman know?

Akliah placed her hand over Baraqua's mouth. "You think of nothing but the man Shai." Her expression softened. "You love the vine dresser as much today as you did the day you came to me in the season of fruit gathering."

Baraqua felt an unexpected relief. Someone knew. She lifted her chin and forced herself to meet Akliah's eyes. "It's true; I do love him. But since I cannot have him, this is what is left to me and I will conquer my feelings in time."

Half of Akliah's face was now in shadow. "To stay among us would put your very life in danger," the eldress said.

"My life? Do you speak of the saber cats that prowl above the caves at midnight?"

Akliah tilted her head as though Baraqua was a curiosity. "You have passed half a year among us and you do not yet understand the true nature of what we do here."

"I understand well enough," Baraqua said, wishing she did not sound so wary. What was Akliah trying to say?

"Our lives are spent in perpetual battle against the fallen cherubic being known as Lucifer, whom the archangels cast down from heaven on the day of his rebellion. Only those of undivided heart have strength to bear such difficulty."

Baraqua felt the prick of pride. She would not admit that she did not understand. She would not be treated like a child.

Akliah pressed her hands together. "Tarah the shepherdess joined us the year the elders first pitched their tents in the clearing and established the full cycle of holy feasts and Sabbaths." She walked a few paces into the birches and turned back. "Tarah engaged in the battle carelessly, thinking she was a conqueror without the character to support that. During a long and arduous fasting vigil she was strangled by one of Lucifer's minions and none of us could prevent it."

"I have never heard Tarah spoken of," Baraqua said. How ignorant she was of much of the clan's history.

"Few speak of it," Akliah said, "though her father raised a monument of rose marble over her grave, just below this glade." For a moment the eldress looked small, standing among the quivering birches with her prayer rope held tightly in both hands as though she thought it might fall to the ground. "Do you think I bear this vocation naturally?" she said.

Baraqua was surprised at the woman's candor. "I assumed—" She had never thought about why this daughter of Adam had abandoned the Sethite camp.

"In order to survive here, one must have no earthly attachments," Akliah said. "After breath left my good husband Gabril's body, I felt as though I too were bound in the shroud of death. But I waited until my son Abel, named for his righteous uncle who was Adam's second son, decided to cloister himself." She hesitated. "And my daughter Benaiah—" Her voice caught. Baraqua knew the story of that girl who had left the mountain of God years before to cavort with the godless in the valley once known as Havilah.

"May your heart be comforted in the loss of your children," Baraqua murmured, a common courtesy. She paused a respectable moment. "I admit I am both unworthy and unprepared," she finally said. "But since my father has forbidden me to marry Shai, what else am I to do?"

Akliah's voice was firm. "Don't doubt your father's direction, for divine wisdom guides a parent's mind. I was a far greater fool than you in my youth and I almost paid for it with my life."

Baraqua was taken back. She knew Akliah had once been in love with her evil brother, Cain. Surely the eldress was trying to help her understand something important. But a desperate loneliness filled her. She did not want to live without Shai, but she did not dare contradict this one who had been hospitable to her for half a year. "Very well then, since you do not want me, I will return to my mother's tent for the remainder of my life," she said in resignation. She was too weary to argue more. She straightened the belt of the robe she had worn in the caves. An ache settled in her throat. Everything was so unfair.

She raised her chin. Maybe she would not resign herself to the humiliation of her mother's tent. "Perhaps, since there is no place allowed to me, I will journey into the east and live among the people of Nod as you did," she said.

Akliah gripped her wrists tightly. "You speak like an impulsive child, not a woman of good rank who has spent months in supplication before God." She stepped back. "Forgive me, but you are as unstable as a handful of sand," she said. "In one breath you speak of shouldering the mantle of prayer and in the next you babble about living on the steppe of Nod where devils thrive like weeds."

Baraqua rubbed her wrists where Akliah had grasped her. The woman was surprisingly strong. She did not care if Akliah thought she had injured her. To be thought of as so foolish and changeable— She could please no one. Perhaps not even Shai, for why hadn't he come to her secretly during her sojourn in the caves? Had he even tried to plead for her before her father's tent, arguing that traditions like the bride dream were conventions of another time? But she knew the answer. Shai would not show her father disrespect and Rasujal would never break tradition. Sethite ways were too ingrained in all of them.

"I understand your love for Shai better than you think," Akliah said, pulling Baraqua out of her thoughts. "But you must understand, daughter of Rasujal, that this deprivation of the heart will not kill you. God takes away one thing to give another. I know it from my own life."

"Your life is nothing like mine," Baraqua said. Even one who could read minds would never understand her love for Shai.

Akliah held her peace. No doubt it was not worth the woman's time to say anything more to the girl before her. Her mind crowded with the decisions she must make. She would leave the mountain, with or without Shai, for to live unmarried in her mother's tent all her days was unthinkable.

Akliah seemed to hesitate, then spoke. "There is another reason I cannot allow you to take vows," she said. "The stars proclaim that Jared the Seed Bearer, son of Mahal, will soon choose a bride."

"What does my second cousin have to do with me?" Baraqua said, not bothering to disguise the sulk in her tone. Let the educated, high-minded Jared marry as he would. She wanted only to gather her few things and leave the caves.

"Do you think of nothing but your own desires?" Akliah said, exasperation in her tone. "Your cousin's choice of bride has everything to do with you, with me, and with everyone on the earth who longs for the coming of Anointed One."

Anointed One. The Sethites talked of nothing else. Did the lives of ordinary people like her matter? "Well then, may God bless Jared's bride with conception of this Anointed One on the night of their nuptials," she said curtly. It was a common enough bride blessing among the Sethites. But in that moment, she cared nothing for the prophecies of her people. Her love for Shai was all that mattered.

"Since you are neither betrothed nor under a vow, you are among the women Duma the dream angel will consider," Akliah said. "Nothing can change what lies in the stars regarding the Seed Bearer's bride." She sat back down on her stool and motioned Baraqua to sit at her feet. Baraqua reluctantly obeyed. "Three days ago, the elders entered their prayer tents and have not taken food or drink since," she continued. "They know Jared will have his bride dream before the stars turn again."

"These traditions are amusing," Baraqua said with a hard little laugh. "But how can Jared be allowed to marry when he hasn't even spoken forth his virgin Seed Bearer's prophecy?"

"It was the same with his father, Mahal," Akliah said with a slight shrug. "Dinah was given to Mahal in marriage years before Mahal's first vision filled him, and on the very day Jared was born."

Baraqua tried to remember what Mahal's vision had been. Songs had been written of it. All she remembered was that the people had always been uneasy about it and few songs were sung at counsel fires about Mahal as compared to the other elders.

"The stars are impatient and we will soon know of the woman the dream angel has chosen," Akliah was saying.

"Indeed, the stars are impatient," Baraqua echoed bitterly. They were impatient for everything but helping the love-sick daughter of Rasujal. "I'm sure he'll dream of Tamara's rare beauty or of the skilled scribe Solanj, daughter of Yacob." Solanj's knowledge of the sacred writings and *Chronicles of Adam* was as thorough as any man's, and she was sturdy enough to bear Jared all the sons he wanted, anointed or not.

The sun slipped farther between the trees and Baraqua's spirits sank lower. She wanted only to be the wife of Shai and live in the vineyard. She would make a fine producer of wines. She got up and turned toward the caves. "I must go before the sun turns its back on us for the night," she said.

But Akliah stood up and put her hand on Baraqua's arm. "I must show you something first." She drew a length of woven cloth out of a basket beside her stool and held it up. The square had been separated prematurely from the loom and was riddled with mistakes, as though a girl of eight had been making her first sampler. Baraqua stared. Why would the eldress show her such a thing?

"Do you understand?" Akliah said.

Baraqua ran her hand over the uneven texture of the undyed linen. It could not be Akliah's work, for her weaving was renowned. This cloth was worth nothing but to mop up a spill.

"Is there a child under your tutelage?" she said.

"This is my work," Akliah said simply. "It was to be your prayer mantle. But the loom faltered and the shuttle broke several times. I used thread from last year's good flax harvest, yet nothing would alter the result you see." She lifted Baraqua's face to meet her eyes. "This ravaged project is the final sign that you are not meant to live here."

Baraqua forced herself not to change expression. The piece of linen was a mockery, a symbol of herself as a tangle of disorder and weakness that had been fated by some devious force locked within stalks of flax and a loom's caprices. She threw down the cloth that had decided her fate.

Akliah's voice was gentle. "Do not regard its appearance in the obvious way, but as a way to remember your time with me."

A way to remember? Baraqua did not dare make a response. It was getting dark. She would sleep somewhere on the mountain until she could sort through what to do. She would need a boat, a week's provisions, and a brimmed hat for the journey over the sea to whichever country she decided to explore. The story of the cursed prayer mantle would eventually reach the Sethite camp, but she would not be there to bear the mortification.

"I cannot carry this sorrow for you, but I will pray that you find the right path to walk upon," Akliah said. An evening bird squealed softly in the tree above them. All nature was preparing for the night.

Baraqua said nothing. Let the eldress think her rude.

"I know only this," Akliah said with finality. "You were formed for love, not solitude."

Chapter 6

*Because of these three things came the
flood on the earth; namely, the fornication
that the Watchers committed... when they went
whoring after the daughters of men, and took
themselves wives of all they chose, and they
made the beginning of uncleanness—*
BOOK OF JUBILEES 7:21

Semjaza, high chieftain of the angelic Watchers, paced impatiently outside the throne room of God Most High. From beyond the jeweled gate that separated the antechamber from the throne room came the sound of a multitude of the heavenly host praising that One who had no beginning and would never cease to be, who had formed the cosmos by a mere Word of his mouth. The sound repulsed Semjaza. The Watcher glared at the arched door and at its guard, the mighty celestial, Sabaoth, whose incorporeal form shone with unbearable fervor. Semjaza moved to the outskirts of the chamber. He must be as far from Sabaoth as possible as he waited for his audience with the Throne. That he had been allowed to appear in the seventh heaven at all had been a great surprise, now that he was entrenched in the pathways of Lucifer. Though this would not be the first time Semjaza had stood in this antechamber during the eons when he had served God, it would be the last.

In his Luciferian state would he be able to bear the Presence? So much had changed since he had stepped into the dark way. He imagined the uncreated light that emanated from the Throne perpetually, and the gleaming river called Life that flowed from beneath that place of authority. He considered the celestial chorus in numbers beyond count whose vocation was pure adoration. Would its intensity destroy him when he entered?

But no. He had the emblem of pride upon him, Lucifer's great breastplate, a remnant of Lucifier's original authority as the highest in rank of any angel in the created order. That remnant of authority would go far in keeping Semjaza intact once he entered the Presence, for God had not withdrawn most of Lucifer's power.

He cast the evil eye on Sabaoth, though the angel was too formidable to be affected. Sabaoth did not matter, for this day Semjaza would ask permission for he and his cohort of two hundred Watchers to do what had never been done in the history of the cosmos: enmesh the seed of angelic substance with that of human women. The desire of his heart was a woman called Baraqua, that maiden of the Sethites he had first seen at the lake in the land of Elda. Soon she would be his. She would love him and bear him sons. She would slake his desire for bodily union, quench his gnawing curiosity about human females.

The girl's beauty had tantalized him from the first instant. Young, softly impressionable, she had reached for him across the water on that night when he was at his normal angelic duties on the earth as one who kept watch over the hearts of men. One look at the girl and everything in him had stirred to possess her. He had abandoned devotion to God in that instant, yet the archangel Michael had blocked him when he moved closer to take the girl in his arms. He and the archangel had sparred, yet Semjaza wore no sword and Michael's was legendary.

He glanced again at the towering Sabaoth. The angel's majesty was incomparable. Semjaza wondered about the appearance of his own incorporeal essence, for he knew his radiance was sloughing away. He drew himself to his full height. He had pushed into the lands of Oblivion and Chaos to test his abilities, those realms where Lucifer sometimes brooded. Rebellion had not cost him strength. He was impatient to state his case and be gone. And he must not arouse the suspicion of Sabaoth.

The chorus beyond the gate swelled, the impact of the sound thrusting a rush of the uncreated light beneath the gates. In heaven, this light was a commodity as common as dirt was on the earth below. The light probed the antechamber and found its way to Semjaza where he cowered. He felt its wooing allure, its warmth against the frigidness of his lost spirit. He recoiled, for he knew the dangerous commodity of pure love was in the light, as always. He would not surrender to that musical love, that coaxing of his Creator. He could not bear the thought of that guileless, childlike God who loved hardened, sinful humanity and even the fallen angels as though they were all still dear to him.

The light receded like a wave and Semjaza sneered at Sabaoth; did he detect amusement in the gatekeeper's countenance? How dull that gatekeeper's existence must be. How much more interesting it was to embrace deviance and damnation. He did not regret his decision, though he knew the price he would eventually pay was the abyss of Tartarus, the lowest tier of the underworld. If he followed through with what he would propose before the Throne, that place would be his eternal abode. But what was ultimate damnation compared to the pleasures that awaited him through the girl, at least for a time?

He remembered the day Lucifer, the most exalted of all the cherubim, had requested a mere share in the Throne. That exquisite bearer of light had vaulted to earth in escape—a dragon spewing fire while stars trembled at his wake. Semjaza had been appalled, but now he understood. He was proud to be in league with that being who was canny as a lion and walked to and fro over the face of the earth to haunt seas, pollute human blood with disease, and undermine devotion to God. Insidious as a scorpion, Lucifer spread jealousy and deceit among people. He spread the lie that man was not made in

God's image as the forebear Adam had always taught, but was little more than a spider in value, a cosmic accident. He whispered to men who would believe it that the cosmos was a vacuous hole without meaning.

"Holy! Holy! Holy! Heaven and earth are filled with your glory!" the chorus harmonized. Semjaza growled. Lucifer should be sitting upon the Throne. "Holiness is mundane," he said with a sneer to Sabaoth. "Darkness is the pathway to life." It was a saying of Lucifer's that Semjaza had adopted. But Sabaoth remained impassive. Enraged, Semjaza spewed a string of curses—at the gatekeeper, at God, and at every pure thing. He would soon show all heaven his audacity. None of these fools would ever forget the day the prince of the Watchers was given leave to defy the natural law.

The gates opened suddenly and Sabaoth gestured that Semjaza should cross the threshold. Clouds of incense affronted him, the sensory representations of prayers that rose from the lips of the pious on earth. He moved forward tentatively. All was as he remembered it. The River of Life still flowed, that water of unimaginable clarity that cast high-arching rainbows into the reaches of space beyond heaven. The rainbows thrummed with the vibrations of a hymn exalting eternity. Endless tiers of angels were at their stations behind the throne, and their joyful clarity stabbed at his spirit. How he hated the love that was stronger here, that force which had no scheme or motive beyond union with its beloved object.

Semjaza stumbled over the translucent golden pavement, righting himself to maintain a semblance of dignity in the setting that now felt completely foreign. Through the pavement he could see the outer boundaries of God's vastness, the extent of his love. How much a novice in evil he must still be to find himself in awe of such things. Lucifer would not have trembled like this. Lucifer would have strutted and laughed in the Creator's face. But Semjaza could not. Not yet.

The fiery, six-winged seraphim fell down unceasingly before the Throne. The stench of prayers grew stronger and Semjaza suddenly rued that he had come. What had made him believe he could survive this? The girl's face welled in his mind, the comely jawline and the hair he could barely resist touching. For her sake he must persist. He was already relegated to Tartarus and had no reason to exist if he could not obtain the girl.

Abruptly, a deep silence fell over the room, the suspension of everything except a palpable awe. The chorus behind the Throne stilled their voices and the angelic harps and glories set down their golden-stringed instruments. He remembered the custom that silence must reign in heaven at times. For it must always be remembered that there was a limit to all creation. But there was no limit to God.

Be still, betray nothing, Semjaza told himself. The silence might last the time it took the sun to circle the earth a thousand times or it might be over in the twinkling of an eye. For there was no passing of time in heaven as there was on earth. All was now.

The silence revealed the extent of dissonance in Semjaza's spirit. He could hear the shrieks of his heart's treachery and rebellion. The thought of being chained in Tartarus mocked and engulfed him. His numerous vices—lust, haughtiness, and derision—ripped through the shadows of his distorted nature, shredding more swaths of what remained of his angelic soul, an ongoing destruction that both strengthened and weakened him.

But as suddenly as it had begun, the silence receded. The harps, glories, cherubim, and seraphim resumed their adoration. Semjaza raised his eyes, despite the scorching light. He was determined to survive this. No matter the outcome, he would make his diabolical request. He would defy God.

CHAPTER 7

A sound like the cry of a nervous animal came from the edge of the birch glade where Baraqua and Akliah stood. Baraqua turned to see her cousin Awan burst from the trees into the clearing, with the girl's stocky husband, Rojj, not far behind. Awan's laugh was like a seed pod rattling in the wind, her eyes darting into the trees and sky as though she could not decide among a banquet of fascinating sights.

"May God Most High have mercy," Akliah murmured as they watched Awan sprint over the grass while Rojj tried to keep up with her. It was common knowledge that Awan lived in the clutches of a madness no prayers or medicinal preparations could cure. Baraqua tried not to show her displeasure as the two stopped running and stood before her and Akliah. Awan was barely panting, while Rojj streamed sweat. Though Awan might once have been considered beautiful, the sickness of her mind had robbed the girl's eyes of brightness and set deep shadows beneath them. Her dress needed washing and her hair, always worn free instead of caught beneath the head covering of a married woman, lay in tangles around her shoulders. Rojj looked more anguished than usual. He was having to spend more time trying to keep his wife out of harm as she careened over the mountain at all hours, lost in her caprices that made the people despise her more every day.

Awan stared at Baraqua as though she had never seen her before. She did not pay the eldress any gesture of respect or greeting. She put her hand to her mouth and giggled like a little girl, then began to recite bits of a children's rhyme about a clumsy bear stuck in a beehive.

Rojj wiped his perspiring face. They would all have to endure Awan's spell, listen to her mumble to people no one else could see, and speak of things that did not exist except in her own fragmented mind. Awan ascribed importance to the shape of clouds or the veins of a leaf and might spend hours examining an ant hill. She kept Rojj's tent poorly, and often the weary goatherd had to prepare his own potage while other men were already on their sleeping pallets at the end of the day.

A prong of geese honked faintly above the trees, dim in the twilight. "The birds wing into the south; I must soon fly with them," Awan said in a breathy voice. She crossed her arms, her hands resting on opposite shoulders. She shivered and stared up at the geese. Her features pinched as she stared, as though to look made her afraid.

The round-faced Rojj greeted Baraqua with a kiss to one cheek, then inclined his head toward the eldress Akliah in the gesture all Sethites showed the women of the caves. For two years Rojj had borne his responsibility stoically. Though he was unoriginal by nature, the goatherd rarely seemed ashamed of his wife's strangeness. People accepted the oddness of their marriage, for who can say what should make up the measure of a man's love? Awan's family was relieved to be rid of her.

But Baraqua felt her own low mood darken further. Her life was in turmoil and Awan had come to make it worse. She looked at Akliah and her eyes pleaded: Don't send me back with them. Let me stay one more night.

Akliah started to say something, but Awan interrupted. "Do I know him?" she said, pointing to Rojj. She seemed genuinely confused. "The elders gave me, not that goat man, the right to fetch you to the banquet." She glared at Rojj and made a face.

"There is a banquet this night?" Baraqua said, though it did not matter. She would be in no condition to feast if Akliah forced her to return to the camp.

"The goat man is your beloved husband," Akliah said quietly, putting her hand on Awan's arm. Awan jerked away, spun, and hugged herself with her crossed arms. "The forest sprites sped me here, but they pulled at Rojj with sturdy cobwebs to show how slow he is." She laughed, and it sounded like something sharp had fallen to the ground and shattered. She shook her finger at her husband. "The sprites must help the slow-witted ones who refuse to repent; that's a tradition."

But Rojj said nothing. Eber the cheesemaker had been thrilled when Rojj approached him about marrying his incorrigible daughter. No other man had claimed a bride dream about Awan. No one would have dared even if her face had come to him in sleep. Rojj had approached Eber without any claim to a dream, possibly under the spell of Awan's fine looks at the time. Since their hasty nuptial ceremony Rojj had attended faithfully to the woman who would never return his love.

"You were kind to accompany Awan," Akliah said graciously to Rojj, to cover up the awkwardness of Awan's comment. She gestured toward the prayer caves. "You've come a long way down the mountain and must be thirsty. Go to my novices and they will give you a cup of orange water."

But Baraqua knew Rojj would not leave Awan for a cup of anything. Night would soon claim the mountain and he could not risk Awan getting away from him.

Awan seemed to emerge from a dense mist of the mind. She put her hands on her hips and spoke with sudden clarity, as sometimes happened. "Jared the Seed Bearer has had his bride dream this very day," she said with self-importance in her tone. "Before the elders, he stood up and claimed Baraqua, and her father agreed." She sat down on the ground and drew up her legs. She smiled at Baraqua, innocent as a child. "The people assemble thick as geese and you will marry Jared in three days upon a throne of snail shells."

Baraqua wanted to show her impatience. People endured far too much from Awan, and Akliah's kindness only made her own reaction seem worse. But she controlled her features. Awan's good husband was worthy of a measure of tolerance. Her shoulders ached. She had prayed almost without ceasing since before the sun that morning and had eaten little. She did not want to listen to Awan's foolishness. As soon as she could she would hide deep in one of the caves, then slip out later to find Shai in his hut beyond the vineyards. The thought of it cheered her slightly. She now had a plan.

But Rojj put up a hand. "It is as Awan says, Baraqua. It was your face that came to Jared's dream this afternoon."

Baraqua stared. Rojj would never lie. Awan giggled, elated to see Baraqua so shocked. She began to tap the tips of her fingers against her thumbs, which she sometimes did for hours. Had Awan tapped those thumbs as many times as Baraqua had prayed for release from love of Shai?

"Are you absolutely sure?" Akliah asked carefully.

"I stood with my brothers beyond the tent of Seth as Jared proclaimed it," Rojj said. "When I left the camp the women of Baraqua's family were already setting up the betrothal canopy."

Baraqua looked at Akliah. There was no real surprise in the eldress's face. Awan continued her tapping.

"Curses visit the unbelieving," Awan said in a sing-song voice as she stared at Baraqua, as though they were still children at their games.

Uneasiness coiled in Baraqua's belly. "Well then, Jared should dream of someone else, for I am no Seed Bearer's bride." She could not bear such foolishness on this worst of all days. "Perhaps the eldest son of Mahal has a fever or mistook the comely face of Solanj the scribe for mine in his sacred dream. After all, Solonj and I resembled each other as children." Blood pounded in her temples. It was a mistake.

Awan's face lost its expression of dull musing. She got up and grabbed Baraqua's wrists, leaned back and began to swing her cousin in a circle as they had done as little girls. Baraqua shook off her cousin's clammy hands, barely able to keep from screaming. "Go home, Awan," she said shakily. "The night air isn't good for what's wrong with you." How did the three of them dare to stand and stare at her? Was she to accept this absurdity as though she was a milk cow to be sold?

"Tonight, you will put on the veil Eve wove for her daughter Azura in the ancient day," Awan said in another moment of clarity. "You will sit among rose petals and drink clarified wine while you gaze upon your betrothed. In three days, you will be blessed by the elders and enter the nuptial tent." She giggled. "Your first night will be one you won't forget."

Rojj's face colored. He put a hand on Awan's arm and tried to draw her away. But Awan jerked free. She put her mouth close to Baraqua's ear and the smell of her breath was of molding orange peel and of the bitter herbs Tamara the healer coaxed on her to calm her mind.

"Your days of cavorting in the orchard with the vine keeper are over, cousin," Awan whispered.

Baraqua drew back. She could not suppress a gasp. The thought of Awan spying on her and Shai was revolting. Had Awan seen Shai unbinding her hair? Her voice was too loud. "I cannot marry Jared," she said. "This very night I take my vow among the women of the caves and put on the full mantle of prayer."

Akliah put her hand to her mouth at the blatant lie. Baraqua pushed down her shame and glared at the eldress. "You lied to me. You knew about this," she said, suddenly wild with panic. It was the final crushing of the precious jewel of her love for Shai.

"I knew nothing of what Rojj would say, though impressions have come and gone all day within my heart," Akliah said carefully.

Baraqua gripped Akliah's hands. What if she could not find Shai, or he refused to come with her out of concern for his family's reputation? "I will be a slave to the entire community if you will let me dwell among you," she said.

"Fascinations of the marriage bed await you," Awan said, the annoying sing-song playfulness in her voice.

"Be silent, daughter of Eber," Akliah said bluntly to Awan. "You will show respect to the Seed Bearer's bride." The eldress touched three fingers to her forehead, knelt on one knee and rose again in front of Baraqua, the sign of reverence to an elder or his wife. But Baraqua was thinking about which gown she would sneak from her mother's tent in order to be properly dressed for Shai when they travelled.

The sound of singing and of tambourines was coming from the forest beyond the birches. A group of unmarried Sethite men and girls appeared, bearing a decorated chair attached to poles. Rojj and Awan were right, for here was the party that had come to take her to her bridegroom. The young people filled the glade, their faces charged with excitement. A Seed Bearer's Bride! The sure mother of Anointed One! In their festal clothes, the young men lowered the chair. It was decorated in the Sethite manner to carry a betrothed woman. Other men and boys held torches high and the young women began to dance, tapping tambourines and waving banners of flowing white gauze that undulated like clouds in the growing gloom. Baraqua was too shocked to move. This unbearable fate was being celebrated by everyone except her.

A distant cousin of Baraqua's, tall and with dark, curling hair, stopped dancing and glared at Awan. "We should have known you'd ruin everything by coming here ahead of us," she said.

"Don't speak to my wife like that," Rojj said to the girl, putting his arm around Awan's waist. "It was kind of Awan to think of her cousin at such a time." Awan pulled away from Rojj. She twirled a lock of hair between the fingers of one hand and tapped her belly with those of the other.

Baraqua's sister Bathshae pushed through the group, a wreath of roses over her modest head covering for the occasion. Baraqua felt her breath returning to normal at the sight of steady Bathshae. "Let us have no quarreling on such a day," Bathshae said to the tall cousin. Her voice was many shades of softness, yet everyone heard that command and the tall girl turned away in deference to Bathshae.

The girls began to sing an old Sethite song of marital love. "Fortify me with pitchers of wine and feed me spiced apples, for I am sick with love." Adam had written it for Eve before they conceived Seth, many years after Cain murdered Abel.

Akliah stood near Baraqua and Bathshae, a hesitant joy in her face. "Now I understand why I could not weave your mantle correctly," she said. "The path you are being asked to walk will subdue and buffet you, but its destination will be one of peace." She took Baraqua's hands in hers. "Learn to submit with joy to things you cannot change. Find happiness as the Seed Bearer's bride."

Happiness? How much people dared say when it was not their destiny at stake. But Baraqua kept her face composed as the eldress offered the well-meant advice. There was no more time to think, to scheme of a way to disappear forever from the mountain. She could not see a way out of the labyrinth she was lost in. Bathshae's arm was around her waist, leading her to the flower-draped chair. Two of the men helped her into the chair and one of the youngest girls pressed a cluster of water roses into Baraqua's hands and kissed her cheek. "May the womb of the mother of Anointed One be blessed," the girl said tremulously, then twirled away with the lissomness of youth, the energy of an untested life.

They danced again, the girls smelling of hyacinth and roses, the men of cedarwood and masculine astringency. She had loved that scent on Shai's skin after his days among the vines. She tried to nod appreciatively but her neck felt as rigid as a pole pine. Still, she must try. She was the child of a respected scribe, the youngest of a scribe's family whose daughters were honored among the people. She had been brought up to respect the traditions. She willed to see Shai among the familiar faces. He was unmarried, qualified to be among the men. Where was he at this moment, while the phantom from

Jared's dream worked its will in her life? Glow worms appeared in the darkening air, darting above the girls and their tambourines. A memory flashed, of fireflies beneath a lake, a man's cold hands and irresistible essence. She had barely been a woman.

The girls' eyes shone as they admired the men, their faces high in color. They knew the power of their femininity and believed without question in a pleasing future with one of those young men, only because in their youth they had no capacity to believe otherwise.

Akliah squeezed between the dancers, a stark contrast in her shapeless brown robe to the girls' youthful splendor. She reached up and put something into Baraqua's hands. It was the square of ineptly woven cloth, the embryo of the prayer mantle Baraqua would never wear. Baraqua fingered it, an ache in her throat. "You consider me weak and frivolous and want to remind me of my failings," she said. "Yet I know I could have succeeded here. I know it."

Akliah gripped Baraqua's hands tightly. "I do not think of you as weak," she said fervently. "Your destiny is other than here, yet God is but a breath away, mighty to save. Trust him."

Baraqua turned her eyes from the eldress. How was it possible to believe the God the Sethites worshipped cared? He might save someone else, but not her. She would have to do that herself.

The young men hoisted the chair and moved out of the birch grove and into the ancient Trail of Weeping that led up the mountain to the Sethite camp. Long ages past, Adam and Eve and their first children had climbed that trail each Sabbath out of the meadows of Havilah to sacrifice a lamb near Eden. Adam had been faithful to the ritual every week since his exile.

Baraqua observed the young men as they climbed. The muscles of their half-bared arms gleamed in the torch light. They were heady with the importance of this night of nights as they smiled on the girls, each hoping for a bride dream soon for himself. They were envisioning even now the pleasures of a new wife's embrace in the nuptial tent and the slaking of the need that had haunted their loins since the budding of manhood. These men did not yet understand how easily such pleasure can be corrupted. They did not know that the women they married might someday destroy them with a look of disrespect which turned to disdain and finally urged the women to turn away in the night from those men's eager hands. They did not know that all too soon their waistlines would thicken and their shoulders stoop under field work or the shame of rebellious children, while the passing of too much time would dim their thoughts until they no longer remembered or cared about the starry night they had carried the Seed Bearer's bride to her destiny.

Baraqua wondered how she saw it so clearly, how she knew, while knowing little of the caprices of life herself. The awareness must be merely a place to thrust her own sorrow.

The procession moved up the trail. The girls were singing the old prophecies of Anointed One. "His head shall bruise the Serpent's heel! He shall trample upon the enemy of God!" The hymn was as old as Eve, as weary as the world. But the young people had put new harmonies to the strains, and the tone of the hymn was bright.

Baraqua straightened the folds of her borrowed prayer robe. There had not been time to retrieve the clothes she had arrived in six months before. Would any among the ecstatic young people consider that she was the least worthy of all the women Jared could have dreamed of? Her eyes scanned the sides of the trail for a glimpse of Shai. But she knew he was not there.

At the first switchback above the prayer caves Baraqua looked back. Akliah was almost invisible in the darkness, her hand raised in the gesture of leave-taking. Baraqua raised her hand in parting as well. It was not right to resent Akliah. That good woman would always symbolize the great battle Baraqua had waged—waged and lost to a life far more devastating than wrestling spirits in damp caves would have been.

The voices of Awan and Rojj wafted from farther down the trail. "I was the one the elders sent to bear her home," Awan was bellowing. "I will bind them with cobwebs for stealing my mission. I will put them to sleep at the edge of a cliff."

"My flower, you only imagined they sent you, so please let it be," Rojj pled in a strained voice. He sounded like a man bowed over a graveside, reciting a lament for the dead.

CHAPTER 8

These are the names of the holy angels who watch: Uriel...who is
over the world, turmoil, and terror; Raphael...who is over the spirits
of men; Michael...set over the virtues of mankind and over chaos;
Gabriel...who is over Paradise and the serpents and the Cherubim.
I ENOCH 20:1-8

From high in the stars of the constellation known as Bethuleh,
the virgin, four archangels looked out over the earth.
Michael, Gabriel, Raphael, and Uriel were observing the
young woman whose face had come to Jared's bride dream. The
daughter of Rasujal the scribe was being moved up the mountain in
the throne of a betrothed woman, misery in her face.

"We must trust Duma's choice, for the dream angel feeds on the
mind of God in these matters," Michael said. Yet he was uneasy, for
the girl's distress was profound and he sensed that her resistance to
her duty was extreme. Such distress would not dissipate just because
Jared the Seed Bearer would be a kind and intelligent husband. The
labyrinth of this woman's soul was more complex than most.

As captain of the archangels, Michael's aura was a scintillating
red, a cautionary reminder of his infamous strength and the power
of the sword that had ousted Lucifer from heaven with a single
stroke. The image of stately Adam was emblazoned on the

archangel's breastplate, the man into whom God had breathed his own life and whose people Michael had been entrusted as guardian.

"Her rebellion puts the future of the Sethite lineage in peril," Uriel said. As usual, there was gravity in Uriel's tone, for as keeper of the gates of Sheol, the underworld, Uriel kept much company with the dead. The association had marked him, and his somber gray breastplate was emblazoned with a scarlet cross no one but he and God Most High knew the full meaning of.

"We pray it will not be so," Michael answered, his long hair undulating like flames of fire. He was as concerned as Uriel, but as captain of the archangels he kept much of his burden to himself. He was glad for this moment of respite in Bethuleh, which wordlessly prophesied of the young woman who would one day bear Anointed One. In a time of trepidation, even the holy archangels needed reassurance that God's plan would unfold.

"She has barely been told her destiny and already she plots her escape," Gabriel observed of the chosen woman. The swiftest of all angelic messengers, Gabriel rarely rested. His calling was high attention to the voice of God, that he might immediately do his bidding. The marble-white angel held a silver trumpet, symbol of that readiness to proclaim. "I will descend to her side this instant, my lord Michael," Gabriel said. "I will whisper the consequences if she does not marry Jared."

"But we know nothing yet for sure," Raphael said. "We must think well of the girl and believe that in time she will see what she must do." Raphael was the gentlest of the four. He radiated the healing colors of verdure and gold electron and his breastplate was engraved with the flowers of medicinal plants and with the image of a freshwater spring. His vocation was to bend over the dejected and succor the sick.

"She has no right to disrupt the prophecies manifested in the stars," Uriel said. He had little patience for human beings who sought their own will over the divine. He saw too well the outcome of godless lives at his post outside Sheol.

"I had expected Duma to choose gentle Solonj," Gabriel said. "Scholarly and quiet in spirit, she has loved Jared since her babyhood."

"God has reasons unknown to us." Raphael's voice was musical, brimming with healing tones.

Michael fixed his eye on the star Tsemech in the left hand of Bethuleh, represented as a stalk of wheat in the prophecies. Tsemech represented Anointed One himself. "The One who sits enthroned never lies and all true prophecies will one day manifest," he said. "Nevertheless, the daughter of Rasujal will be a challenge."

"This trial is an occasion for the healing of her soul," Raphael said brightly.

"But will she choose the healing way?" Uriel said. "Love of self is an unkind master. If allowed, it will bind the soul forever."

"Love of self and Lucifer's low lures combine in lethal ways," Gabriel agreed.

"Do not doubt it," Uriel said crisply. "Sheol is glutted with those who loved on a whim where they should not have." He turned to Michael. "Let Gabriel go to her. She is too blinded by infatuation for the vine keeper to grasp the importance of this."

"Be at peace, Uriel," Michael said. "Your duties among the dead make you anxious for the living. But since the fall in Eden people crave what damns them and look for meaning amidst the rubble of the fallen earth." He paused. "She will suffer enough without too much interference from us."

"Suffering requires time," Uriel said firmly. "She might learn the lesson too late."

"But the prophecy is fixed, as Bethuleh is witness," Michael said. "We must trust."

"God will not stop her if she deserts her duty," Raphael said softly, as though to remind himself. "Free will is divinely given, and never rescinded."

It was Michael's hour to move among the Sethites. He prepared to rise out of the constellation.

"Don't go before we discuss Semjaza's audience before the Throne," Gabriel said.

"God has revealed nothing to me yet," Michael said. "But we can imagine how it went." He made a bow of reverence to Bethulah and descended. The Sethites would be gathering for the betrothal ceremony of Jared and Baraqua. He did not know what he would find.

CHAPTER 9

And in the eleventh jubilee Jared took to himself a wife,
and her name was Baraka, the daughter of Râsûjâl, a daughter
of his father's brother, in the fourth week of this jubilee—
BOOK OF JUBILEES 4:16

A hundred pitch torches lit the camp of the Sethites as Baraqua stepped down from the chair that had brought her up the mountain. The people lined an aisle she was to walk, to where her parents stood at the end. The women hailed her arrival and waved palm branches and branches of rosemary to scent the air. She had never seen so much light or such adornment of the camp, or the people so well dressed. Every eye was on her.

"All good fortune to you, Bara," shouted a cousin from the crowd, his arm around his young wife. How loud people's voices seemed, how bright the light after six cycles of the moon spent in silent caves. She had reentered a world that now felt unfamiliar. She did not belong to it any more than she belonged in the prayer caves. Her heart beat hard. There was nowhere to run. The people pressed around, smiling, delighted. They seemed not to notice how miserable she was or how dingy her gown.

She peered down the aisle at her parents, Rasujal and Gayile. How unhappy they would be if they knew her true feelings about Jared, about Shai, and about Akliah's reasons for refusing her entrance into the prayer community. She would keep it all within until she knew better how to manage the situation. Her father stood splendid in his finest scribe's robe, and a sickening prick of doubt came to her heart. Surely her father did not love her, or he would not appear so pleased, knowing her feelings for Shai as he did. Was he calculating the life of increased prestige he would enjoy when she became the Seed Bearer's bride?

Baraqua's sister Bathshae squeezed through the crowd and took her arm. "You are radiant, even without the garment of your betrothal."

How could Bathshae be so blithe when Baraqua was bleeding to death? "Go tell our father that I must wait a half moon to prepare myself," she said to her sister. "This is happening too fast." But in half a moon's time she would be far away. It saddened her to think of being apart from Bathshae.

Bathshae's forehead creased. "But the betrothal must take place before the wandering stars change their positions," she said. "You will adjust." That was it; even Bathshae was blind to her misery. She must truly believe that Baraqua would be happy because she herself was content with her lot and could not imagine any other state.

"I won't adjust," Baraqua said, desperate that Bathshae understand. But she kept her face composed so that no one would suspect her unhappiness.

"May your son soon throw open the gates of Eden," the women were singing. It was a new song, bright and confident. The women had twined orange blossoms into their hair, leaving off the modest head coverings for this night that would not come again for a generation.

"He is a good man, this son of Mahal," Bathshae continued. "My Obadiah sits at fireside with him often enough. He knows the star stories perfectly and he speaks wisely on all things."

Stars. She wished they would fall from the sky and leave her free. She fingered the smooth river pearl at her neck and scanned the crowd. *Where are you, Shai?* The coarse, oat colored prayer robe scratched her ankles as she walked, Bathshae's arm linked with hers. The hem of the garment was deeply stained with the sepia dust of the caves. She would refuse to change her gown or anoint her face before coming to the son of Mahal. Let him find her unwashed and silent. Then he would tell his father that the dream angel had made a mistake.

Baraqua walked slower, her thoughts swirling. She had known girls summoned from the vine gardens or the kneading trough to recite the betrothal vows with dirt or flour still on their hands. Why was human will of so little importance compared to the leading of the heavenly bodies with their cold, shimmering points?

Flutes began to trill and the rhythm of the women's tambourines beat against her ears. A bright celebratory fire blazed ahead, with the scent of cinnamon and cloves steaming in pots among the coals to the air.

A woman on the right side of the aisle spoke distinctly enough for Baraqua to hear. "She is not a flawless beauty like Tamara, but their children will be fine looking enough."

"Not fine looking at all," the woman next to her argued. "Her sons will be sickly, for the youngest daughter of Rasujal has always been pale and her blood is too thin to bear Anointed One." The woman snorted knowingly. "Her mother tried to get her to eat beet root as a child, but that stubborn girl refused and this is the result."

Baraqua moved on with Bathshae. She tried to picture her cousin Jared. She had not seen him up close in several years and could not picture his face.

And then she was before her parents and Bathshae moved away. Over his best robe, her father Rasujal wore the long, black-trimmed vest of an honorable scribe. He was a man of strong features, his forehead perpetually creased in concentration. Though he had no doubt scrubbed his hands for the auspicious event, Rasujal's fingers were deeply stained with the ink of black walnut shells, the fluid of his trade. He took Baraqua's hands in his and he and Gayile embraced her and whispered the blessings parents since Adam and

Eve had murmured to their children on the eve of marriage. Baraqua had never seen them so content. Gayile's finely formed face was flushed in the heat of the torchlight, and though she wore a single strand of lapis beads as an ornament, her expression was as though the gold in every mine belonged to her.

The words came against Baraqua's will. "Why didn't you let me return from the caves in my own time?" She regretted her words immediately. She had vowed to keep everything within.

Rasujal frowned. "You did not receive my permission to go the caves, so why would I need your permission to call you back?" he said. Gayile's high color paled. "Your own time?" she echoed. "But the bride dream—"

"You both taught me that our first allegiance is to God, not other people," Baraqua said. "I was deep in prayer when Awan and Rojj came to fetch me home." She did not care that it was a lie.

Gayile pursed her lips. The wife of Rasujal was not one to analyze what lay beneath the surface of a matter. Her daughter's response was too complicated. "Do not shame us with ingratitude," she said.

Baraqua bit down a response. She was too tired, too dirty, and too overwhelmed to resist the power of everyone else's happiness. Even Bathshae could not see her anguish. Her plump oldest sister Basmat came to her side. Basmat was deep in her twelfth pregnancy, her round face a mass of smiles and chins. She laughed and squeezed Baraqua, her little sister. Basmat was always laughing. She lived life as it came to her and made no complaint, as long as good food and good company were present. "It is time to dress and anoint you," she said to Baraqua with a grin. She gestured toward the betrothal tent where the women would prepare her to meet her bridegroom.

Bathshae squeezed Baraqua's hand. "Obadiah just brought me news that Obed has taken a fever and I must return to him," she said. Four years earlier, Bathshae had given birth to her first child, a boy who still could not walk, talk, or control the movement of his eyes. Baraqua forced down panic. The night would be even stranger without her favorite sister. But she could not argue that Obadiah should care for Obed on this auspicious night. Obed was the center of Bathshae's world.

The tent of preparation, smoky with incense, was crowded with Baraqua's relations. Gayile and Basmat led Baraqua to a cushion and sat on either side of her. The others gathered where they could. The women smelled of cooking spices, fresh bread, and the dusty scent of newly threshed barley. They smelled of the oils they soothed their babies' rashes with, and of fire and smoke and work. They smelled of comfort. Baraqua greeted her sisters Havah and Eha, who lived on the other side of the camp where their husbands drew jewels from the River Eden for the adorning of the elders' liturgical vestments.

"You see, love for her bridegroom is already in her eyes," Basmat said, pleased to announce this requirement for every bride.

"She pined in the prayer caves as she waited for her bridegroom's call," Eha said with a sigh. "They say she danced with joy when the news reached her."

Baraqua forced herself to remain seated, though she wanted to run from the tent. Her life stretched endlessly before her, suckling babies in the tent of Jared and cooking his potage. To the others, she was now the center of their hopes for their own futures. She was the affirmation of Eve's ancient prophecy. Everything the Sethites lived for hung on this marriage.

Her younger cousins patted their ears with delight at what Baraqua's sisters had said. They kissed Baraqua, pressing white roses into her hands, stroking the course prayer robe with curiosity. Everyone wanted to be chosen to bathe and adorn the future wife of Jared the Seed Bearer. The little girls leaned against their mothers, taking in the excitement of being in the presence of such an auspicious bride.

Basmat held up a shawl of finest hooked lace. "I have worked on it for many months, awaiting the nuptials of my youngest sister," she said, and Baraqua forced a smile of thanks to her mouth as Basmat pressed the delicate garment into her hands.

Someone was pushing against her from behind. "Move over, simple one. I can't get by." It was Awan, squeezing between Baraqua and her mother. A lopsided wreath of twigs and wilted red amaryllis lay over Awan's tangled hair, and she paused to straighten the childish ornament with a self-satisfied look as she settled into place.

"Do you wish the daughter of Eber to remain among us?" Gayile said tersely to Baraqua as she glared at her niece Awan.

Baraqua studied her rude, unpredictable cousin. How unaware Awan seemed of how little others enjoyed her company. But she wondered if the girl had felt Gayile's meaning. Did Awan hide the rejection she felt? The crown of limp flowers slipped from her head.

"Forget-me-nots mean don't forget me," Awan said in a childlike voice. She clasped the wreath to her heart. Baraqua remembered when they were children, when Awan's eyes had focused on real things before her, when her mind had been lucid. She had been mistress of games, and the fastest runner of all the girls.

"They aren't forget-me-nots, Awan," Eha said impatiently. "Don't you know an amaryllis when you see it?"

"Since Bathshae cannot be here, Awan must stay to bless us in her place," Baraqua interrupted. Awan's presence seemed fitting— a madwoman attending the preparations for a mad, loveless marriage.

Awan looked quickly at Baraqua with eyes that swam with sudden tears. She turned her face down and began to play with the hem of her garment. But when the rituals began, she calmly held the drying cloth while Eha and Basmat washed Baraqua with warm water scented with blue tansy and jasmine. Gayile even allowed Awan to pass her the vials of sacred oils that she smoothed on Baraqua's belly to prepare her womb to conceive a child.

As Gayile and Havah drew the gauzy white betrothal gown over Baraqua's head, Gayile's hand brushed against the pearl at her throat.

"Where did you get such a lovely thing?" Gayile said when the bodice of the garment was in place. Baraqua could not tell if her mother guessed something.

"A gift from a friend," Baraqua stammered, resenting the rare moment when her mother seemed intuitive.

"Shouldn't you remove it, now that you are to marry?" her mother said.

Baraqua raised her chin. "The good wishes of the giver go with me into my marriage," she said as calmly as she could. Someone asked Gayile a question and she turned away. The moment was over.

Did Shai truly wish her well? Baraqua wondered what she would do if he refused to leave the mountain with her. But there was no time to ponder this. The women crowded near, happy for their kinswoman who was chosen through the mystery of a man's dream. They asked Baraqua and each other a hundred questions but seemed to have no patience for the answers before they pounced on the next speculation, chattering now about the sacramental mystery that bound a man and a woman together in flesh, just as Eve had come out of Adam's side to establish the union of one-making for all couples who followed in marriage.

"Her hair takes the braids in perfect submission," Basmat said as she and Eha plaited Baraqua's hair into the intricate betrothal style. The braids would remain in place until Jared unloosed them in the nuptial tent. Havah began to apply henna to Baraqua's arms, carefully drawing dew flowers and a bird-of-paradise intertwined with flowering vines along her fingers in black, crimson, and cerulean. She let them do as they wished. When she was gone would they think back on this labor of love as a waste?

Basmat crossed her legs, her belly bulging with the promise of her twelfth child. "I remember the night of my own nuptials as though it happened yesterday," she said, and grinned above the soft folds of her chins. Baraqua had not even been born when Basmat married.

The women laughed and patted their ears in encouragement, for Basmat was a good storyteller, especially the story about her own wedding night which she told at every gathering of women.

"Well," Basmat began slowly, pretending it was hard to remember. "You all know my husband Jocbed well." The women laughed knowingly. Jocbed was pious but lusty, ever eager for an hour with his wife in their large tent.

"Jocbed had eyes only for you from the day he was weaned as a baby," Havah said as she dipped her henna brush into one of the pots of color. "He went straight from his mother's breasts to longing for yours."

Basmat looked at her sister with mock impatience. "Is this my story, or shall you tell us your own version?" she said.

"Your story, my flower, always yours," Havah said with a wave of her hand.

"Well, Jocbed could barely keep his hands from my bodice, so the elders gave permission for a short betrothal," Basmat continued, and Baraqua shifted on the cushion. The tent was too warm, the sequence of rituals too long. She remembered when she had thought her sister's story fascinating.

"Jocbed's father put him to the plow from before the sun until after twilight just to keep him away from me before the day," Basmat continued. The women leaned forward hungrily, as though they wished their husbands had such desire for them. "Once in the nuptial tent, he unloosed my braids faster than any man ought to be able to. He unfastened my gown like he had done it a thousand times, and I didn't have a moment's rest until the rising sun finally put the man to sleep." She sounded out of breath, as though remembering brought back the exertions of that night. "Our first child was born exactly nine cycles of the moon later. I am surprised I didn't give birth to triplets instead of one tiny girl."

The women laughed as though they had never heard the story before. Havah patted Basmat's swollen belly. "And handsome Jocbed has not wasted a moment since." They teased Basmat this way every time the story was told.

Someone refilled Baraqua's wine cup, which she drank in two draughts and despised her forced merriment. She did not want twelve children, only one who looked like Shai.

"The veil," Gayile said. Someone handed her the shimmering betrothal veil, and Gayile placed the ancient head piece over Baraqua's intricate braiding. The veil's origin was known only to Eve, and she would tell no one how it was that shadow and light moved together in such mysterious contours within its folds.

"Come, Anointed One, we pray," said Gayile, her hands on Baraqua's head. "Quicken my daughter's womb."

The lady Eve entered the tent. Baraqua was made to sit in a low, carved chair to receive the forebear's blessing. It was a great honor to be attended by that mother of all living. Eve's dark robe was embroidered with the tree called Life. Its threads were bleached with aphron, pure as clouds. Her hair, legendary in its beauty, was never shown. Strict propriety in her appearance was part of Eve's repentance.

Eve stood before Baraqua and began to pray. Part of her words were in Edenese, and the rest in the universal language. Baraqua would never remember what Eve prayed, but she knew it had to do with a fruitful womb.

When the prayers were completed Eve drew a transparent vial the color of sky from a pocket in her gown, half full of a richly colored oil. "This is the precious rose-of-paradise God gave me on the day of my expulsion from Eden. It was to sustain my heart in the fallen world," Eve said. She tipped the vial to release one drop and touched Baraqua's forehead with it. An exquisite aroma permeated the tent, and every woman became still.

"This oil is but a vague remembrance of the bliss of paradise," Eve said with wistfulness in her tone. "May its powers bring you delight."

Baraqua hardly dared breathe. She wished the others would leave and she could confess all to the forbear and ask her a thousand questions. But such a thing would never happen. She was being compelled along a prescribed path she seemed to have no power to break out of.

A man spoke from outside the tent. "The bridegroom waits."

"The bridegroom waits?" Basmat echoed in her hearty voice. "Only one night in every generation do angels choose a Seed Bearer's bride. We women will enjoy every moment until we please." The stillness Eve's presence had cast within the tent was gone.

Baraqua studied her sister. Basmat rarely cared what other people thought. But she would care very much when Baraqua was gone in the morning. Only love for Shai would compensate for the humiliation her family would bear at her absence.

She stood up suddenly, knocking over the henna pots. She must find Shai now.

"By the altar, what is it you do?" Gayile cried out. "The veil is not arranged properly."

But Baraqua would not heed her. She must leave now, while boldness was in her. "I must use the privy," she said. She pulled back the betrothal veil and went out. She would run east and follow the path behind Eden to the clearing where Shai and the other vine dressers lived. *Shai, I come.*

But in front of the tent stood Mahal and Dinah, the revered mother and father of Jared. Dinah's delicate face was rosy with excitement and she looked beautiful in a gown adorned with a few small river pearls sewed into the bodice. Mahal was tall and somber in his elder's robe, the look of Seth and Adam strong in his face. She had not been this near the elder and his wife in several years. She lowered her eyes, trying to appear docile.

"You have lifted the veil before the time," Mahal said, but his eyes were merry. "Our son must not see you so before the ceremony." The dignified elder's words sounded practiced, an attempt at a lighthearted tendency that was not in his nature. He was obviously nervous. And why wouldn't he be? His precious son was soon to be joined to a woman he probably believed was without remarkable qualities.

Dinah put her hand on Baraqua's arm. Dinah, *God will judge.* Her renown was of a woman wiser than her years who bore all suffering with utmost dignity; one whose prayers before the incense burners might last all night. Dinah's face was open, artless, and Baraqua knew the woman would accept her new daughter-in-law without question because Dinah completely trusted divine movement. She spoke to her husband in soft admonishment. "It is improper to tell a woman how to arrange her veil."

Mahal ducked his head in the way of men who are helpless against their wives' wisdom. Yet on his face Baraqua saw absolute adoration for Dinah.

"He does not embarrass me," Baraqua said quickly, politely. She did not want to hurt them. Since it was now impossible to escape to the privy or anywhere else, she would leave a slightly favorable impression of herself with Jared's long-suffering parents. Shame would come to them as well for what she planned to do.

Dinah took Baraqua's hands in hers and Baraqua was surprised at how rough they were. Dinah never shirked duty just because she was a Seed Bearer's wife. She was often seen in the open fields, her face streaming sweat as she beat out new flax with the others.

"We praise the God of heaven and earth that you were sent to our son's dream," Dinah said with absolute sincerity. "We have prayed since the day of his conception for the perfect bride."

Baraqua started with surprise. These people had prayed for her. Her despair deepened. How unhappy Dinah would be if she knew how wrong the dream angel's choice had been. These guileless people deserved someone better.

She heard herself speaking. "I... to marry your son is—" She could think of nothing else.

"Words are unnecessary," Mahal said. "You are truly lovely, and we are proud."

Dinah lowered the veil and arranged it around Baraqua's shoulders, then she and Mahal put their arms through hers on each side and guided her toward the brightly lit perimeter of the betrothal canopy. Baraqua looked neither to the right nor left, numb with trepidation. Why did Shai not step out of the crowd and claim her? Could she throw off the veil and declare to the entire clan that she could not be united to Jared in good conscience? But she did not know how to do this. Dinah and Mahal guided her to the tall young man beneath the canopy. Jared was splendid in the robe of a bridegroom, as though he had been born to wear it. She forced herself to look at him through the delicate veil. She saw something she had not expected. In Jared's eyes was suffering.

CHAPTER 10

The sons of God saw that the daughters of men were fair—
GENESIS 6:2

The sun was high when Baraqua woke in the betrothal tent. She threw off the thin linen covering, willing herself to alertness. It was the custom for the betrothed woman and her mother to sleep within that tent every night until the nuptials, but Gayile was not there. Baraqua heard voices outside the tent: Gayile, Basmat, and Havah. It must be almost midday and Baraqua bit her lip in frustration. She had been so sure she would wake in the night. She had packed a few belongings, and it would have taken only a few minutes to arrive at Shai's tent. They could have been far out to sea in the old fishing boat by now.

She quickly put on the betrothal gown she had taken off the night before. The scent of the oils of preparation from the night before were still strong on her. She touched the mass of braids that ringed her head. The first thing she would do once she left the mountain would be to comb out her hair and bury her betrothal gown. Let the despised garment be food for worms.

There was water scattered with rose petals in a basin. She washed her face, rubbed oil of gardenia into her wrists, and rinsed her mouth with water and soda rock. Then she picked up her cloth bag of belongings and stepped outside. The women were sitting on low stools, carding wool. Several of Basmat and Havah's younger children played with puffs of wool at their feet. She stifled her frustration. She would have to be canny if she wanted to get away. There was never solitude for a betrothed woman or man until the nuptials were completed.

Basmat smiled up at her out of her perpetual contentment, wool and children all around her. "You are the envy of every virgin in the camp," she said, as though the very thought of it brought her even more contentment. Life was one long stream of contentment when one was Basmat.

"The oils of preparation are having their effect," Havah said. "See how her countenance radiates desire to conceive her husband's son."

The others raised palms in agreement. "So God Most High has ordained," murmured Gayile happily, without a trace of acknowledgement that she even remembered Baraqua's words from the night before. Other women began to arrive. They brought food and handiwork. They would eat and offer advice the rest of the day. She must leave while she could.

"Come eat some fruit, daughter," Gayile said, gesturing to a large bowl full of fragrant pomegranates. No one seemed to notice the cloth satchel across Baraqua's shoulder.

"Where is Bathshae?" Baraqua said.

"In her tent with Obed, as usual," Gayile said, and sighed. Gayile kept to herself what others could only guess she believed, that Obed's misshapen body and dim mind must be the result of hidden sin in Bathshae or her husband.

"I must see her about a matter," Baraqua said, and ran out of the clearing before anyone could protest.

At the less populated eastern border of the camp was the tent where Bathshae lived with her husband Obadiah and the child Obed.

"Sister?" Baraqua called out as she stood a few steps from the tent.

"Enter with the blessing of God," Bathshae responded and Baraqua ducked inside before Bathshae's neighbors could notice her. The inside of the tent smelled of unaired bed coverings and of lamps that needed cleaning. Because of Obed's limitations Bathshae had little time for the exertions of housekeeping. She sat on her rumpled sleeping pallet with the little boy on her lap. Obed stared at Baraqua out of watery eyes as she approached and sat down. Then he recognized her and smiled broadly, revealing severely crooked teeth. He would be Bathshae's baby all his days.

"Blessed be the womb that will soon carry Anointed One," Bathshae said with a warm smile. She touched her fingers to her forehead in deference.

"Don't do that," Baraqua said in rebuke. "I am and always will be unworthy." She felt for the thousandth time the sting of contrast between her own restless, self-preoccupied character and Bathshae's serene and generous one. "It's too bad you are already married," she said crossly to her sister. "You would be the perfect wife for Jared."

Bathshae laughed in her open way. "What a thought!" she said, clearly intrigued. A strand of hair slipped from her head covering and she pushed it back. She had been lovely on her nuptial day, but constant care of Obed had made her fatigued and thin.

Baraqua gripped her sister's hands. "I have something to tell you that no one else must know of," she whispered. She hoped sharing her great secret with Bathshae was the right thing.

"What then?" Bathshae said, her brow creased in concern.

"I leave the mountain this very hour and will try to persuade Shai to come with me. I will never return."

Obed smiled even more broadly. He put out a soft little hand, groping for Baraqua's hand. Baraqua pulled her hand away as subtly as she could. She would admit to no one that she never wanted to be near Bathshae's son.

Bathshae looked more confused than Baraqua had anticipated. "I did not realize accepting your duty was so repulsive to you," she said simply. Baraqua saw the disappointment in her sister's eyes and it made her want to contradict what she had just said. But her despair was too strong. She had to face what had become her reality.

"I cannot marry the Seed Bearer and I know no other way out since we are already betrothed. I will leave whether Shai is with me or not."

Bathshae opened her mouth to speak, but at that moment Obed's face began to redden. Bathshae pulled a small earthen pot toward her. She lifted Obed's tunic and set him over the pot. A foul odor filled the tent as the child eliminated, his short, malformed legs stretched before him. Bathshae covered the pot with a cloth, set it outside the tent, and rearranged Obed's tunic and undergarment.

"You believe my lot in life is too difficult," Bathshae said.

Baraqua was caught off guard. Bathshae had never challenged Baraqua's loyalty to the little boy. Bathshae began to stroke Obed's thick, tangled hair. "You and I have always vowed not to hold secrets from one another, yet I never confessed to you that I did not love Obadiah when he first set the laurel branch before our father's tent and professed his bride dream."

"I would never have guessed," Baraqua said, genuinely surprised. "Why did you never tell me?"

"Because I decided to trust the dream instead of my feelings," Bathshae said. "I feared I would lose my resolution if I spoke of it to anyone, or that discontent might begin to gnaw at my heart like a rat among apples. I went under the nuptial canopy believing that the Creator still guides the hearts and dreams of men and that he knew what I needed." She looked down almost shyly. "I never wanted to marry at all. I dreamed of joining Akliah in the prayer caves." Her voice was so low Baraqua could hardly hear her.

"But you looked so content that day," Baraqua protested, remembering Bathshae's rose-tinted cheeks as she stood before her bridegroom. She felt a surge of anger. "Why didn't you tell our father of this higher calling in your heart? He would have allowed you to go to the caves." But would he have? He would certainly have opposed her going after he refused Shai to her. She was glad she had made the choice to go without his blessing.

Bathshae rummaged in a basket, brought out a piece of bread, and gave it to Obed. The child began to gnaw, still staring at Baraqua through his odd, bright eyes. Limited though he was, she sometimes wondered if Obed could read her heart.

"My mind does not work apart from the traditions of our people like yours does, Baraqua," Bathshae said. "I accept what must be while you fight for what you want, even if it is not possible to obtain." She looked down, as though she was embarrassed that she had said so much. "It has always been so with us, this difference," she continued. "Remember the man at the lake? You spent too many hours after that night pining on those shores in Elda for a creature that could not have been human. It is as though you cannot receive the world as it is, as though only the unobtainable is acceptable." She wiped saliva from Obed's chin. "I think that season after the lake set your heart to seek your own way. It is transferred now to your determination to have Shai at whatever cost." She rearranged the child on her knee. "Do you think it is by chance that the wound in your ankle healed poorly and that you still bear the scar?"

Baraqua stared at a broken oil lamp in the corner of the tent. "Wounded ankle, wounded heart," she said.

"It was a danger to your soul, that small rebellion," Bathshae said. "Forsaking duty will not heal either of those wounds."

Baraqua's gut tightened. In the white betrothal gown, she felt even more like a picture of pure deceit than she had the night before. What a waste the people's trust in her was. Bathshae's intuition about her had always been correct. Today, her sister's counsel was strong, and Baraqua hated it. "It was easier for you to obey the bride dream because you are naturally sweet and good," she said to her sister.

Bathshae took Baraqua's hand. Her grip was unusually tight. "Sweetness does not matter. We must each respond to what we have been given. Loyalty is everything."

"You truly believe that?" Baraqua said. "You would have me play wife to one I don't love?"

"I do not call it play." There was firm conviction in Bathshae's tone. "You don't know the future or how things will change between you and the man Jared. I learned to love Obadiah." She scowled, then ordered her expression. "And no matter what our mother thinks, I believe Obed is a gift."

Baraqua felt ashamed. She would never tell Bathshae that she almost agreed with their mother.

Obed leaned toward Baraqua. It was his sign that he wanted his aunt to hold him. Reluctantly she pulled the unwieldy little body onto her knees and Obed looked up, adoring and happy. She turned away. The child's blank innocence was a terrifying contrast to what she knew she was.

"I admit that I am skilled in very little; that is no secret to anyone," Bathshae said quietly. "Yet a quiet heart is worth something, and I guard my heart by yielding joyfully to what must be."

"Who is to say what must be?" Baraqua said. She paused. "Will you despise me when I leave?" she whispered.

Tears rose in Bathshae's eyes. "When you are far away and believe yourself happy, will what I think matter?"

CHAPTER 11

At twilight on the evening before her nuptials, Baraqua slipped from the tent of preparation. Her mother had gone to help a niece laboring in the birthing tent, and Havah and Eha had finished their final anointings of Baraqua's body in preparation for the next day. Dark elation seized her as she ran toward the vineyards. Except for the plaited hair and white betrothal gown, she felt like the girl she had been on those evenings she and Shai had met, cherishing their secret meetings. The familiar scents of misted grasses and of angel blossoms half closed against the coming night brought back the excitement of those days just before she had entered the prayer caves, a lifetime ago it seemed.

She kept to the low foliage until she reached the vines that gave the best fruit on the mountain, for it was there that Shai often worked past twilight. He was digging among some of the newly pruned vines, for the grape harvest had passed. She stood a little apart to watch the way hair curled at the nape of his neck and the muscles of his arms tensed as he turned over the earth around the plants. How she still loved him—

Shai looked up, leaned his tool against the arbor, and looked at her without a word. It was already too dark to see fully what was in his eyes. He did not come to her as he would have before. "You risk much on the eve of your nuptials," he said, and the old warmth was not in his voice. "There are people everywhere, Baraqua. Your cousin Awan has a hundred eyes."

"I don't care," Baraqua said as she came closer and stood before him. "Kiss me," she said. "Make it like it was before."

"Like it was before?" He said it as though he did not know what she spoke of.

"That old boat is probably still beached just below the cliffs," she said. "There will be enough moon tonight to find our way to the foundations of the earth like we always talked about."

"You scheme like this on the night before you marry?" He took up his tool again and poked at the soil around the ancient vines. "You've already taken the purity baths and your womb has been nourished with strong teas to receive the sacred seed of Jared. Would I dishonor him by stealing the purity of his betrothed?"

Baraqua put her hand to her throat where the warm pearl rested. "Through this jewel you pledged yourself to me," she said. "You unbound my hair, the privilege of a husband. You dishonor *me* if you do not keep your vow."

Shai reached out a hand as though to touch her, then drew it back. "You speak like one of the foolish women," he said. "I will spend the rest of my life regretting that season when my words ran as freely as an undammed stream." He stabbed the air with a finger. "I choose to do no more wrong than I have already done. I will live alone in my hut to the end of my days, but at least I will have my integrity."

"But you vowed—" Her stomach sickened. All those lonely months in the caves, begging God... for what? She had not considered that her prayer might be answered in Shai's change of heart instead of her own.

"Be at peace, Baraqua," Shai said, more gently. "Everything has changed with Jared's angelic visitation. Both of us are now responsible to something higher than ourselves."

"Our happiness matters, not responsibility to some tradition about stars and angels," she said, and felt the bitterness in her words.

The elders preached on the higher duties, but she would not accept it from Shai.

"You have been given a great gift, daughter of Rasujal," Shai said. "We all hope fervently that you will bear Anointed One."

She knew her voice was cold. "My name is Baraqua, not 'daughter of Rasujal.' And I say, let someone else bear Anointed One." Had what they shared meant anything to him?

"I feel the presence of a strange evil these past days, something that I've never sensed before," Shai said with fervency. Things are changing, though whether in the heavens or on the earth I do not know." His jaw worked. "We need Anointed One now."

"So," she said tightly. "You have bartered me for the mere hope of a man to lead you back to Eden."

"That is not what I meant," he said. He gestured toward the vines, gnarled and spare from the pruning. "Take a lesson from creation. If we don't prune these vines, next season's fruit will be meager."

Vines. Pruning. How she hated the way he was talking. She felt exposed, naked in her longings. How stupid she had been to believe he would fight to keep her. Instead, he talked as though he were her father. She knew she should walk away, dignified in her betrothal finery, the future wife of the most important man in the clan at that moment. But she could not make herself walk away. She raised her chin. She would try one more time. "It can be some of what it was," she said. "I will give myself to you unwedded. You may even take me now if you wish." She reached into her hair and tore out one of the fastenings that kept the braids in place. The unleashed hair rippled down her bodice. "I can conceive by you and everyone will think it is Jared's child."

Shai took up a blade of grass and twirled it between his fingers, his eyes fixated on it. Was he thinking of the nights he had run his hands into her hair? Had he wanted to cleave to her then?

"I have never seen you so beautiful as tonight," he said. "But forbidden fruit is never what one thinks it will be, as the forebear Eve can tell you." He raised his digging tool to his shoulder as though preparing to leave. "This day I choose what is right instead of indulging in ghosts of the past."

Her hands tingled with shock. It wasn't possible. "At least tell me you will always love me," she said. She thought of the man who had walked to her on the lake all those years before. The memory often came to her when she was lonely. Bathshae's strong words came back to her. Had she only traded that mysterious man for Shai? Had her mind been right when she had believed Shai loved her?

"None of us belongs to ourselves, Baraqua," Shai said. "The plants I tend depend on me for their life. They belong to me and I to them."

What were these high-minded musings when there was love to be partaken of? she thought impatiently. "I belong to myself and no one else," she said. She felt helpless against all the talk of duty and self-sacrifice, shamed by it. How could any person live beyond the confines of their own inclinations?

"The bride-dream owns you, whether you understand that or not," he said. "Tend the dream and produce fruit. Besides, I am not worth squandering your honor for."

"True, you aren't," Baraqua said impulsively, glad to hurt him. She yanked the pearl from her throat and held it out to him. He would not dare take back the symbol of his pledge. He folded her fingers over the white jewel on its slender strand and pushed it to her heart. She felt her heart quicken at his touch. *Love me,* she pleaded silently. He turned and disappeared into the trees. The pearl felt suddenly too heavy to bear.

CHAPTER 12

Observe everything that takes place in the sky, how the lights
do not change their orbits, and the luminaries which are in heaven,
how they all rise…and do not defy their appointed order.
I ENOCH 2:1

Michael hovered in his accustomed place within the constellation of Bethuleh, observing Gabriel's grace as the archangel spanned the dome of the sky like a blast of light. No shooting star could outpace the great messenger, though some on earth had mistaken his form for that cosmic phenomenon. Would that every creature was as quick to obey as Gabriel, Michael thought as the great messenger came to rest beside him near the star of Tsemech.

"Do they descend this night?" Michael said. There was no reason to ask, for all heaven knew by now what had taken place when Semjaza went before the Throne. But he would hear it from Gabriel himself, who himself had just come from the seventh heaven.

"Yes, this night," Gabriel said. "All two hundred in the cohort swear allegiance to the plan and will descend to the Mount of Ermon." The archangel's expression betrayed the intensity of his grief. "Semjaza feared facing the fires of Tartarus alone on the final day, so insists the others vow to bring all to completion." Gabriel was a sparkling eddy of movement, as though he were already restless for another divine errand.

Michael gazed down on the earth where half of the flat disk was shrouded in moonlit darkness while the orbiting sun brought warmth and life to the other side. "I'm sure making this pact is no great sacrifice for the others, for, like Semjaza, they are already in bondage to their lust," Michael said. He wanted to weep at the change in Semjaza's glorious cohort of Watchers. It would be humanity's loss, for the celestial beings who had once watched closely over their souls would become enemies.

"They forfeit much," Gabriel keened. "The day of the damned has begun."

"I saw the change when Semjaza began to keep company with Lucifer," Michael said. "I told myself that his association with the great rebel was for some purpose known only to God. I should have challenged our friend before bitterness began to darken his countenance." He returned his gaze to the earth. To mourn too deeply would help nothing; Semjaza had made his choice. Because his sin was angelic, committed out of complete awareness of what he did, his damnation was fixed and there was no chance for repentance. This was unlike the human condition since human beings, by their nature, could be drawn to sin from sources outside themselves. Human sin was therefore imperfect and their souls redeemable.

"What were Semjaza's demands of the Throne?" Michael said.

"Permanent access to the earth, promising he would draw humanity closer to divine will," Gabriel said.

Michael sighed. "As though God did not see through the lie. We all know Azazel was probably nearby, giving Semjaza strength in the fullness of evil he does not possess yet."

"If Azazel descends with them—" Michael could not finish, for the thought was appalling. The Watcher Azazel had turned from God long before Semjaza, shadowing Lucifer like fumes above a sulfurous lake. He imagined Azazel, Semjaza, and their ilk burrowing like moles into villages and tents, plumbing depths of depravity they could never accomplish without taking the form of men. It was against the natural order, but it would take place.

The light within the constellation increased as Uriel and Raphael appeared, Uriel exuding righteous indignation and Raphael diffusing healing scents. "High captain," Uriel said to Michael. "This very minute the Watchers take council at the ceiling of the sky. A day of heavenly mourning has been declared in the heavens."

"I marvel that God Most High would allow such an unholy breach of cosmic law," Michael mused. Yet he did not question it. The Creator's scrupulous respect for the free will of his creatures was immutable. He gazed beyond the earth to the uninhabited worlds that stretched beyond the sky dome. God had planned for human beings to explore the cosmos endlessly. He had laughed in his joy when the week of creation was complete and the cosmos brimmed with mystery and beauty. But the sin at the tree in Eden had greatly decreased man's ability to move beyond the range of birds. And it had not taken long for most of them to become too ignorant to care about God's original intentions. They spent their petty lives of less than a thousand years content with the dust beneath them instead of the star fields beyond their sight.

"Indeed, it is a breach of cosmic law," Gabriel said. "Yet we have all taken the form of men when appearing to human beings, especially in the days when Adam first came out of Eden, helpless against the wild, broken world. But to violate the boundaries between flesh and spirit in such a way is not—" He broke off, as though to say more would be a blasphemy in itself.

Michael put his hand on the hilt of his sword. "We will not defile ourselves with thoughts of where this will lead," he said.

There was a sudden commotion in the vitreous firmament above them.

"That is the cohort at their vile council," Uriel said. "Prepare yourselves for the sullying of heaven."

The four spirited upward where the three lower heavens joined the higher levels, where laws of time and place had no governing power as on earth. At the floor of the fourth heaven a swarm of coarse looking, hulking creatures jostled for places around one of the portals of descent in the River of Stars, that thick band of celestial bodies that spanned the sky. They bore thin resemblance to what they had been, and where they had gathered, a tarlike substance oozed over the crystalline pavement, the offscouring of their sin.

"A pathetic remnant," Uriel said. "To give up glory for the pulsations of the flesh—"

"Do they see what they have become?" Gabriel said.

"The wicked are blind to their own rot, whether human or angelic," Michael said. He stared in revulsion at the once-brilliant angels who now writhed, shadow-like, jostling for position at the lip of the portal, casting their vacant eyes on the earth below to better see the women they lusted for. "Though they have made themselves repulsive, they will appear extraordinary to human women who want more in a mate than the frailty of the human male. Those females will not discern that by taking the Watchers into their embrace, they damn their own souls."

Michael suppressed a twinge of dejection at the sight, for that gesture would be unseemly in a noble angel. Even in his mourning over the Watchers, he knew the divine scheme would not fail.

CHAPTER 13

*And they were in all two hundred who descended
in the days of Jared on the summit of Mount Hermon, and
they called it Mount Hermon because they had sworn and
bound themselves by mutual imprecations upon it.*
1 ENOCH 6:6

*Look at what Azazel has done, who hath taught
all unrighteousness on earth and revealed the
eternal secrets which were made and kept in
heaven, which men were striving to learn.*
1 ENOCH 9:6

Semjaza the Watcher peered through the River of Stars, that dazzling wonder of the lower heavens. Far below rose the wide, lush summit of Mount Ermon, where shepherds groveled at their lowly vocation. Once he and the others touched the mountain, he would seek out the woman called Baraqua. Before the night was over her womb would nest the embryo of one of the new lords of the earth, who would take the place of Adam's lineage. How delicious victory was. He had received from the Throne everything he had known enough to ask for. The anticipation of what was ahead was a pleasure in itself.

He studied his cohort, gathered in cacophony around the portal. The sight was a startling contrast to their formerly peaceful cooperation. He had not counted on such disorder. Would he be able to take the earth without disciplined collaboration?

"Odious scum!" Semjaza shrieked in the manner of human men berating their slaves. He enjoyed the shock of the insult on the faces of his chiefs and their underlings. "Where is the lookout who is to announce the coming of Azazel and the key?"

Armaros spoke, eleventh among Semjaza's chiefs-of-twenty. "I have flown to and fro throughout the outer heavens this night and know that Azazel still rides with Lucifer on the backwinds of Oblivion," he said. Armaros's once-musical voice sounded like a wild dog with the foaming sickness. His appearance was of a trunk of deadwood that burns from within and perpetually collapses to ashes and regenerates.

"Azazel keeps me waiting to spite me," Semjaza said with a growl of rancor that surprised him in its force. "If he did not hold the key, I would descend without him." He gave vent to his rage in a dance, transforming to a writhing fire of demonic splendor, a glorious demonstration of his transmutation. The others scuttled cockroach-like away from the portal, staring at their chieftain out of the spheres of what had once been angelic eyes that blazed with compassion and righteousness but now pulsed with the wretchedness of ghouls.

"We must obey Azazel's authority," rasped the chief-of-twenty called Baraqijal, as clumps of maggots fell from his mouth.

Semjaza stopped dancing. "Do not lecture me about authority. It was I, not Azazel, who risked all to obtain permission for this deed. While I braved the Throne, that leech cowered out of sight. Whether Lucifer's lapdog comes with us or not, you must show your allegiance to my plan by swearing with me, agreeing to the deed we undertake."

"We are helpless against our desire for women and must swear with you," said Araqiel, another of the chiefs. "For the men of earth have bred copiously, and their daughters are comely and alluring. There are enough of them for us all." Araqiel's voice sounded like a cold wind that scrapes a sandy wasteland. He had once reigned over the shining dome of the earth and the glowing stars imbedded in it, so that men might always look upward in awe of God's majesty.

"Swear then, for I must hear it from your mouths. I will not take the chance of bearing the consequence alone," Semjaza said.

"Tartarus looms!" the two hundred keened in unison. "Yet we are compelled to go with you, for shackles already hold us."

"Give me a sign, each of you," Semjaza said with a snarl. One by one, starting with the chiefs-of-twenty and then the chiefs-of-ten, the members of the cohort came forward, offering into a heap before Semjaza some manifestation of what he had once been and now rejected: shards of holy light; the remnants of voices of unspeakable beauty; shredded wings of swift obedience; cast-off garments of purity. When they had finished, Semjaza tossed the remnant of his own chaste heart onto the heap and fire from his own mouth devoured the offerings. "It is finished," he said. The floor of heaven shook and from higher up was the sound of a mourning hymn.

A presence of unspeakable darkness descended over the horde and Semjaza's confidence drained away like water. It was Azazel, more versed in Luciferian mutiny than any other fallen celestial being. The potency of the Luciferian force within that arch-Watcher made all of them recoil. But Semjaza stood firm, his head high. All he wanted from Azazel was access to the summit of Ermon. He, Semjaza, must be first to descend, woo, and wed. He wondered if droplets of water still beaded like liquid silver along the girl's smooth arms as she swam in the lake of Elda. Surely she was waiting for him.

Semjaza drew himself to his full, towering height. "I am impatient to be gone from here," he said, avoiding Azazel's eyes.

"Do not challenge me, for I can unlock the portal or transform you all to dust as I will," Azazel said. His voice was so ominous that Semjaza could barely keep to his place.

He forced stability to his tone. "You cannot undo our immortality, no matter what your powers are," he said.

Azazel laughed, and in the sound Semjaza imagined a million wind-bleached human skulls clattering over a cliff.

"Unlock! Unlock!" the cohort screeched in unison. "We burn to take women tonight!"

"I will do all in my good time, you nest of stench. And not doubt that I will take more wives than all of you together," Azazel growled, while vipers dark as ash mingled with the words from his mouth. The angel produced a key of what looked like earthly, rusted iron and with a careless laugh tossed it through the River of Stars and disappeared after it.

Semjaza spewed a curse on Azazel, the power of it sputtering across the sky and dousing stars. I must be first! To diffuse his rage and humiliation he plunged through the portal and felt himself falling down the vault of the sky, unable to move as freely through the air as he had before. He seemed to be half-captive now to the laws of falling bodies that governed the earth. He was changing and he must accept it, for this was what he had pled for at the Throne. The others were also descending and Semjaza watched them transform to shafts of light that ripped against the airs of earth, turning like wheels of fire, writhing like serpents as they hurtled past moon and sun. The summit of Ermon was growing larger. He watched what appeared to be fleshly feet appear at the extremity of his form and make contact with the summit of the mountain. He felt the sensation of the grassy earth beneath him. This was what it was to have human senses, to abandon his former estate and take upon himself human design. The others touched down around him, and as they did, dense stands of trees bordering the summit exploded in torrents of blue flame. He felt a flush of power, his essence drawn into the confines of earthly time and space. He cried out in elation, and the power of that cry split the cliffs that flanked the mountain.

Sheep careened down the slope and the summit exploded in flame. The bodies of what had been three men lay silent, burning like stalks of dried flax. A crevice opened out of the ruined cliffs and from the slit in the earth teemed a throng of fiends, prancing over the carnage with the laud of death in their mouths.

CHAPTER 14

Baraqua felt her bridegroom's hands tremble as he lifted the crown of white ginger blossoms from her hair. She did not look at him as he set down the bridal wreath on one of the fresh reed mats that covered the floor of the nuptial tent. So, it was done. She was now the wife of Jared the Seed Bearer. Shai's rejection the night before had left her in such shock that she had not found courage or clarity of mind to leave the mountain on her own. Shackles could not have made her feel more imprisoned than she did now.

According to custom, she would live with Jared in the lavishly embroidered nuptial tent for the first forty days of their marriage. She did not raise her eyes, for Jared was no fool. If she looked at him, he would see that she did not blush with anticipation at the lovemaking to come, the obligatory act that would seal their union for as long as they lived. He would know in her eyes that she longed for someone else's arms.

Beyond the clearing where the nuptial tent was pitched, the Sethites danced. They would celebrate half the night among the glow worms and sparks flying from the fragrant fires. Melodies from flute and harp wafted through the trees as the young men sang a new song about the woman who would soon bear Anointed One. The tent itself was a masterpiece. Eve had sewn and lavishly embroidered it long ago for the marriage of her son Seth to his twin sister Azura, for to marry one's sister had been the custom in that early era when few inhabited the earth. That was in the time when Eden still glowed with heavenly beauty and the tree Adam called Life still flourished at its center.

Baraqua turned her eyes to the embroidered mural on the wall beside her. The body of Eve was depicted emerging from the side of Adam on the sixth day of creation, fashioned from a bone of his body. The teaching was everywhere in Sethite life: woman receives her life from man and man is incomplete without woman, for his bone is the source of her body and then her body bears the bone of a son. Male and female together composed the image of God.

She glanced at Jared and away. There was nothing false or forced in his smile. "You are lovely," he said. He leaned toward her and began to unloose her hair. He smelled of clean linen and sandalwood. His hands were bigger than she had thought, and warmer. He took his time, sliding his fingers into the long waves that fell across her shoulders and along her back as lamplight caught in the shining mass. "I had no idea you were so beautiful. What an honor to be first to see the full glory of your hair."

Baraqua recoiled inwardly at his touch but forced herself not to move. *You are wrong in this, son of Mahal. Another has put his hands into this hair on a day as white as a pearl, a day sealed in my heart that someone like you will never understand.*

He caressed her cheek. He was a good man, well-favored in face, form, and mind. His breath was sweet, there was nothing coarse or obtuse about him, and his education at the feet of Adam and Seth had been impeccable. He knew every intricacy of both stars and trees, the meaning of times and seasons, and all the rubrics of Sabbath worship. He had been groomed to perfection for a Seed Bearer's duties.

"Don't be afraid, my beauty," Jared said. "We will make a great son together this night."

"I'm not your beauty," she said hastily. She regretted her bluntness immediately, but how could words be anything but awkward at such a moment? She had to prevent the consummation, that one means she had available to have the marriage annulled.

Jared began to untie the fastenings at the front of her gown. With each one he whispered, "Come, Anointed One." Tradition; the inevitability of stars; the hasty dreams of mere men. Was that all she was worth? He pushed the nuptial garment from her shoulders, and she wanted to weep with the unfairness of it. This man deserved a wife who adored him, while she was destined for Shai. If she showed no interest maybe he would become discouraged and lie down to sleep with the intent to resume the consummation later.

But it was as though he read her thoughts. His expression changed and he leaned back on a cushion and took a handful of berries from one of the trays of fruit Baraqua's mother Gayile had left in the tent. "Shai is a good man," he said abruptly, studying her face.

"What do you mean?" she said carefully, trying to control her surprise. She had not counted on this. How could he know about Shai?

Jared popped a berry into his mouth. "Just because I've spent my youth preparing for the life of an elder and prophet doesn't mean I don't notice who moves the heart of a beautiful woman," he said. "If we had a choice—" He paused. "But neither of us has a choice, Baraqua. All we have is this night and each other."

Baraqua flushed. He sounded like Shai the night before in the orchard. Duty. Destiny. Did these men truly believe there was no room for the inclinations of the heart? Let them think as they would. The imagination of prophets and the tracks of sly stars had tried to seal her destiny, but she could change that.

Jared was staring at the pearl in the hollow of her throat. She had meant to throw it into the river in her anger the night before, but could not do it. She would tell this man nothing about the pearl or the one who had given it to her in pledge. All that should concern him was impregnating her.

"I'm not going to take you against your will, if that's what you're assuming," he said calmly. "Until you no longer love another man it is senseless for us to become one flesh."

She could think of no response. She felt flustered, cornered. She and Shai had always been discreet about their times together.

"Do you think it is only a son I want?" he said. "Your love is as necessary to me as a dozen sons."

"No man thinks like that," she said, trying to cover her astonishment. She fastened the bridal gown quickly. He had seen her nakedness but was not going to implant his seed. She was still free. The lamplight made shadows and light of his even features, the physical perfection of those in the direct Sethite lineage. There was nothing of common lust in his eyes. One side of his mouth turned up slightly, as though he wanted to smile but thought better of it. "Let us speak now of that man who sits unseen between us. We will talk of him and then put him aside forever," he said.

"You believe it to be that easy?" she said. "You know nothing of such things." For the second time she rebuked herself. She had just vowed to give no hint, but in a few words had told Jared far too much.

"How then will we live in peace together?" he said. She hated his forthrightness compared to her conniving to hide the truth. She wanted only to be in Shai's arms, to feel his warmth and devotion. She wanted to be anywhere but facing Jared the Seed Bearer, her husband by her own choice, however unwilling. She thought of the moment of hush in the betrothal tent when Eve had anointed her with the sacred oil of Eden. The precious fluid had been wasted.

"Perhaps you too love another," she said. She would not let him keep the attention on her.

"Whether I do or not, it is we two who have made vows," he said. He took up a piece of purple fruit and ate from it as though he was ravenously hungry. She could read nothing in his face now. "Very well, wife," he said when he had tossed the pit aside. "I will neither ask nor expect anything from you on this night of nights." He looked confident in the way the privileged always do, his garment perfect in fit across his shoulders and the shape of his neck and jaw as regal as Adam's. Maybe he had said this because he was already deciding she was unsuitable. Perhaps he himself would annul.

He wiped his hands and beard with a scented napkin and sat up straight. "Since you aren't interested in receiving my seed and won't talk about the vinedresser, I will tell you about myself," he said.

So— Jared wasn't inflamed with desire for her after all. He too was shirking duty. Hers would not be the story of so many women who whispered with nervous laughter in the weeks after the nuptials about their bridegrooms' vigorous ways. She would have no story like her sister Basmat.

"I spent my youth in the tents of Adam and Seth, as you know, learning the mysteries of the cosmos in the manner the Creator taught Adam and Eve," Jared was saying. "My Edenese was so fluent I dreamed in that language of paradise."

"It is a language beautiful to the ear," Baraqua agreed carefully. She cared nothing for Edenese. But she would listen for the next hour if that was what he wished to drone about. He would fall asleep eventually. She would go to Shai one more time, and if he would not come with her, she would descend the steep trail beside the western cliffs and find the fishing boat herself. She must force herself this time, for the moonlight would still be adequate. Tomorrow would be too late.

"Once I asked Adam why knowing Edenese was important," Jared was saying. "After all, the garden is forbidden to us now and the people of earth speak another language. But Adam would always say, 'We must keep the ancient tongue alive so that when Anointed One appears the people will already know the words of paradise.'"

He paused as though to discern her interest, but Baraqua kept her expression bland. The people would forget her on the day Jared stood again beneath the canopy with Tamara or Solonj. Wasn't any womb adequate to nurture a Seed Bearer's sons?

"Later I learned to write our present language in the cyphers my grandfather Kenan and aunt Zyla developed," Jared continued. "If I could choose, I would be a scribe."

"My father is chief among scribes yet did not take the time to instruct his daughters in the art of writing," Baraqua said. She did not resent it. She had no passion for cyphers as some did.

His smile was wry. "Sometimes I resent my childhood. But I spent hours listening to Eve's stories of the days in Eden when she and Adam co-ruled with God's divine council there before they ate of forbidden food." He stared at one of the oil lamps. "She would weep when she recounted how that exquisite garden was suspended above the earth in those days as a kingdom of its own, long before the regression of the cosmos and the spread of shadows."

"You speak as though I know nothing about our people's history," Baraqua said.

"Very well then, my bride, shall I speak of matters of the heart, which is usually of interest to women?"

"Why would you tell me what lies within your heart when you accuse me of loving another?" She would not say Shai's name within this tent. If only Jared would grow tired.

"What if my heart did tumble in my chest at the sight of some of you beauties?" he said. "I knew I would have no say in the matter. The dream angel would make the choice."

She reached for a fig, peeled it, and took a bite of the sweet, gritty fruit. "You always seemed indifferent to the life of the camp," she said.

"The nature of my birth made my parents too anxious about my safety. Perhaps their overprotection made me shy," he said.

Something rang at the back of her mind. *The nature of my birth. Safety.* She thought of the ballads about Adam, Seth, and the other Seed Bearers sung on feast days. But there had been something odd about the first vision of Mahal, Jared's father. His was not a story made much of like the others were. And why didn't they sing more about Jared? Many did not even call him by his name, addressing him as "son of Mahal." It had never occurred to her until now that this was unusual.

"You were born in the woods, midwifed by your father—" She tried to remember more. There had been something about foreigners attending the birth.

He looked suddenly uneasy. "Yes, I was born in the manner you say."

"And weren't strangers on the mountain that night?" Something perverse in her wanted to make him speak of what she could see bothered him. *Jared.* The name did not have the same sound as the other elders' names. It was Edenese. "What is the meaning of your name?" she said. She heard stealth in her voice and felt the prick of intuition. What she learned might benefit her.

He tried to take her hand, but she drew back. "Is my name's true meaning that important to you?" he said.

"Yes." She would insist. He looked like a boy half afraid.

But he continued to resist. "It is far more important that, out of all the women of our clan, your face came to my bride dream," he said. "With you beside me I won't have to bear the imminent evil alone." His eyes seemed to plead.

The night was very warm, but Baraqua felt suddenly chilled. "What evil?" The word hung in the air like something with power to bring alive the shadows in the corners of the tent. Her heart pounded. She must have known the meaning of the name, once, but something had made her forget. She knew if he told her now, it would change everything. Sometimes shadows must come to life.

Jared spoke in a rush. "Forgive me; I shouldn't have said anything about this tonight. This was to be a night of rejoicing and… love."

"But it isn't either of those things, is it?" Baraqua said. She wondered why she felt so frightened.

"The meaning of my name is no secret for those who pay attention," Jared said dully. "Jar-ed means 'In his day they shall come down.'"

More fragments of the story rushed together in her mind. "Yes, it was the morning of your birth and your father hid in a whirlwind with you beneath his arm and received the name."

Jared sounded suddenly exhausted. "Yes," he said. "My father saw unimaginable horrors from within the whirlwind. Not even Adam can decipher the vision's meaning and the people do not wish to think of it." His lips tightened. "And I may as well tell you that yesterday I received my own virgin prophecy. What I saw as I prayed and fasted in preparation for our nuptials confirmed my father's vision."

"What did you see?" Baraqua said, her voice rising. Why had he kept this from her?

"I wish you would just let me comfort you with my love," he said with the same pleading look. "We have the rest of our life together to speak of what came to my vision."

"I am not a child you must protect," Baraqua said. She made her voice calm, but she was hot with anger. "Why didn't your father assemble the people to announce your vision, as is the custom?"

He threw up his arms in frustration and let them fall. "Can you imagine such a thing as gathering the people in their festal garments while they prepared for the celebration, to tell them an enemy from the sky might soon invade their lives?"

"Enemy? Of what do you speak?" She said each word slowly.

"Out of the heavens will descend an incursion of—" His lips were ringed in tension. "The earth will be visited by… something… contrary to all that is pure and holy, the anti-glory of God." His voice trailed. He tried to begin again. "These beings will change what it is to be alive on earth. They will change how people think and what they worship. Those who love truth will be greatly tested."

She stared. How was it possible that she was now united to a man whose very identity bore such woe? If these ones from the sky were truly evil they would target the ones whose vision had foretold their coming. As part of Jared's family, she too would be in danger. Her throat tightened. She thought of the words she had repeated beneath the canopy. They bound her to this prophet of disaster for life.

"Why didn't you tell me about the vision when it happened?" She did not care if she sounded accusing.

"I tried. I searched for you last night until long after the sun hid its face."

Regret rushed in to replace her anger. What a fool she was. He had searched for her while she stood with Shai in the vineyard, begging him to love her again. Had he found her sitting like a proper maiden in the betrothal tent and told her the vision, she would have had a legitimate objection to the marriage. Her father would have insisted, on grounds of distress of soul.

"The angel of the bride dream should have chosen more wisely," she said. "I am not willing to bear this with you. You could have told me even under the canopy if necessary."

She thought of her hours with Shai; her defiance of her father and the escape to the prayer caves; the coming away in confusion and panic; marriage to one who would become the prey of a powerful adversary. Her life was unraveling.

"My father encouraged me to keep silence until after our forty days of lovemaking," he said. "I sensed you had gone to Shai last night, but I did not want to shame you by searching the vineyard. I have violated your trust and I beg you to forgive me."

"What kind of leader is more concerned with not upsetting his people than with their safety?" she said. "What kind of man disrespects his wife in this way?" The words gave her uneasy pleasure. He was not the perfect Seed Bearer after all.

"I have no defense," he said without hesitancy. "My father judged the matter wrongly and I was unwise to agree to it."

Your mistake has cost you, just as mine has cost me, she mused. But she felt lighter than she had since the moment Awan and Rojj brought her the news of Jared's bride dream. When this was over, she and Shai would be free to love again. Her father would see Shai's superiority over the duplicitous Jared.

"What is your plan when these beings arrive?" she said. She was biding time. She hardly cared what he said, for it would not involve her.

"I told you, my father thought it better to wait instead of devising strategy on the eve of my nuptials," he said. "And if I were to say I've thought of nothing but the vision it would bruise your feminine vanity."

He was right. Despite her own feelings, she would have resented it if his mind had been full of plans for a defense against the invasion instead of a new wife. But none of that mattered. Her objective was to break free. "I thought you Seed Bearers were supposed to be special, anointed," she said with a hint of mockery. "I see now that your minds tend toward the expedient, like everyone else."

He sounded discouraged. "Another man would have done it differently. But I am like my father, who has always preferred the company of his lovely wife over typical masculine pursuits."

Baraqua wondered how he could speak with such resignation when so much was at stake. She got up and began to pace. "I barely dare believe what I am hearing," she said.

"Please sit with me, Baraqua," Jared said. "I need you with me through whatever may happen."

She whirled to face him. "Sustain you? How can I respect a man who begs a woman for strength?"

Jared looked stricken. He licked his lips and stood up. "You assume the worst of me. But I still maintain that the dream angel makes no mistakes." He paused. "I confess that I have admired you since we were children."

"This is not the time to tell me this," she said. She relished the hardness in her heart and voice. "I married you out of obedience but without knowledge of a grave truth."

"You came to this tent with your own secret," he said.

"My secret, as you call it, bears no resemblance to yours," she answered. "I came to you a virgin, which satisfies the tradition."

"I did not suspect you were other than pure," he said. He drew back the door flap and stepped outside the tent. An owl called to its mate from a treetop and Baraqua heard the flutter of its wings as it left the tree. She felt an odd loneliness. Had her father been among those who knew of Jared's vision? A leading scribe would have been required to record from either Mahal or Jared what had taken place. If Rasujal did know and had chosen not to protect his youngest daughter from a risky union—

Traditions were everything to these men.

She left the tent and stood beside Jared. "I'm going to the privies," she said. This was her chance. She would have to leave the mountain in her nuptial gown.

"I'll go with you. White bears live in the cave not far from there," he said.

"I'm not afraid," she insisted. "I need time to think." She had decided she would not go directly to the elders. She wanted first to tell Shai the news and discuss what they would do.

A flash of light filled the clearing as though it were midday. A roaring sound filled the sky, the rumble of a rockslide. The light and sound dissipated as quickly as they had manifested.

"It came out of the skies to the west," Jared said. His hand went to his waist, but his flint dagger was not there. The sky lit up as bright as day again and the thunderous sound returned.

"This was in my vision," Jared said. His voice was hoarse. He took her shoulders in his hands. "Baraqua, they have come."

CHAPTER 15

...and the angels which kept not their first estate,
but left their own habitation—
JUDE 6

Jared's face was white as aphron. He gripped Baraqua's wrist and began to ran out of the clearing toward the western cliffs.

"I will not partake of this with you," she shouted. "I will live my own life." His hand on her arm hurt. A thorny branch ripped her nuptial gown as they ran into the trees, tearing the garment at the knee. The old wound in her ankle began to throb and her unloosed hair whipped at her face as she tried to keep stride.

"I have already played the coward by not warning the people," Jared shouted over his shoulder. "I will not fail in my duty now."

"May the shadows of the underworld swallow the people," she hurled back, furious, glad he did not seem to hear her blasphemy.

They passed the clearing where a silent angel had helped Adam build the first sacrificial altar on the day he was exiled from Eden. They ran alongside the vineyard where Baraqua had sought out Shai the night before, then tramped through a field of tender barley shoots.

"I hate you, I hate you," Baraqua repeated under her breath. If she fell, she feared Jared would drag her, oblivious of her difficulty to match his stride. When she thought her lungs would burst they reached the edge of the cliffs that overlooked the sea below. Jared stared, clinging to her hand, and Baraqua forced herself to look at the phenomenon in the west. Something like wheels of fire were spinning earthward through the stellar dust. The wheels seemed to unfold and became shafts of unearthly, frigid light as they descended against the backdrop of the night sky.

Jared's face was slick with sweat. "God of Adam, show mercy. How will I protect the people?"

"They seem... alive," Baraqua whispered. She hardly dared to breathe. The shafts of light disappeared over the western mountains and an explosion of fire rose into the night sky.

Jared's breath was sour with fear as he faced her. "This is the foment of my vision. Now you see why I could not explain what neither my father nor I understood ourselves."

Something was coming near the cliffs like a shooting star. In an instant a man's form with feet of fire and skin that glowed like the moon was hovering beyond the cliff where they stood. She looked at Jared to see his reaction, but he did not seem to see. The face was Shai's. "It is the man who walked upon the lake," she said, her voice breaking, going to her knees. Was this why she had loved the vinedresser, because as an adult he looked like the lake man of her youth? She had never been able to remember that face, only the eyes and the essence of his presence.

She laughed nervously. The man's form was coalescing further. He appeared more human every minute. It *was* Shai.

"I have found you, beauty of the lake," the man said. The voice was definitely Shai's in intonation, but the cadence of his speech was different.

"Someone is here, but I cannot see him," Jared said, looked wildly about him. How insignificant he looked beside the perfection of the being before her in the air. Jared's ordinariness, his earthliness suddenly repulsed her.

"It is my destiny to go with him," she said to Jared, gesturing to the man. "I only thought I loved Shai. It was the man on the lake all along."

"Who are you talking about?" Jared cried and clutched at her arm.

Baraqua shook him off. "The one I have waited for has come. You are destined for Solonj, not me."

"Are you mad?" Jared shouted. "My prophecy is fulfilled before my eyes and you speak like a frivolous girl."

"I am no girl, but a woman who understands love," she said. She would step off the cliff and Shai would catch her. She would be free. But when she turned to speak to the man again, no one was there.

Men and women were running out of the wood with torches. Their night garments slid from their shoulders and Baraqua could hardly identify some of the women with their unbound hair hanging around their faces. At the head of the group were Mahal and Dinah. Dinah was still in the gown she had worn for the ceremony and Baraqua guessed her new mother-in-law had been cleaning up after the feast, long after everyone else had gone to their tents.

"You are not injured?" Dinah said as she took Baraqua's hands in hers.

Baraqua could not think how to answer. What did Dinah want to hear? Some of the women began to weep, and men spoke loudly among themselves, disputing what was actually happening over the western mountains and what should be done. Some crowded at the edge of the cliffs to better see the violent conflagration creating a glow high into the sky, while others prayed on their knees.

Mahal ran to the edge of the cliff. His eyes were wild and he looked older to Baraqua than during the ceremony when he had lifted the cup of blessing over her and Jared.

"Now you see that the whirlwind spoke truth," Mahal wailed. "Now you will believe what I saw the day Jared was born. Yet now that it is upon me, I have no wisdom to apply the knowledge that has weighed on me all these years."

Enosh went to Mahal. He was the only one who seemed unphased by the what was happening across the sea. "But grandson Mahal, these who descend this night are heavenly beings sent from God. They mean to help us."

Mahal got to his feet and faced Enosh. "*Your* first prophecy was of a new method to bring up water from the ground when the wells went dry. Judge not therefore, for you have not endured the nightmare I have."

"I meant no disrespect," Enosh said, taking a step back.

"You insult God himself by suggesting that he sent this, for both I and Jared know great evil lies within these beings," Mahal said. Baraqua had never seen the mild-mannered elder angry. He stabbed a finger into the west. "Would God destroy his own mountains?" He was shaking violently, and Adam went to him and drew him away from the precipice.

"The mountains of Ermon were named 'place of the serpent' even in the era when Eve and I made our abode in Eden," Adam said. "Tomorrow will be a day of fasting as we all beg God and the holy angels for wisdom."

"What will become of the earth?" Baraqua heard her mother say from where she stood with Basmat and Eha beneath the trees.

"The earth will go on as before," Enosh said, gesturing expansively, his voice smooth with reassurance. "Things will be better, for beings of higher intelligence will be among us." He looked around the crowd. "I tell you, anyone who considers this a misfortune is a fool." But Baraqua heard gasps from some of the women.

"Do you defy the prophecies of your fellow elders?" Adam said. "It will not be the first time."

"Mahal and Jared are only men and whirlwinds can mean many things," Enosh retorted.

"Only men, Enosh?" Jared said. "A prophecy is valid when what it predicts takes place." He pushed his chin toward the raging fire. "Do your eyes deceive you?"

Enosh's face darkened, but Adam spoke. "Ermon lies on the thirty-third line of the earth, the number of the serpent. Lucifer is in this conflagration."

"Thirty-three is a number like any other," Enosh said, and Baraqua was astonished. Why would the son of Seth argue about such a matter as the table of numbers? It had never been done.

"I must beg forgiveness that I did not tell the people of my virgin vision yesterday," Jared blurted out. "But it concurs completely with my father's." His voice carried to the edge of the crowd. "Now I pledge myself to do all that I can." He groped for Baraqua's hand and she did not pull away. He was trembling. "My father chased dark forces from the cave on the night of my birth, and these who come out of the stars this night are of the same ilk. To fight them will take all our resources of prayer, fasting, and great cunning."

This was not the man who had pleaded with Baraqua for wisdom a few minutes before. And she knew he was not revealing all he knew about the incursion. He would hold it within, or the people might become too frightened to act.

"The son of Mahal does well," she heard someone in the crowd whisper.

But Mahal was staring at her. He no longer looked wild of eye but strode to her with strong intent. It was an expression very different from what it had been when he blessed she and Jared during the nuptial celebration.

"Though your hair is loosed of its plaits, you still wear your bridal garment," he said accusingly. He turned to Jared. "And you still wear your nuptial garment as well, something neither man nor woman ever puts on again after uniting in flesh." Sweat was beading on Mahal's forehead and the people's faces became even more grim at the sound of his accusing words.

The elation she had felt at seeing the face of Shai beyond the cliffs drained from her heart. Life on firm ground was a harsh contrast.

"You went to the nuptial tent hours ago," Mahal continued, focused on Jared now. "There was plenty of time for what needed to take place." He lifted his chin, his expression harsh as he addressed Jared. "We stand on the verge of a nightmare, yet you did not implant the seed of a child to ensure the safety of our lineage."

"Father—" Jared raised his hand with the intent to speak.

But Mahal was rounding on Baraqua again. "I blame you over my son, for it is a woman's duty to draw in seed through her allure." He ran a hand over his perspiring face. "Through a miracle, my son Jared has lived these sixty-five years unharmed. Then God gave him a bride unworthy."

Unworthy. Baraqua took a step back. Her father Rasujal pushed through the crowd to her side. "I call shame on this saying, for you, an elder of our people, heap slanders upon my daughter without knowing the matter fully," he said.

"Don't defend your willful offspring, scribe," Mahal said sternly, though tears were on his cheeks. "She has been a rebel from her childhood and did not have the light of love in her eyes under the canopy this night. She has defiled the nuptial vow and because of this incursion of evil she might never have another chance to conceive."

"You must say no more," Rasujal insisted, and Baraqua felt relief. Her father did love her, despite it all. She bowed her head. Let them think what they wished of the woman who had been thrust into a union with a man she did not know or love. Mahal would be sorry he had spoken like this when she, the one he called unworthy, could not be found on the mountain the next day. Any hesitation was gone. She could not leave the mountain fast enough.

"Do not speak like this to my bride," Jared said to Mahal. "Such harshness is unlike you and I bear full responsibility for what happened."

"And as Rasujal has said, husband, we know nothing of what passed between our son and his wife," Dinah said, taking Baraqua's arm. "Women are not as bold about lovemaking as men. We must be patient."

But Mahal still glared at Baraqua. "My life-long trepidation over my son's safety and the continuance of the lineage has been for nothing."

He sounded far away, but she heard his final words, like a hammer striking a seal: "Baraqua's pride may have cost the world its savior."

CHAPTER 16

And they were in all two hundred who descended in
the days of Jared on the summit of Mount Hermon, and
they called it Mount Hermon because they had sworn
and bound themselves by mutual imprecations upon it.
I ENOCH 6:6

The shepherd Rapivab snored in the grass between his two sons, clenching his shepherd's staff. A lifetime battling wild beasts had trained every sinew of his body to stay on guard against black-humped wolves, even in sleep. The family's ample flock of curly-horned ewes and rams completely covered the broad peak, the highest in the region. The ewes had lambed vigorously that season. There would be plenty of rich mutton stew next time Rapivab slaughtered for his wife's iron cooking pot.

The old shepherd stirred. He was dreaming with unrestrained pleasure of Magda, his oldest son Ashur's young wife. He was enclosed in her tent, finally conquering that girl of flawless skin, finding her yielding kisses more than sweet. He had desired her night and day for far too long. He did not care what his hunched wife thought of the way he stared openly at the girl across the evening fire. That beetle worshipper had not satisfied him for years anyway. Magda deserved a lover like him instead of cold-hearted Ashur. Perhaps he would even seed another child for his legacy in his daughter-in-law's fresh young womb. After two years of marriage, Ashur certainly had not.

But something was not right. Magda seemed to be slipping through his arms, her face and long hair dissolving. He clenched his staff tighter, but the girl was being swept from the tent in a sudden gust of wind. He clamored after her, clawing his way out of the dream and scrambling to his feet. Magda was nowhere to be seen and he was standing on the open mountain with nothing but his sheep and his sons around him. The wind that blew was not the usual warm, spicy breeze that wafted up from the cassia forests below Ermon. These were currents as hot as the air near a cook fire. The mighty spruce and cedar trees further down the mountain—some of whose trunks spanned the circumference of fifty men's arms—were bending like willow saplings. He swore aloud by the beetle spirit, the god of his wife, wondering if the hot wind was a portent of good or of evil. Then he cursed the wind because it had wakened him from his pleasure.

Suddenly the sky lit up like noonday. Rapivab turned his face upward to see what looked like pulsing pillars of lights high above. The shafts of light hurtled earthward, but something about them made him gasp. "They are living beings!" he cried. He staggered and dropped his staff, and the sheep began to awaken and struggle to their feet. The shepherd remembered an ancient legend some foreign balladeers had once sung at his fire, a story of gods that would one day come to earth to reward good men. He ran to where his son Ashur lay and shook the young man. "They come!" he shouted, his voice still gravelly with sleep. He went to his other son, Relenz, and kicked the boy where he sprawled in the grass. "Get up, fools! Don't you know the day of the gods when you see it?"

Ashur and Relenz stood and stared into the sky. Ewes and rams bleated frantically and stumbled about, trampling their own lambs as they began to run down the mountain.

"Be still, you stupid beasts," Rapivab shouted. "The gods have finally come to give Rapivab his heart's desire, and I must make a sacrifice of the fat of your haunches." He smoothed his graying beard and straightened the stained sheepskin garment that covered him to the knees. The pillars of light were nearer now. They would stand before him and ask what he wished, and he would breathe out, "Magda." He would lose himself with her day and night while Ashur wasted away with jealousy. Through his daughter-in-law's body he would raise up sons who would increase his flocks. He would become the richest shepherd among the people of the region of Ermon.

Ashur sprang to his feet. Terror was in his face as he held up his arms and clenched his fists as though ready for a fight.

"Don't stagger like a blind man, you impotent blight," Rapivab snarled at Ashur. "Show respect, for they are sky deities."

Ashur's eyes darted wildly as he looked at his father. "The mountain burns around us, and you call gods what will surely destroy us?"

"What, afraid of a little fire?" Rapivab mocked. How dull his oldest son was. And the younger was far too religious. Magda's sons alone would make him proud.

Ashur put his hand to his face where a moment before a thick beard had grown. The beard was gone and fire licked at his skin. He covered his eyes with his arm and began to plunge down the shepherds' trail between some spruce trees, tripping over a large ram that darted across his path in the turmoil. He sprawled and was thrown heavily against a large rock, striking his head. The ram fell hard against him, then got up and kept running. But Ashur did not move.

Rapivab turned away from the sight of his motionless son. He did not need him anyway. He wheezed with excitement, finding the hot air harder to breathe now. He knew this was a test so that the gods could find him worthy. He did not want to miss a moment of this marvel he was privileged to experience.

Relenz's skin streamed with sweat. But he did not cry out or run away, only looked calmly into the sky and betrayed neither fear nor wonder. It was as though he had expected the invaders.

"Your senseless brother has fled, but you will stand with me to receive the blessing of the rulers of the sky," Rapivab said to Relenz. "Rejoice with your father, for I have found favor with them and can ask whatever I wish."

Relenz looked at Rapivab with that independent expression Rapivab hated. He felt somehow diminished whenever his younger son was nearby.

"These beings are not here to satisfy your lusts, Father," Relenz said calmly, breathing hard with the heat. "Fall on your face and beg God's mercy for your sins. Perhaps the One who created heaven and earth will yet spare you."

Anger surged in Rapivab. He wanted to strike his son with his staff, but it was no longer in his hand. The boy's eyes were unflinching, as though he waited. That fool had spent years trying to convince Rapivab that men were responsible before their Creator. Even now, he looked as though he could wait an eternity more for his father to agree with him.

"Your false piety has blinded you to what is true," Rapivab said with practiced bitterness. "This is no day for begging mercy. It is the day of my reward, as it should be."

Relenz said nothing in response but knelt and bowed his head. He would no doubt be praying to the invisible god of his great-grandmother, that deity the old woman used to claim had once lived on earth in a garden of delights and walked with a man and a woman as though they were friends. Rapivab had always despised that forebear of his mother, and he despised men like his son who followed such teachings, for the god of Relenz insisted on fidelity to the tent of one woman and fairness in business dealings. He admonished men to care for orphans instead of lingering over meat and mead at their firesides. He, Rapivab, the proud shepherd, would never serve a god like that.

The sentient creatures had almost reached the mountain. Rapivab grunted with effort to remain standing. Surely the heat would subside when the test was complete. But they were instantly before him now, tall, fierce looking men with faces like burnished bronze and white-hot eyes that did not look into his. He wondered if these gods spoke a different tongue than his, though he was determined to speak.

"I choose my son's wife as my reward," Rapivab said in the only language he knew. He wondered why his throat was so dry. He gasped for another breath but could not inhale. He resisted the impulse to drop to his knees like Relenz. No, he would not submit just because the moment seemed impossible to endure.

"Come to my tent to break bread, my lords," he thought he said. But he knew the words were only in his mind this time. He wanted to tell them that though his wife was half bald and her face coarsened with work, she could prepare a seasoned lamb for the spit better than any woman in the vale. But the words would not find their way out and his torso felt as soft as beeswax under the midday sun. He watched as a tongue of fire from the mouth of one of the gods struck Relenz and the boy fell on his side and stared with unseeing eyes. He has died making his pathetic prayers to a god who could not save him, Rapivab thought smugly. He was accustomed to such uncharitable thoughts. Relenz deserved them. Yet he looked into the boy's empty eyes with a sudden pang, wondering why he wanted to stretch forth his hand and touch his son. He did not understand why he wanted to tell the boy that he loved him. Had he ever loved anyone?

But it was too late to do anything. His body was slipping to the ground and he could not stop it. It seemed to take a very long time to fall, as scenes from his life moved before the eye of his mind full of sun and mountain wind and futility. His cheek was burning against the charred earth. Rocks and trees exploded around him and fire gnawed at the rich grasses where ewes had lain peacefully with their lambs while he dreamt of Ashur's wife. He knew he was badly injured and would not be fit to sneak back into Magda's tent today. But when he healed, he would wash and anoint his face and go to her again. He would ply her affections with the red jewel he had taken from the tent of Luz the potter the week before, a polished garnet as red as the girl's lips.

He heard something split open very close to where he lay. He realized it was his own skull.

CHAPTER 17

The sunrise was an ochre band at the horizon when the four archangels arrived on the charred hump of Ermon. Lament was strong in Michael's spirit, for the entire summit, once the pride of the northwestern lands for its grazing meadows, was blackened by fire to a wilderness. Smoke rose in whisps and a landslide had already carried part of the mountain down the crumbled cliffs. Michael had heard the rock crack when Semjaza set forth his victory call, the conquest of a coward.

The archangel had not expected this magnitude of cruelty so early. Why such utter destruction of a beautiful place on the earth the Watchers were so eager to occupy? It was still difficult to think of Semjaza as anything but what he had been originally, scrupulously obedient to divine ways and a lover of both earthly and heavenly beauty.

Michael moved nearer the deeply burned bodies of three men, devoured by fire almost beyond recognition. He and the other archangels bowed low before each body, honoring the cosmic principle that no human being should be deprived of angelic presence in the first hours after death.

Raphael's hand of blessing went to the forehead of each man, his prayers fervent as he committed their souls to the mystery of death.

The warm jacinth stones of the archangel's breastplate radiated hope for even the most forsaken or reprobate.

Uriel's face blazed. "I do not have your impulse to heal and restore, Raphael. I see too much evil in the place I serve. The souls who clamor in Sheol are like this vile shepherd, lost in self-preoccupation even in death. Or they are like the man Ashur, calloused to what is precious."

"Perhaps if I guarded the underworld as you do, I would be as you are," Raphael said.

"Both outrage and compassion are justified in this hour," Michael said. He settled near the remains of the young man called Relenz. The expression of final agony that was usually present at a death by burning was not on the young man's face. "He sleeps in peace," Michael said. "He was one of the few in the western lands who still loved the Creator."

Raphael touched the head of Relenz and the body began to emit the scent of sweet myrrh. He breathed on the blackened face and the ravages of the fire disappeared. "May the holy souls welcome Relenz to their bosom," the four intoned.

Uriel hovered near the remains of Rapivab. "Raphael, do you have a prayer even for this soul so lost in darkness during his life?"

"I see a hint of repentance at the end," Raphael sang, sprinkling water from the wells of heaven over the body. "God's mercy has no limits."

"And now," Michael said when the short ceremony for the dead was completed. "We must go forth and try to weaken whatever the Watchers inflict upon humankind." He spoke to Gabriel. "Report to the Throne all we found here. Recruit as many angelic heights, chariots, thrones, and principalities from among our brethren as you can. There will be much to do."

Gabriel rose into the morning sky, white as a dove against the veils of soot rising off the mountain. Michael spoke to Uriel. "Alert the harps and glories to mourn forty days. It is no small thing that two hundred of the holy have given themselves to damnation." He looked toward the trail that led up from the village below. "The kin of these men are coming. Let them wonder at the renewed face of the one whose righteousness they mocked. His mother will suffer the grief that leads to death, though she will not turn from worshipping the beetle god." He sighed. "But there is light in the heart of the woman called Magda, who has known men to be nothing but licentious or indifferent. God will not forsake her."

The young woman running up the trail was already weeping, her legs below the garment of animal hide blackened with soot. She paused and turned her eyes into the sky where patches of blue shone beyond the smoke. Someone was singing up there, to the thrum of a harp that could not be of the earth.

CHAPTER 18

And Azazel taught men to make swords…
and about metals of the earth…Semjaza taught
the casting of spells and root cuttings; Armaros taught
counter spells; Baraqijal taught astrology; Kokabel
taught the portents; Ezeqeel, the knowledge of the clouds—
1 ENOCH 8:1,3

And when they wished, they made themselves appear as men.
1 ENOCH 17:2

Semjaza stood in a grove of massive angel oaks in the land of Nod. The mist-shrouded forest was the perfect setting for his school of Luciferian craft, the study of the cauldron. The limbs of the broad trees creaked, moaning under the wind, weeping with secrets. The Watcher formed a slight smile in the human way. It was the expression the man Shai used. It was no great thing for Semjaza to take on the appearance of the vinedresser, nor his expressions and traits. Centuries of observing human beings made them simple enough to imitate. The trait of duplicity was easiest of all. Semjaza was becoming adept, in the clumsy human way, of saying one thing while meaning another, of feigning sincerity or benevolence while his heart was poised to destroy or abuse. A turn of the eyes or a change in voice tone was all it took to fool most people. Before, his presence on the earth had been mostly unseen. Now he could appear or disappear as he wished. He could play any role he chose without consequence. Manipulating human lives apart from the blessing of God was thrilling.

He would pose as the intelligent but humble Shai to obtain the woman from the lake. Baraqua would be his queen and become immortalized, just as he had become humanized. That she was newly wedded to Jared the Seed Bearer was not important. Human men were frail, despite their masculine delusions of vigor and prowess. Though an elder of the Sethites and protected by several august angelic guards, with a bit of strategy that man could be as easily disposed of as any other. A malicious germ could be sent to paralyze his lungs; a misplaced foot at the edge of the sheer western cliffs could quickly become a fall to the death.

As an angel, Semjaza was allowed at times to see the golden cords that bound a husband to his wife and she to him. Between some, the cords were thick as ropes, the couple's faithfulness to each other impenetrable. Between others, a thread as fragile as a cobweb could hardly be discerned. He had not yet been able to tell what the strength of Baraqua's union with her husband was. His sight had somehow been obscured, but he would see it in time. She had been magnificent in her bridal robes the night he had descended. He had been sick with desire for her. She had looked troubled, like one who longed to be free, and he had departed until a better time. From what did she wish to be free? She was steeped in the Sethite beliefs about the true God. She knew the prophecies about the man of the future they called Anointed One. Through Jared's seed she might receive that highest honor on earth as his mother. Semjaza must make himself highly attractive and move quickly to woo her, for the woman must not draw closer to Jared. Anointed One must never be born.

He looked around the grove. The school would be renowned in the earth. He would make a name for himself in the teaching of magic and he believed one day Baraqua would be impressed. People would eagerly accept what he taught, for most humans chose the easy way over of the sacrificial path of moral devotion and repentance. He chuckled, that human indication of amusement or satisfaction. He would soon be instructing beautiful women in the cutting of roots to divine the future. Those more adept would learn to read future events in the patterns of falling leaves or the way sprigs of tea leaves rose to the surface of a cup. In iron cauldrons, his cleverest initiates would boil bat blood, holly leaf, and rare dittany under the chants of a language he had created full of obscure and oval sounds. Yet these arts were but trifles designed to distract human hearts from divine love. Pure worship of Lucifer was another matter for another time.

He left the grove, trailing mist. It was the hour to take counsel on the windy steppe with some of his chiefs-of-ten-and-twenty. He had sent a few to mark out boundaries for a city to commemorate the enclave of black stone that Lucifer's first human servant, Adam's first son, Cain, had built centuries before to honor the succubus Lilith. The old beliefs about association with dark beings must be revived and the murderous spirit of Cain unleashed again. The peoples of the earth would forget they had been created in God's image and likeness. They would fall from any remnant of divine love they still held into magic, spells, suspicion, and the arms of the succubus.

He stared at the river called Euphrat whose headwaters bubbled out of Eden, flowing eastward through Nod. The flow marked the passing of earthly time, that accumulation men call history. How different earth was from the heavenly realms. In heaven, the slight movement of a meadow lily marked neither time nor place. Movement in the high heavens had neither beginning nor end. All was eternal.

Semjaza's chiefs walked among the stakes that had been driven into the virgin sod so as to appear like any other building site. They spoke and gestured as though they were normal men at work. Yet on closer look, Armaros, Baraqijal, Kokabel, and Ezeqeel were taller, more formidable, and more richly dressed than any human chieftain. Semjaza studied Armaros and was impressed with the angel's transformation. The eyes of Armaros had become unfathomable, dusky as polished ametrine. He wore a robe of subdued yet shimmering fabric that suggested an exotic origin, the garb of a prince, and he cradled a small harp out of which he drew complex and melancholy songs about fleshly exploits, imitated by many young men in Nod and beyond. Already Armaros had a reputation as a master of seduction. He had seeded dozens of his female admirers but had not yet taken a woman to wife.

Semjaza did not trust Armaros. He trusted none of his cohort since the descent. He knew his ability to manage those under his own authority had become stunted somehow and that true harmony among the two hundred was gone. He had not expected to feel so estranged from the others or such a confusing solitude. He had not expected loneliness.

"Why are the city's boundaries not set where I ordered them?" he barked to Armaros in the human way. "This enclave must be thriving with inhabitants within a week by the reckoning of the sun. There is obsidian aplenty to the north to build both walls and habitations. The students from my school of magic will live here, so as to be near the oak grove."

"Though I live only to do your will, my lord, we have been hindered," Armaros replied, and Semjaza heard the hint of mockery in the rich voice, flawless in its mastery of the universal human language yet highlighted with angelic nuances that added to his exotic guise.

"You live for nothing but to chew the cud of your own lust," Semjaza said with a leer, to hide his own unease. A volley of agreement erupted from the other chiefs. "Our lust! Our fierce and brutal lust!" They sounded like restless wolves crouched beneath a Noddish moon.

Semjaza glared. "You yelp like animals instead of celestial beings a thousand times superior in intelligence to human men. Will you rut in the fields like beasts instead of wooing with refinement?" He tried to hide his contempt. "Do you think I care how many virgins you impregnate?" he said. "But at least feign elegance, for that will set us above other men in the eyes of women."

"Most women don't seem to care," Armaros said. "Their carnal fires burn as high as the men's. They do not even require marriage in exchange for our prowess over them."

Semjaza narrowed his eyes. "Still, you must each take a wife in the proper way, for this provides a veneer of respectability. Our sons must be held in honor by all, the better to conquer the earth. They will thwart God on the day he tries to hurl us into Tartarus."

The tilt of Armaros's mouth was cunning. "You still believe that rumor of divine punishment for our deeds?"

Semjaza drew taller. He knew the comment was intended to make him look weak for requiring the mutual pact on the night of descent. He wondered if Armaros had seen the woman Baraqua yet. He must win her before any of the others tried to claim her.

"I jest," Semjaza lied. "Tartarus is an illusion of fools." But he heard his own apprehension. He must keep what he felt strictly to himself.

The Watcher Baraqijal laughed, bitter as Tartarus itself. He wore the elaborate garb of the new order of sky priests. In the southern desert he had built six observation towers of pure marble. Through his diligent teaching, many now believed the stars and moon were lights that ruled the earthly night. He had convinced the people that to worship the stars as gods was noble, and that to predict one's life tendencies through the arrangement of the constellations was desired. He taught that the constellation Bethuleh was a harlot instead of a pure virgin, and that Dahrach the dragon had ultimate power over human affairs instead of the archaic deity known as God Most High. Semjaza gladly anticipated the future of Baraqijal's influence; star towers as gateways to eventual worship of Lucifer himself; the greed for silver that diviners would earn for their star predictions without care for the souls in their charge; emptiness of soul for the devoted. He welcomed the degrading of humanity in any way possible.

"You know as well as anyone that Tartarus will claim us one day, Armaros," Baraqijal said. "Yet we will take our pleasure on the earth for many centuries yet."

"Carouse where and how you will, but take legal wives," Semjaza repeated. "As husbands you will inherit lands and wealth in dowry." He smirked. "There is no need to steal these things if men are willing to give them to us."

"And you? Have you taken a woman?" Kokabel said. A former governor of heavenly portents, Kokabel's earthly vocation was to thin the barrier between human and angelic substance so that the Watchers might possess people's bodies and make them slaves in every way.

Semjaza shrugged in the way human men showed ambivalence in matters of the heart. "I've impregnated a pretty wench of no consequence, yet her spawn will be great among our offspring," he said. He would not allow the image of Baraqua's face to come to his mind. None would guess his passion for her. None would find a woman to match her. He would be utterly secure in power once he established his kingdom with her.

"My sons will be greater than yours," Ezeqeel said. "It is my family who will reign in titanic glory above all others." Ezeqeel's appearance was as fog on a mountain, his robes deep folds of gray and holding a demeanor of irresistible pathos. His new vocation was to spread the pall of melancholy and encourage self-murder.

Baraqeel snorted. "You, greatest? You governed mere clouds in the former time and now change shape at whim like a coward."

"The art of despair demands this," Ezeqeel said defensively. "But one day I will dispense the slanted hail to destroy crops and bring famine, which is the true mother of suicide."

"Enough of this," Semjaza said. "We all have our place in the new order. Tell me why the city's foundation is hindered?"

Armaros affected a human scowl. "The archangel Michael prevents the boundaries you commanded. He will not allow the number thirty-three in our calculations."

Semjaza's anger sparked and he noticed that the archangels Michael, Gabriel, Raphael, and Uriel had positioned themselves at each of the four staked corners. He recoiled at the unflinching holiness in each countenance. He had not calculated such interference.

"By what authority do you challenge us?" he roared at Michael.

"Use caution when you address him, my lord, for Gabriel has already injured me this day," Ezeqeel said sulkily.

"Hail, fallen one," Michael called out brightly to Semjaza, amusement in his eyes. "Have you forgotten that there are still people on the earth who fast and pray to the true God?" The archangel's radiance was so strong Semjaza averted his eyes.

"Indeed," Michael continued, clearly enjoying this impediment to the Watchers' plans. "Human interventions change outcomes just as angels' actions do. The prayers of babes and sucklings have decreed that your foul city must be built smaller than you wished. And it must not be built of black stone but of ordinary field stone set without mortar."

Semjaza lunged at Michael, his hatred for the archangel raging as he clawed his way to an attack. But Michael's sword and strength were ice, fire, all things impenetrable. The two wrestled, sparred, but Semjaza could not prevail. Kokabel and Baraqeel rushed at Uriel but were no match against the authority embodied in Uriel's sword as well. They tumbled back into the long grass.

Semjaza backed away from Michael. "You weaklings still suckle at the teats of cherubim while we Watchers embrace freedom," he said, hoping he displayed Lucifer's dark aura.

"Fine words from a molting vulture," Uriel said with a laugh, never one to countenance blasphemy. He plunged the tip of his sword into the grass and white light spread outward, cracking the earth with fiery rays. The Watchers scrambled like wounded dogs.

Three farmers plowing a field just eastward looked up. Something that looked like daggers of fire ran across the field, yet the grass was unburned. They dropped their hand plows and ran.

Michael spoke. "Despite the freedom you have been granted, the laws of the cosmos still stand. Do not expect the pious of the earth to give up their inheritance easily."

"Inheritance?" Semjaza echoed with a sneer. "The earth belongs to those with power to take it."

"Adam was given authority over the earth and that authority is not rescinded," Michael said. "The prayer of the humblest gleaner is a blade that can pierce the sky." The signet of the Throne glowed from the archangel's brow and Semjaza trembled. He had seen the lady Eve intercede before an incense burner in the night, drops of blood falling from her brow in the agony of her intercessions. Lucifer hated Eve above all people, and so Semjaza must.

"Cursed be the greedy God of the seventh heaven who kept bright Lucifer from sharing the Throne," Semjaza shrieked. "I will do everything to render the earth the opposite of what God intended."

But Michael was no longer looking at Semjaza, just as Sabaoth had not paid him any attention that day in the antechamber of the throne room. The archangel's gaze was upward, rapture on his face, for it was the hour the heavenly host sang lauds. Something pierced Semjaza's heart. He could no longer hear the music of the heavens. He felt another level of his inner essence decay, and with it came a sense of deprivation he had not counted on. It was a loneliness so profound he almost cried out.

The heavenly song soon ceased, for in a moment Michael turned again to Semjaza and sighed, as though Semjaza was an annoying afterthought. "I leave you to the dry chaff you have chosen," Michael said, as though he read Semjaza's mind. Then he and the other archangels disappeared into the vast cerulean sky.

A fisherman was casting his nets off the river. He hauled at the loaded net and hailed Armaros with a friendly gesture. Armaros made a sound like the prick of a scorpion's tail. "I sat at that fool's fireside last night in the guise of a philosopher, listening to his ignorant notions of the cosmos. His nubile daughter cast her eyes on me, and the father was too full of his pontification to notice. I will humble the girl tonight in the high grass and then desert her. Let her bear her child alone while the father recedes in shame."

"Go then and whore," Semjaza said. He was surprised at how unnerved he felt after the encounter with the archangels. Truly, prayer was in the land. Some men would oppose him and the others. And Michael was no one to trifle with. He wanted the others gone from his sight so that he might contemplate what to do next.

His chiefs erupted in human-sounding laughter at some comment Armaros had made. Their forms dissipated. Semjaza might not see them for some time. Only when they were gone did he notice that another of his chiefs-of-twenty stood a short distance away. It was the silent Kasdeja, whose vocation as an obedient Watcher had been as a guardian of pregnant women. Even then Kasdeja had been different from the others, created to be unobtrusive and gentle, to better observe women during childbirth and quietly coax their children into the world.

But Semjaza recoiled at the sight of Kasdeja. Evil had sent its tentacles deep into his own spirit since his rebellion, yet something about the absolute permeation of wickedness that seemed present in Kasdeja set that Watcher apart from the others, and Semjaza was appalled. It was understandable that the attendant of women had not taken on the exaggerated masculine beauty or appearance of high culture or mystery the others had, for his strength had always been a superior intelligence, not aspect. But now the once-peaceful face was emaciated to the point of appearing skull-like, and the eyes were the lifeless ones of a human being in the moment the spirit separates from the body at death. How would this gaunt, visibly unappealing anomaly in his close-fitting white garment make an impression with the people of earth? The sun glinted on something the angel held in long fingers, which were yellowed at the tips like those of a corpse. It was a small scimitar, almost as slender as a blade of grass and lethally sharp. From the tip of the scimitar a drop of blood fell.

147

CHAPTER 19

And the fifth was named Kasdeja; this is he
who showed the children of men... the smitings
of the embryo in the womb, that it may pass away—
I ENOCH 69: 12

Semjaza was strangely sickened at the profound wickedness he felt in Kasdeja's presence as the two stood on the windy steppe. His chief-of-twenty seemed to have deteriorated faster than the others since the descent, like a weanling of hell itself. Instead of base lust or greed for lands, at the core of Kasdeja's essence Semjaza sensed only a deathly, appalling stillness. He boldly probed his subordinate's thoughts but sensed no cacophony of earthly desires. Then an image came to the eye of his mind: hill upon hill of tiny graves where tatters of wind moaned between the headstones.

He steadied himself. What was at the root of this most subdued of his chiefs? But all was blackness.

"And who will you take to wife?" Semjaza said. But he knew somehow that Kasdeja was not interested. It was as if he valued no identity beyond the tool in his yellowed fingers. Let the interaction be quickly over, Semjaza thought. Kasdeja's nearness was suffocating. Need for the body of the madwoman who carried his child was also stirring in him and he wanted to go to her quickly. He did not care if Kasdeja disappeared and he never saw him again.

Kasdeja sniffed in the way of old women who have listened to gossip they disapprove of. "Let the others forfeit their dignity in this matter," he said. "The thought of stooping to female flesh repulses me."

"But you bound yourself to our agreement before the descent," Semjaza said, hoping the other's answer would offer a clue. "We must take wives, even if by force."

"I came to accomplish Lucifer's mission, not sire sons." Kasdeja's voice was like frayed rags drying in the wind, soft as a rotting melon.

Semjaza wondered if he had ever really known this angel. "What, no curiosity for carnal pleasure?" he said with forced lustiness. Behind the openings that passed as Kasdeja's eyes he saw the pulse of some monstrous destruction. He was angry that Kasdeja mentioned his allegiance to Lucifer instead of to his own chieftain.

"Rutting like any common field worker is not worth my time," Kasdeja said, disdain in the flaccid voice. "I have had enough in the past of seeing those worthless worms that emerge from gushing female wombs. Children are insignificant, greedily seeking the teat and gulping earth's precious air, better reserved for the beasts of the field." The angel caressed the scimitar, his counterfeit breath like a death rattle. Two trim vipers sidled through the grass and disappeared beneath his spare garment. The lipless mouth twitched at one corner.

"But you would bear brawny, mighty men, not human children," Semjaza said, feeling foolish to be arguing with this skeletal specter. "Through your sons you will be infamous in the earth."

Kasdeja's expression was sly. "I will have infamy enough in what I have chosen," he said. "And as to children, Azazel and Armaros will make up for my lack."

"What art do you propose with that scimitar?" Semjaza said. He should not have to glean information from his underlings. It was Kasdeja's role to inform him of any and all plans out of respect.

Kasdeja's expression became starker still. A gleam came to the lifeless eyes as he held up the shining object. "A way of death far more sophisticated than Azazel's stumbling, chaotic wars, I assure you." He drew a vial of murky liquid from a pouch at his waist and held it into the light. "Whether through potions or by silent blade, I will change the way the women of the earth feel about the inconvenient bulges that push against their waistlines after men have come in to them after the way of all the earth." He swirled the vial between the corpse-like fingers and Semjaza thought of his own hybrid child, restless in the belly of the madwoman. The girl might not survive the full pregnancy, for the child was already enormous. What if she and others pregnant by the Watchers chose the relief of Kasdeja's methods?

"That will not be a problem, my lord," Kasdeja said, as though he knew Semjaza's thoughts. The rotting melon voice cracked open, oozing the odor of despair. "Those who bear the sons of angels will consider doing that a privilege, whereas I will seek out only the womb worms of ordinary women. Within a generation the sound of a baby's cry will be a rarity on the earth."

"May your plan prosper," Semjaza said almost shakily. After all, to rid the earth of most human beings by any method could only be good. A few left to be slaves would be all that was necessary. He felt unschooled beside Kasdeja, lost in his simple reveries about Baraqua, clothed in the tunic of a workman. Kasdeja had apparently planned carefully, while he was caught between two women and had just had his plans for the city drastically modified. He would cancel the building of it so that none of his cohort would lose respect over its reduced size. Kasdeja dissolved into the tall grass without another word. He was relieved. Death was one thing, but the cutting of children in the womb was something even Semjaza's deteriorated mind had not strategized.

He began to walk toward the mountain of the Sethites, using the muscular legs that were like those of the man Baraqua loved as he moved through the steppe. How limited the human body was, how humiliating its heaviness as it plodded over the ground. In the distance the mountain was as vividly green as a tourmaline jewel—the pride of the earth, God's former home. Impatience seized him; his longing for the girl's body could not wait. He rose into the air and moved faster than sound. He would take her to the cave below the mountain where bats clung to the walls. He would enjoy her humiliation as she lost herself in his embrace, calling him lord and believing every absurd word he murmured about their future together in order to heighten her passion. But there was no future for him with such a woman. She had served her purpose.

He materialized not far from Eden. The scent of God was still on the Garden despite its decline. He remembered the sixth day of creation when he, a pure, joyous Watcher, had marveled over that paradise along with all celestial beings. He remembered his horror when the rebellious Lucifer had lured Eve to eat forbidden food from the center of the Garden. He had wept with the others at sunset when she and Adam were driven out by cherubim with flaming swords, both clothed in the fur of a yearling lamb God himself had slaughtered. He had hated Lucifer with a righteous hatred that day, but now he understood the fallen cherub's jealousy and cunning. He understood and reveled in it, for it had made so many things possible.

He found his distended consort lying beside a stream, her hair a dirty tangle down her back. She babbled her joy to see him, and the sound was a cacophony to his superior senses. He took her to the cave and abused her all night, trying to satiate his lust. But he was finding that once the fire of carnal desire was ignited, it was never satisfied. He wondered if the madwoman knew or cared that he was not a real man and would never love her. They must all be like Eve had been in Eden, easy to deceive.

The four archangels looked on in anguish as Semjaza moved high in the treetops above the Sethite camp with the woman Awan in his arms. The Watcher's wingspan was as broad as the mountain itself, and a semblance of the man Shai was in the humanized features the fallen celestial had assumed. The Sethites who were at their work sowing barley, suckling children, or drawing water would not hear the shuddering of those wings, nor hear the cruel laughter of a being who had once been holy but was now debauched beyond redemption.

"God's ways are beyond knowing," Gabriel said as Semjaza arced the mountain with his prey. "It will always be a mystery to me how evil is so skillfully woven into God's will."

"Evil will have its place until the sky rolls back like a scroll and our God makes all things new in heaven and on the earth," Michael said.

Yet one person on the mountain did sense the travel overhead. Rojj the goatherd, squatting near his flock, looked into the sky. "Awan, do not forsake me," he shouted until he was hoarse, then paced stiffly as though he was sick of mind himself. He came to the edge of a steep slope and began to shake with sobs.

"His heart knows," Raphael said. He moved near Rojj, wafting healing color.

"Is there a faithful woman on the earth?" Uriel said sternly.

"The actions of one do not make all guilty," Michael said. He followed the line of Semjaza's flight until it disappeared. "Awan represents all that will take place under the new order of the Watchers."

"She will be the first of many," Gabriel agreed.

Michael was somber. "Why are people so eager to embrace what seeks to destroy them?"

CHAPTER 20

For this cause ought the woman to have
power on her head, because of the angels.
I CORINTHIANS 11:10

The light before dawn was as clear and sharp as sapphire as Semjaza settled near Baraqua's tent. The Seed Bearer's bride knelt before the fire ring as a spark from her flint bit into the tender. She exhaled into the wisp of smoke. The spark fed on her breath and brought up a flame. That breath—Semjaza drew as near as he dared without her detecting him. Regret pricked; he had been impulsive in aligning with the madwoman. It had been beneath him. If only Baraqua had been receptive and alone that night at the cliff. When she was his he would do things differently. She would refine his humanized traits. But he could not allow her to sense him yet, though even if he walked through the camp in visible form few would see him, for the people of earth no longer expected to see celestial beings except in their stories.

Jared's bride was dressed in a work frock, for today she would beat out flax in the far fields with her sisters. She had not yet bound up that glorious, knee-length hair beneath the head covering. He touched the hair, that crown of a woman's beauty. The strands were as smooth as the waters of the fourth heaven. She brushed her hand over the place he had touched and looked around as though she wondered about something.

"Shai," she whispered, and bit her lip. She gathered the mass of hair into a braid and tied it with a thong of hemp, then took bread dough from a bowl and began to form bits into rounds. Was she making a meal for her husband because she loved him, or out of duty? She did not look happy when she was near Jared, Semjaza had observed. Soon he, Semjaza, would deliver her from the drudgery of mere human life, elevating her to the new order. *When you are mine you will never cover your hair,* he vowed. He would lose himself in her beauty day and night. She would relieve his loneliness and dispel the fear of Tartarus. Her lips parted and the slanted sun of morning cast a glow on her cheek. He gazed on the smooth, small hands crafted from the miracle called flesh. He did not share Kasdeja's revulsion about the feminine. Pale blue rivulets ran beneath the surface of her skin, those conduits that moved the mystery of blood through a human body. It was blood that set mortal beings apart from the angels; blood, and the divine breath that made them bearers of God's image, which Lucifer had coveted. What would the children of mingled blood and spirit be like? He would find out soon enough, for the gestation period of his son would be much shorter than that of humans.

Baraqua was heating fat beans spiced with cardamom in a crock set among the ashes. How menial human life was, a never-ending round of tasks that, left undone, could lead to death. Fire must be kindled, food eaten, the body washed and rested, children nourished and looked after. Yes, he would make this woman's life a dream of pleasure. She would be almost as he was.

The man Jared came out of the tent, cinching his work tunic and yawning. Envy of his access to Baraqua's beauty gripped Semjaza. He eyed Jared's throat where the pulse of life throbbed. He could snuff that pulse any moment he chose. What a fate for the great Seed Bearer, a death so mysterious the Sethite minstrels would immortalize it in song.

But he cast the plan aside. He would woo rather than kill. Let the man die of broken pride when his woman abandoned him. He wondered if Baraqua was already with child. If so, the ghoulish Kasdeja could be sent to remedy that while she slept.

Jared greeted Baraqua with a slight embrace. Blood-warmth was one thing Semjaza would not be able to offer, no matter how masterfully he made love. Would she be repelled by the coldness of his form?

The man and wife sat down together on a bench near the fire. Jared ate of the bread and beans his wife offered and drank tea scented with jasmine from a wooden cup. Baraqua seemed remote and restless, as though waiting for something. Semjaza looked hard to locate the golden marital filaments between them. Yes, now he saw. The cords that attached them were few and fragile. He smiled with satisfaction.

Two men carrying field tools appeared on the trail that ran along that side of the camp. They were the vinedresser Shai and one of his brothers. Semjaza watched Baraqua's face flush and felt her energy surge. Jared stood and greeted the men. They put two fingers to their foreheads and bowed slightly before Jared, and Jared complimented the men on the fineness of the wine served at the nuptial feast.

"We have just come from the amaranth field," Shai said. "The crop is gone, as though it were never planted." He did not look at Baraqua, but Semjaza saw what he guessed was self-consciousness.

"Pest or crow?" Jared said. "It happens from time to time."

"This is nothing like that," the brother said.

"One of the men went last night while the mist was high to test the ripeness of the grain," Shai said. "Someone was wielding a scythe, but when he went near, the figure disappeared."

Jared frowned. "Is anything left of the crop?"

"It is as though the land is virgin, never cultivated."

"How is this possible?" Baraqua said. Her palms were pressed hard against the bench where she remained seated.

"I spoke with our scouts yesterday," Jared said. "They have seen no Cainites on the mountain in weeks."

"No Cainite performed this, my lord," Shai said.

"I don't want to accept that this has anything to do with what happened on Ermon, but it was not undertaken with earthly powers, the way you describe it," Jared said.

People were on the trail now, chattering about the virgin field that yesterday had held a crop ready to harvest. Shai and the brother moved on.

"He will always live between us unless we talk about him," Jared said as soon as Shai was gone.

"Why speak of it?" Baraqua said, her voice tight. "You have a legal marriage. Isn't that all you Seed Bearers want?"

"What sort of man do you think I am?" he said. He did not sit down again to eat.

Semjaza drew nearer, taking in each expression and word, filtering it through his high powers. He considered their hearts as they lay close in the night. A human heart was no larger than a hand, beating faithfully beneath bone and muscle with a muffled sound. Whether a human heart beat strong or not made no difference in the great scheme of the cosmos. Yet he wondered if he could mimic Jared's heartbeat when he finally lay down beside this beauty.

Two angelic guardians appeared and stood beside Baraqua and Jared.

"Go now," Jared's guardian said. His garment was of spun gold, the customary garb of those who kept watch over the Seed Bearers.

"I have authority just as you do," Semjaza said with a sneer. "You cannot require me to leave."

"Tartarus cannot claim you quickly enough for me," the guardian said, and blocked the way to Jared's body.

Jared's younger brother, Eli, entered the clearing. He picked up two rounds of hot bread and began to gnaw hungrily. Jared took up his tools and a bag of water and spoke to Baraqua. "Stay near Eli, as I have instructed." Semjaza knew the young man had been ordered to Baraqua's side since the descent. That Jared believed the boy was helpful amused him. How little he understood the power of the Watchers.

Baraqua watched Jared leave and dug her bare toes into the dust in what he thought must be frustration or anger. And then he understood: Baraqua and Jared had not yet lain together heart to heart as he had assumed: they had not consummated their union. Jared the Seed Bearer had no pull on his wife's heart.

Elated, Semjaza rose high into the sky. Victory was near. In mountains and valleys, villages, and on open spaces in the distance he could see shining, exquisite members of his cohort breeding, building, entrenching suspicion and envy between people, charming their hearts with lies about the power of magic, the ease of spells. Few dared approach the holy mountain, for there were too many angelic guardians, and the sword-wielding Michael was never far from Adam's tent. But they were making moral wreckage of the rest of the earth.

Far to the south men and Watchers strategized battles in a colossal arena under Azazel's tutelage. Men were slaying each other even during the war exercises with no apparent remorse. In the towers of Baraqijal's star school men and women jostled to peer through the tubular sky glasses that brought the details of wavering stars closer to the eye. On the towers were inscriptions carved into the stone: *Praise to Ishtar, Goddess of the Sky.*

His plans were unfolding as they should.

CHAPTER 21

And their judges and rulers went to the
daughters of men and took their wives by force
from their husbands according to their choice—
BOOK OF JASHER 4:18-20

The shadows seemed longer than usual for the time of day as Baraqua sat on the bank of the River Eden with her spindle and distaff beside her. Pinpoints of afternoon light plucked at the surface of that most beautiful of the earth's rivers. She wondered what the river that flowed out of this former paradise had been like before Eve ate of the forbidden fruit; before shadow fell into those glades of Eden and vines that had once produced grapes as large as a man's fist began to shrivel.

The air itself was taut, as though the mountain waited for something. She looked behind her. Eli had not returned to his station beneath the giant fir. The young man had come with her as usual, then paced an hour before he blurted, "I thought this incursion would bring strange beings and that we would wage wars. But it's all just a rumor after all." She had sent him back to the camp to fetch food for them both.

But Eli had not returned. She did not want to go back yet as Jared would wish her to. Women would be at her fireside to ask if Jared had had more visions and to wonder aloud what they should do to protect themselves against the enemy who had emptied the amaranth field. She would stay here a while longer and spin enough thread to weave a new undertunic for Jared. It was something she could do for the husband she did not love.

She wedged the distaff between two rocks, then onto the spindle wound a strand of flax from the silky mound at her side. She thought of Akliah's unfinished prayer mantle, the symbol of her rejection. A force beyond the earth had surely ordained the ruptures in the cloth. She glanced behind her again. How easily she startled now. She was not the only one who had seen peculiar gleams between trees and the smoky outlines of creatures that did not look like the innocent animals that lived peaceably on the mountain.

A long shadow fell over the swiftly flowing water and she turned around yet again. "Eli?" she said. But it was her cousin Awan who stood behind her with the sun at her back.

"You frightened me," she said. Awan was the last person she wanted to see. But Awan sat down on the bank and Baraqua studied the face that had once been a fresh-skinned oval. Her cousin had deteriorated noticeably since the nuptial feast. Her eyes still held the glint of sly secrets and her cheeks were flushed with the usual excitement about some personal triumph that would make sense to no one when she told it. Her dress was more unkempt than usual and she smelled. Her hair, unbound as always, had probably not been cleansed with soda rock and wine in weeks. But it was not Awan's face and clothes that alarmed Baraqua. It was the swelling at her cousin's waist. Awan looked to be seven or eight months with child.

"May the Spirit of God Most High be with you—" Baraqua stammered the traditional greeting. She thought back, her mind racing. Had she missed the announcement about the pregnancy? But she was sure Awan's belly had been flat beneath the sash of her gown the night she came with Rojj to fetch her from the prayer caves.

Awan drew up her legs as far as her distended belly would allow. She leaned back on her hands and looked at Baraqua out of those eyes that seemed to see everything and nothing at once. "I wanted you to be first to know," she said. "I will soon bear my lord Semjaza a son." Her voice was not animated, but thick with sobriety.

Baraqua felt a moment of elation, then the bite of apprehension. A baby would bring joy to the tent of Rojj, yet would a child be safe in Awan's care? She spoke as cheerfully as she could. "Finally, a little one for you and Rojj." Perhaps the child would stabilize her erratic cousin. She laughed nervously. "I see you have even created a nickname for your dear husband. What playful secret does the name 'Semjaza' hold between you two?"

"Rojj makes love like a crayfish; I doubt he will ever father a child," Awan said dully. She caressed her mounded belly. "Believe me when I tell you that this child was seeded by a powerful master of the air."

Master of the air. Baraqua stared at the water curling over boulders of pure crystal in its endless flow out of the cradle of the world, trying to understand what Awan meant. That river would create four others, all flowing off the holy mountain. God had set those rivers to water the entire earth. The sun dropped lower behind the pole pines, dimming the clearing. "How is it possible that you are so advanced in your time, since only the span of a moon ago—"

"My child was conceived on the night you went into the nuptial tent with Jared. He will be a mighty man on the earth when he is grown."

Baraqua groped for words. "When will you go to child-bed?"

"You think in the manner of the old world," Awan said, as though Baraqua were unschooled in the simplest things. She paused, then sat up straighter, pride in her face. "The babe I carry is a child of the gods and the one I love is bright as the moon."

Bright as the moon. She thought of the shining man who had hovered beyond the cliff on the night of her nuptials. No, it was impossible.

Awan looked at the river dreamily, just as any woman expecting her first baby would. "My son's name will never depart from the pens of chroniclers." She smirked. "You are jealous because I have been chosen to bear Anointed One instead of you."

"Anointed One?" Baraqua repeated, annoyed at her own confusion. Did Awan actually believe this?

"Eve was given a promise and it will soon be fulfilled," Awan said. "Still, do not think that the savior of the world will act as the Sethites have recorded it. My son will lead the people of the earth into the glorious shadows of the underworld, not Eden's pathetic realm."

Baraqua pulled her shawl higher around her shoulders. "I won't believe these delusions of yours, cousin," she said firmly. "The child is Rojj's, but you have not accepted that."

"I did not expect you to understand," Awan said. "But it will come to pass as I say. The sons of my lord and his legions will make the world a better place than Adam's race has done." A toad appeared where Awan had been sitting, its belly protruding from between spotted legs. The toad's eyes bulged. Its long tongue flicked and drew in a flying insect. Baraqua suppressed a cry, but Awan appeared again where the toad had squatted.

"I will tell you how I met my lord," Awan said.

"I don't want to hear it," Baraqua protested. She wanted to get as far from the river as possible. She wished Eli and his loud friends would crash into the clearing. But something was terribly wrong with her cousin and she must stay to provide what help Awan allowed her.

"Rojj went back to our tent halfway through your marriage feast," Awan said, despite Baraqua's protest. "I could not bear to come with him and feel his paws wander over me one more time. No one spoke to me at the feast, so I walked alone on the mountain. I heard geese above, strange for so late at night. I vowed I would fly away with them before the moon changed, for my life had become unbearable."

She looked out over the water, her face elated at a memory. "At that moment I saw stars drop from the sky like ripened seed pods from a tree. A man who emitted light from within appeared before me. He knew my name and spoke as though I was precious to him." She caressed her belly again, her eyes soft. "How we found ourselves lying on the sand before the sea I do not know. This one who knew my name filled my womb with his seed until daybreak." She smiled shyly and tossed her hair. "I felt the child quicken within me before the night was over." She seized Baraqua's hand and placed it over the bulge. "Feel the life," she said breathily.

Something struck out from the womb, pummeling Baraqua's hand with a strength far greater than that of a pre-born child. Baraqua jerked her hand away with a little cry.

"We must go to the midwife today, cousin," she said. "This is not as it should be."

Awan scowled and moved a short distance from Baraqua, like a child who sulks about a game.

"Something is the matter with your bowels," Baraqua said, trying to sound authoritative. After all, she was older than Awan. She had managed her many times when they were children. She got up from the riverbank. "We will go to Tamara the healer. She will give you a tincture to dispel the bloating."

But Awan remained seated. "Why do you speak to the mother of Anointed One as though she has a mere quirk of the bowels?" she said.

Baraqua forced herself to think sensibly. Adultery was rare among the Sethites. The punishment was fasting and a time of penance in the tent of chastisement, though there had been occasional banishments. The offended spouse could move to a separate tent forever if he or she wished and owed the offender no marital favors. Surely because of her madness the elders would require nothing of Awan. Would Rojj accept the child as his own even if he denied fathering it?

"What does Rojj say about this?" she said carefully. She wondered why this was not being spoken of in the camp.

"I have not been near him or anyone else since I conceived," Awan said proudly, elongating her neck. "You judge me because I spend my nights in the arms of a virile god while you dream of bearing Shai's sons." She sniffed in the way her mother did. "Who is wrong in this, I ask?"

Baraqua felt herself redden. There was no use denying anything about herself. It would only make Awan more obsessed. It had to be accepted that by some allowance of the cosmos one of the beings who had descended that terrifying night had impregnated Awan. The intermingling of earthly and celestial seed was somehow possible.

Awan's voice was gentler when she spoke again. "I came to you first with my happy news because you are one of the few who ever showed me kindness."

Baraqua felt sick with shame. Had they all judged Awan more tainted of mind than she really was? Every soul deserved kindness. How tired Awan looked, and how lonely she must be apart from everyone in the camp. Baraqua saw that her cousin's arms were deeply scratched in many places. The scratches and scabs did not look like the result of work or getting caught in a bramble thicket in the dark. She thought of the round, placid face of Rojj timidly alight when he looked at his wife, helpless against his love for her, forever gentle against her roughness.

Awan gasped and Baraqua heard a distinct growl rise from the child-belly. Awan lowered her head and spoke in a pleading tone. "Not now, my precious brute," she whimpered. "Do not torment me before the time," She began to pant with what must be pain, her features twisting with the sensations. "Give me peace a moment more before you wrack me again," she pleaded. But the creature she spoke to did not comply. Awan began to writhe on the riverbank. The belly heaved and twisted with a life of its own, as though wrestling with itself as well as inflicting pain on its mother.

Baraqua crawled to her cousin. "Jared! Bathshae!" she cried into the trees. Was anyone near to help? Of course not. Jared was in the fields and sensible women would be in their tents as they had been instructed since the incursion. "I will go for help," she said above the suffering girl's cries.

But the pains seemed to subside as quickly as they had started. Awan relaxed and lay looking up at the sky until her breathing returned to normal, then turned to Baraqua. "To be chosen by the gods means both pleasure and suffering. What I endure will not be in vain, for I will be known throughout the ages as the Blessed Mother." She got to her feet suddenly and untied the intricately embroidered nuptial sash that rode high above the swollen belly. She went to the water's edge and dangled the sash over the current. "You are witness that my alliance with the goatherd is now null," she said. "I belong to none but Semjaza, both now and ever." The sash fluttered down and was tugged beneath the surface of the rushing water.

The sound of a man singing in a foreign language came from the other side of the river, at the place where Eden's tangle joined the rest of the mountain. The song was rich with layers of melancholy, smooth and somber, each note beckoning into existence the next one, more beautiful and mysterious than the last as the melody rose and fell. A strange restlessness coursed through Baraqua. It was like the night the man had walked to her on the lake in Elda. She felt a drawing on her heart. Only that singer across the river could complete her. Only that song could satisfy. She understood in an instant how Awan had been seduced.

The man stepped from behind a long-needled pine. His skin shone in the subdued light of the dense wood. He was the man from the lake, from beyond the cliffs. He was Shai.

"My lord, my love!" Awan cried out. Raising her garment above her knees, the unwieldy girl splashed into the river and began to struggle against the current to reach the other side.

"Awan, the water is too swift here!" Baraqua cried, wading in after her. She looked at the man. "Shai, help her before she falls," she cried. But the man was not looking at Awan. His eyes were fixed on Baraqua.

"You call him Shai?" Awan screamed. "Do not try to steal my lord from me, fornicator." She lost her balance and fell into the water. She struggled to get up, hauling at the child-belly. Baraqua splashed to her and grabbed her arm, but Awan struck her in the face and turned again toward the man who stood among the trees and did nothing to help her.

"I will not steal your lord," Baraqua pleaded with Awan. "Only let me get you to safety." But Awan continued to thrash. She slipped beneath the current and resurfaced, coughing up water. "My lord, free me," Awan screamed. Her eyes were wild, her legs splayed as the current took her again.

"What man stays aloof from the distress of a pregnant woman?" Baraqua hurled at the man. She plunged downstream after Awan. Jewels embedded in the river bottom cut into her feet and the cold water stabbed her legs like knives.

"Don't die," she whispered as she reached Awan and was finally able to haul the exhausted girl to the riverbank where the man stood.

The shining man with the face of Shai the vinedresser did not look down at Awan as she clutched at his legs. "My lord, my lord," Awan moaned. The child-belly began to thrash again, knocking Awan on her back. "Leave me, traitor," Awan panted out in her pain, glaring at Baraqua. "My lord Semjaza will fill me with his love."

But the man was probing Baraqua's eyes, forcing her to look at him. They were the eyes she remembered from that night of untrained, blushing youth— "I have loved you from the foundation of the world," he said.

The foundation of the world. She and Shai had talked of visiting the foundations of the earth. Were they the same? How free she had been that night, her lithe body knifing the water; the glow of a thousand lights above and below her; the sense that she belonged with that man whose eyes consumed her and her innocent heart responded to his presence.

But the man picked up Awan and walked into the trees. There was deep contentment on the girl's face. Baraqua stared into the dark wood until they disappeared, then waded back into the water, picking her way around the crystal boulders. On the opposite bank she looked back. Did she expect him to be standing there waiting for her?

She felt a sudden, perverse gladness for her cousin's happiness, and at the same time jealousy. Truly, the gods had descended.

CHAPTER 22

And to Seth, to him also there was born a son; and
he named him Enosh. Then began men to call on
[Heb: huchal "call on to profane"] the name of the Lord.
GENESIS 4:26

Rojj was not with his spotted goats on the eastern flank of the mountain. The young boy minding the flock blushed when Baraqua asked the goatherd's whereabouts. "They've all left their fires unattended and gone to the elders' clearing to see what will happen to those girls."

"What girls?"

The boy ducked his head shyly and blushed. He got up to run after a few animals that were straying from the others. "The daughters of Yusuf the ink maker have gotten themselves huge with child," he said.

Baraqua wiped sweat from her face, stunned. The run from the river and the impact of the boy's words made her weak. The twins Yammah and Yarih had always been steady girls, recently betrothed to two pious keepers of the sacred writings. Those men would not have claimed the girls' virginity before the traditional pitching of nuptial tents and the ceremony beneath the canopy. She must find someone who could tell her more. But first, she must find Rojj.

She ran along the trail that led into the camp. The image of Awan in the shining man's arms was like a specter before her mind. His eyes had been on her, not Awan. Just like the night of the descent when he hovered before the cliff, that being had made it clear he had come for her. She felt sick for her cousin, for she knew Awan's life was in danger, if not from the shining man, then the powerful baby within her body. She both loved and hated the unholy thrill the man's desire for her brought. There was power there, excitement that could not be had with a human being. If she was clever enough, she might possess a form of Shai in that shining man. Would that be adultery, since the man was not of the earth and adultery was an earthly offense? To have access to some semblance of Shai— No wonder the elder Enosh viewed these invaders as an asset to the people. No one could deny their allure.

She reached Rojj's tent and pushed back the door flap. The inside of the untidy dwelling smelled of goat milk and of soured lentils left too long in their soaking water. Awan's few gowns lay folded and stacked in one corner, and one of two sleeping mats was rolled up beside the clothes, a forlorn and inevitable sign. Baraqua's heart mourned for Rojj. The goatherd would never be a highly respected scribe or a craftsman of renown. But did Rojj know in his quiet spirit that his strange wife was not returning to their tent?

She dropped the door flap and walked between rows of stately date palms that would take her to the heart of the camp. Though most of the evening fires had gone out, she smelled baking bread from one direction and turned into the clearing where the elders' wives sometimes pitched small tents during the season of gathering the yellow fruits that ripened on that side of the mountain.

Naom and Dinah sat before Naom's fire. Dinah stood up and greeted Baraqua with her soft smile. Jared's mother was always the same, accepting and without guile. Baraqua felt even more guilty about her lack of love for Jared when she was near Dinah.

But Naom did not rise. She remained seated near her bread oven and gestured vaguely as Baraqua approached. Something like fear played at the corners of the deep-set eyes. With a sharp stick Enosh's wife jabbed at food inside her baking oven. She had a perfect memory, knew by heart every account written within the scrolls of the *Chronicles of Adam,* and had dictated many of them to the scribes when Eve or Adam were occupied. It was rumored that her eyesight might be as powerful as Seth's, with the ability to see into the outer star fields. But she was an unassuming woman and not inclined to speak much, for she believed a person could learn more by listening than by talking.

"Rojj's boy told me the people are in the elders' clearing because things are not right in the camp of Yusuf the ink maker," Baraqua said.

"You call them people?" Naom said. There was disgust in her usually measured voice. "They have forsaken the dignified image of God within to run from their firesides and gawk at men from out of the sky." She took up a fistful of ash from the fire ring and sprinkled it over her head. It was the sign of deep anguish.

Baraqua let out her breath. So, others had seen the shining men. Could it be these who had impregnated Yusuf's daughters?

Naom was weeping openly, tears mingling with ash on her face. "These corrupt ones titillate the eye but have no glow of righteousness within. Why would a woman give herself to them?" She speared a round of bread in the oven and tossed it onto a rock to cool. It skidded into the fire and the edges began to blacken among the embers. Naom's eyes narrowed. "Do you think I am becoming dim of mind to say these things?"

"No," Baraqua said.

Dinah put her hand on Naom's arm. "Mother Naom, Baraqua does not yet know what these men are."

"But I do know," Baraqua blurted out. "Awan is with child by one of these creatures Naom speaks of. He is beautiful beyond belief, so why wouldn't she desire him?"

Naom squinted in her direction. Could she see her attraction to the sire of Awan's child?

"Take heed, Seed Bearer's bride," Naom said slowly. "In Eden, Adam's face shone like the sun. But not all that shines is good."

So the eldress knew. Yet she did not look at Baraqua with disdain. When she had told the women briefly about Awan and the man at the river Naom covered her face. "Evil has come to our mountain and may never depart." She looked like she would begin to keen, but spoke instead. "Nothing you can tell us is as bad as what I must tell you both now," she said, her voice breaking.

"Of what do you speak, good eldress?" Dinah said, alarm in her voice.

"To my great shame, my own husband Enosh now keeps company with these men from the heavens. He turns his ear toward their voices. He agrees with their plans."

Baraqua sat down on the carved ironwood bench across the fire from the women. Three days before she had heard Enosh scoff openly at Adam's precautions for safety since the incursion. During Sabbath worship the elder's eyes seemed everywhere but on the sacrificial lamb.

Naom swiped at her tears. "My husband encourages alliances with the shining ones and will no doubt rejoice that Yammah and Yarih have been taken. He believes the superiority of these beings will improve the stock of the Sethites and give us a name on the earth."

"We have a name already," Dinah said with great feeling, then blushed. "Forgive me, Naom. I meant no disrespect."

"There is no need, Dinah," Naom said. "I know better than anyone that a strong delusion has taken the mind of my beloved." The circle of bread was now a charred disk. Naom stared at it sadly. "Enosh will find nothing at my fire to eat this night, for I will no longer prepare food for a traitor." She sighed. "There, I have said it. I will not keep faith with a husband who betrays his God and his people."

Dinah knelt and put her arm around Naom's shoulders. "Perhaps there is a misunderstanding, for how could our lord Enosh be all you say? she said.

Naom patted Dinah's arm. "You want to think that all bees seek pure nectar, Dinah. But I have watched my husband. He will no longer hear reason." She stood and straightened her gown.

Dinah placed a log of cedarwood on the fire and the low flames licked around it. The increased light seemed to bring a small amount of cheer.

But Naom was not finished. She gripped the top of her outer garment and rent it to her waist. "May God Most High have mercy on a people whose elders embrace ghouls," she cried. Then she ran toward the elders' clearing.

"I was cruel to rebuke her," Dinah said after a moment, watching the log burn.

"You are never cruel," Baraqua said. She felt strongly the contrast between herself and this woman who had suffered and yet remained tender and hopeful. Dinah would never think disloyal thoughts about Mahal as she herself did about Jared. She felt soiled by her attractions to both Shai and the shining man, yet helpless against what she felt. What could the dream angel have meant by choosing her for Jared instead of a worthier woman?

Jared's mother raised her chin. "I must speak my heart on a matter, though I will not insist on a response from you," she said.

Baraqua gestured her agreement, though she feared what the question might require of her.

"It has been some time since your nuptials and you have resided with my son as his wife," Dinah said. "But though you wear a married woman's sash and head covering, you do not have the look of a girl who is one in flesh with her husband." She turned away as though embarrassed at her audacity. She jumped up, knocking over the bench. "Please, love my son," she cried. Then she was gone.

Semjaza was having his way with the madwoman. But though he absorbed the pleasure, the Watcher's mind was not on the object of his lust. Through slices of shadow and light within the vast prisms of his angelic mind he saw three of the Seed Bearers' wives speaking together, with Baraqua among them. He could see the color of the women's essences as they sat at a low fire. Baraqua's aura was a dim violet. Character was weak in her and she struggled in her conscience. He smiled in the way of a cynical man. At the river he had seen that she desired him, hesitant though that desire was. Her conflict amused him. It was becoming harder to feel real ardor or compassion, even for Baraqua. He would have to adjust to this devolution.

The aura of the woman Naom was different, clear as a diamond of many facets, cultivated by years of attention Godward. She understood his origin and that of his cohort. She would fight against her own husband to thwart them. He would never be able to reach her.

The same intensity of virtue was in the heart of the mother of Jared, whose rock-like character had been formed by years of prayer to keep Lucifer from destroying Jared. The sight of Dinah within his mind made him feel momentarily weak by comparison.

Naom was running, her robe rent. Her warnings would be heeded by some but not all. Semjaza and his cohort would be irresistible to many because they promised the illusion of freedom that compliance with Adam's God could not. He and his cohort would conquer God's chosen people. They were, at their root, no different from the other tribes, willing to walk the easy path.

He pushed the madwoman aside. In her drugged state she was not aware of him. She sang incoherently of an opulent birthing room in a celestial castle. In reality she wallowed in bat guano and might die before she gave birth, for her child-belly had grown to an impossible size. How altered the wife of Rojj was from that first night he had seduced her in the outpouring of his sensual hunger.

He located the mental image of the elders' wives again. Let them weep or preach, let them struggle and storm. How little it would matter. Fatigue, hunger, and confusion were the daily norm for most human beings. Age gripped their bones too soon for them to aptly apply the wisdom they might accumulate over the years, and youthful heat soon faded to apathy. Less than a thousand years of life was allotted to these creatures in whom the breath of God resided. Ashes to ashes, dust to dust was the story of human existence.

How magnificent it was to be immortal. As an angel in the dark glory of the fallen state, the earth was Semjaza's for the taking. He would use the girl's strong attraction to both himself and the vinedresser to snuff that violet-hued aura from the Seed Bearer's bride.

CHAPTER 23

The generation of Enosh approached him and asked, "What is the name of your father?" to which he responded, "Seth." "The name of your grandfather?" "Adam." "And what was Adam's father's name?" they asked. "He had no father," Enosh explained. "G-d created his form from the earth and then blew into his nostrils a living soul." They said to Enosh, "Demonstrate how it was done." Enosh then took a handful of dirt and formed the image of a man, and the evil spirit entered into its nostrils and he became alive. The people declared this being as their god, and they believed in it.
from MIDRASH AGGADAH

When Baraqua entered the elders' clearing it was fireless, like a face without eyes. There was a hard, tense feeling in the air as people held torches against the gathering night and clustered near the carved thrones where the elders and their wives sat; Dinah white-faced and still, her arms clutching the arms of her chair; Eve composed, with the circlet of silvery mystery on her brow; Azure with the usual look of pleading in her face that people live in harmony. But Naom was not on her throne. She stood before the elders and heaped more dust on her head. Her rent gown fell off one shoulder. The chair beside Jared's new throne was empty, and Baraqua's heart beat hard as she realized it was for her. She must sit beside her husband, but she did not want to upset Dinah more at the sight of her. What misery, to know that your child is not loved by his own wife. Still, she must make some show of duty.

She circled the perimeter of the clearing and stepped onto the wooden dais that set the thrones apart from the area where the people gathered. She sat down on the new throne with its scent of freshly planed cedar, feeling for the first time the real privilege of her position. Jared put his hand over hers. "Pretend they aren't there," he said with a slight tilt of his head toward those who stared. Baraqua was glad when Naom spoke again.

"Turn from this fantasy before you destroy your soul, husband," Naom said.

Enosh's voice was harsh. His hands were clenched where they rested on the arms of his chair. "You, my own wife, think to shame me for wanting a better life for our people." He looked around the throng. "Not even Adam will dissuade me from mingling with the shining ones. Just one trek into Nod proved to me their intelligence and advancements in many trades that will enhance the lives of the earth's people. They are friendly toward us, and whatever their shortcomings might be, they are willing to share much-needed innovations with our people. The houses in some of their settlements emit the red light of orichalcum, beneficial to the spirit. They easily pump hot water from deep within the earth in which to bathe. And they teach the higher arts that raise human awareness." Enosh stood up, animation in his face. "These men are our future, and we Sethites must come into their circle of light with all the other clans and peoples of the earth, if we wish to advance."

Adam stood and faced Enosh. "Anointed One is our future, not the minions of Lucifer," he said firmly. "These men take women against their will. The 'higher arts' you speak of require calling on elemental spirits of Lucifer's lower realms. I do not call these things mere faults."

"It is not completely as you say regarding the women, forebear," the man Yusuf said, pushing through the crowd and gesturing respect to the elders. "Though some women are taken by force or beguilement, my daughters Yammah and Yarih went willingly, intrigued by promises of status and houses of marble. They have freely chosen to bear sons to the shining one who seeded their wombs."

"They share one man between them?" Adam said, stunned.

Yusuf bowed his head. "It is their way. Remorse will be my garment from this day forward, for Yammah even told me her sons will never come up the mountain to seek their grandparents' blessing."

Seth looked hard at Enosh. "So, men who take two wives and dishonor the rights of a grandfather are the future of the earth?"

Enosh's jaw was rigid and he did not respond to Seth. How different he was from the brusque though amicable elder of mere months before. "Your daughters are courageous for embracing the new way," he said to Yusuf. "Perhaps one of their sons will be our long-awaited Anointed One, for surely a man with enough influence to lead the earth back to Eden must possess some celestial origin."

"The house of Enosh lies under a dark sky," muttered a man near Baraqua, and the people began to whisper. Seth thrust his elder's staff into the ground. "This is a blasphemous saying and shows you are deceived, son Enosh," he said, and his voice trembled with anger. "Years ago, you said in the hearing of the people that you doubted Anointed One will come at all. Now you say the savior must have celestial origins."

"We cannot intermingle with these men," Adam said sternly. "They have left their original habitation to live double lives on the earth."

Enosh's face darkened. "I believe God will accept all this as part of his his established order. Did he not create angels just as he made humankind?"

"God's revelation as inscribed in the *Chronicles* does not change," Adam countered. "Angelic beings and human ones are not to intermingle."

"You only assume that," Enosh said.

Jared stood, and after him his father Mahal, as though they read each other's minds. Mahal spoke. "In our visions, my son and I saw nothing holy or good connected with the beings who descended. The vision offered their clear intent of evil, so much that we still wake in the night, floating in our own sweat at the memory of those visions."

"It is as he says," Jared added. "Anything these shining ones offer must be opposed."

Many of the people began to beat their ears in agreement at the elders' words, though some looked confused. Naom's eyes were still fixed on Enosh. Baraqua wanted to go to her side and tell the people about Awan and the man at the river. Perhaps this would alert Enosh. But she saw Rojj's face across the clearing, barely discernable in the dim light. She would not publicly humiliate that one who had already borne the unbearable for too long. And to her shame, she wanted to keep the story to herself for a while, to savor the memory of how the man had looked at her, wanted her. *Shai*—

"Come, wife," Enosh said to Naom, taking a step toward her and extending his hand. "I go now to my new people and you must follow where I lead."

Naom took a step back, her face drawn in disbelief. "Did you hear what the prophets just reminded us about this?" she said. She looked from Mahal to Enosh and back again. "You betray heaven and I no longer call you husband."

Enosh dropped his hand, disbelief in his face. No elder's wife had ever contradicted her husband before the people. There had never been need. "Then it will be as though we never stood beneath the canopy," he said slowly. With one heave he pushed over his heavy throne. The sacred symbol of his authority hit the ground with a sickening thud. He spit upon the throne, glared briefly at Adam, then disappeared into the trees, his son Tarshish behind him.

CHAPTER 24

And I continued south and saw a place which burns day and night,
where there are seven mountains of magnificent stones—
I ENOCH 18:6

...Uriel, one of the holy angels, who is
over the world and Tartarus—
I ENOCH 20:2

And the angels which kept not their first estate...
he hath reserved in everlasting chains under
darkness unto the judgment of the great day.
JUDE 6

Semjaza stood on the icy roof of the underworld, the very narthex of hell. He had come to the desolate plain of Dûdâêl at the far extremity of the disk of the earth to glimpse his destiny. Here the sun crawled low on the horizon day and night and not a blade of grass nor the smallest creature lived within the windy ice fields. Below him, sea waters lapped at the foot of the towering ice wall he stood on, holding intact the earth's waters.

He tried to remember: had God really said hell was his destiny? Perhaps Tartarus was not real after all. Could a holy and benevolent God be capable of creating such a place? To find out he would have to face Uriel, the archangelic guardian of the underworld. His pride barely endured the thought. But he must know if his name was truly in the register of the inhabitants of the pit. Perhaps it had been there once but was now erased. God had surely seen how competent Semjaza was in his new role on the earth, using the gift of free will to accomplish much. Surely all expression of moral freedom glorified God in some way.

Screens of undulating light of many colors shimmered across the sky that stretched beyond the seven jeweled mountains of Dûdâêl. The mountain range was a legendary cache of jacinth, pearl, and redstone, free to any man who dared navigate the frozen seas and climb the ice wall. The highest peak of the seven mountains was formed of crystal antimony, gleaming under the weak sunlight, radiating the energies of the perpetual sunset that ruled this boundary land of the earth.

He dreaded what he might find beneath the ice. God had not intended any being to inhabit the underworld. But Lucifer's rebellion in heaven and the human sin committed in Eden had changed everything. Already Sheol contained the souls of both righteous and wicked people, awaiting future judgment. But Tartarus was a place apart, set aside for the Watchers. He must see what it was like. Perhaps he could destroy it.

He had not started out that day to think obsessively about Tartarus. He had moved as usual among his apprentices in the grove of oaks. Powerful talismans hung from mossy branches and the incense whose smoke could alter the mind's perception filled the air. His students pored over gilt-edged books and drew the captivating Luciferian lessons into themselves. His female students were becoming accomplished in spellcasting and the reading of root threads. At the corners of the eyes of his favorites he set star-like buds of power and put wands of enchantment into their hands. He had been instructing an especially lovely girl in the pretention of knowledge of the future when he had heard the sound of weeping from the heavens, the sound of a grief unabated. He had spewed a curse. God Most High was grieving a great loss, and Semjaza knew it was him. Though he was hardened to the divine he had acted on a sudden compulsion to find out if Tartarus was truly his fate.

He gazed on the junction where the domed sky rose behind the seven mountains that lined this outback of the earth. One day he would bring his mighty sons here to shatter that glassy firmament and open up the vastness of the space that lay beyond it. What an affront to God that would be. The enthroned One would regret he had denied Lucifer a share in his power. He would regret that he had kept the chieftain Semjaza waiting in the antechamber.

He materialized before the forbidding gate set in the flank of the first of the seven mountains. An appalling silence issued from behind the gate that led down to Sheol. It was worse than the moaning of the incessant wind. The archangel Uriel stood quietly by, that solemn keeper of the bowels of the earth whose brilliance contrasted with the darkness behind him. Semjaza eyed the archangel's sword and the scepter the colossal being held as a symbol of his authority. Though permeated with God's righteousness, Uriel's countenance was also taut with anguish. Uriel never stopped grieving the fate of the inhabitants below. Yet Semjaza could tell that Uriel had no respect for him.

"Have you come to be tormented before the time, traitor of God Most High?" Uriel said with contempt in his tone. The archangel's eyes blazed and the gleam of the mysterious, fiery red cross on his breastplate forced Semjaza's eyes away.

Semjaza felt a pang of sudden envy. Why hadn't God granted him the power of an archangel as he had Uriel? To have authority over the underworld was a considerable honor. "I offer you a bevy of soft-bodied women for a day at your station," he said impulsively. He would like to discover whether he had the power to harrow the depths of hell as Uriel did.

But Uriel was not listening. His attention was directed toward the sound of heavenly praises erupting before the Throne high above, cherubim and seraphim falling down as they sung the thrice-holy hymn. It was too bad, Semjaza mused, that one couldn't live between good and evil, using whichever source of power suited the moment.

But Uriel had discerned Semjaza's jealousy. "How strange that you desire a station where utter allegiance to God is required." With his scepter the guardian of the underworld gestured behind the gate. "Go then and see what has been reserved for celestials who break the laws of the cosmos to cavort with flesh and blood."

Semjaza felt a stab of fear. Would he survive the journey? Tartarus would be empty; there would be no one to help. He took a last look at the curtains of light in the southern sky and descended into the cavernous void.

He soon found himself at the head of a vast cavern with something like cliffs rising on either side. On the left, faint rays from some eerie light source barely illumined a throng of opaque human beings who huddled behind large boulders or struggled to climb from steaming pits, sliding over each other like newly hatched lizards. The features of these people were obscured by devouring worms that covered their eyes and mouths. Occasionally one of the stronger ones would pounce upon what must be an adversary. But even they did not seem to have enough strength or skill to inflict real harm. Curses followed these attacks, but the words were uninspired, vapid punctuations that fell like feathers from molting birds, the same words repeated again and again without effect.

"I take— I hate— I defy—" the miserable souls moaned. Among them were some whose hearts Semjaza himself had tried to instruct in the days of his service to God. How futile his work had been, for those he had tried to nurture ultimately preferred darkness to light. He drew himself up smugly. He was glad for their demise. He would work to bring many more souls to this place. If he must spend eternity here, so would they.

The other side of the chasm was slightly brighter and the ground contained no rough places or steaming pits. The faces of the souls there were clear, without the devouring worms. Their expressions were serene as they spoke to each other or stared across the chasm, wiping what might be tears from their cheeks as they viewed the chaos and suffering. Semjaza recognized some Sethites among them, as well as people of other lands who had obeyed their consciences without clear knowledge of the God of the Sethites. Near the edge of the cliff on that side was an altar of white stones on which something that looked like a lamb lay and before which a man prostrated himself in an attitude of worship.

A man on the left side of the chasm was staring across the chasm at the man before the altar. He had no arms and only one eye. Despite the distortion of his face because of the worms, Semjaza knew the man was Adam's son Cain, the earth's first murderer, and that the man at the altar was his brother Abel.

Abel put his hand on the lamb's head. A shaft of white light rose and an aroma like myrrh permeated the stale air of the cavern. At the sight of the fire the creatures on Cain's side began to moan. They turned their faces from the fire and the lamb and some crawled beneath stones. But Abel and the souls near him began to sing a hymn. Semjaza cringed. Even in the underworld, God Most High was praised.

Hate flashed in Cain's face and he staggered to the rim of the cliff. "I would murder you again if I could, simpering excuse for a man," he hurled across the abyss. The voice sounded more like a dying animal than a man.

Abel walked to the edge, as though trying to get as close to Cain as possible. "I have forgiven you for the stone you brought down on my skull, brother," he said in a voice like music. "I have forgiven those arms you no longer possess that performed the murderous deed. I will never stop loving you."

Cain shrieked, overcome with rage as worms fell from the semblance of his mouth. "Even in death you are a fool, for you continue that foul sacrifice. You know nothing of the glory of hatred, but I will feed you with mine through all eternity."

"It is the sacrifice of the lamb that takes away all hate, Cain," Abel called out, and the music of his voice was more somber.

Semjaza would hear no more. Their fates were sealed and he had his own to contend with. He turned from the souls who had given themselves to darkness in their earthly lives and from those on the smooth side who had walked in the light of conscience. He submitted himself to the space between the cliffs; he must descend further. He did not know how long he fell, for, like heaven, there seemed to be no passing of time. The abyss was unutterably dark and even with his strong discernment he had no idea where he was in relation to the rest of the underworld.

The air began to press tightly around him. He felt no actual restraint yet realized suddenly that he could not move. He was suspended now within what he knew instinctively was absolute nothingness, an anti-presence without reference point. He grappled to understand; he was in a place that was not a place, a limbo apart from creation, utterly without significance, future, or challenge. He called out, but no creature answered. And then he knew. This was the utter absence of God.

CHAPTER 25

And Azazel taught men to make swords, and knives,
and shields, and breastplates, and made known to them
the metals of the earth and the art of working them.
I ENOCH 8:1

Semjaza moved quicker than light away from frigid Dûdâêl. That he had broken free of the shackles of Tartarus had been the doing of Uriel, though he would never acknowledge it. He had forgotten to look in the book to see if his name was there. He did not want to know. The memory of that horror would haunt him always. He brought up the image of Baraqua to stabilize his mind; her face soft in the light before dawn as she tended her campfire; her hair catching the morning sun; his own anticipation of her arms around him. The thought cheered him in his humiliation.

But what had he expected of the deepest pit of the underworld? He had survived it and would not be frightened any longer. Through Baraqua he would sire a thousand sons. When she finally succumbed to death, he would take other women to bear him more. Those mighty men would protect him on the day God tried to punish him. There had to be limits, even to God.

He moved over churning seas that teemed with brightly colored sea creatures. He passed steaming jungles and gentle meadowlands through which rivers of perfect clarity wound, so clear under the sky that they seemed to reflect the wonders of the seventh heaven itself. Undulations of warm, sunlit air blew from the treasure houses of the winds. Earth was a good place to conquer.

Suddenly the angel Hadriel blocked his pathway through the sky as he moved toward Nod. "Woe to those who seek dominion over what has been given to others," the keeper of the east wind said in a voice as changeful as wind itself. "Repent; no one knows how far the mercy of God may extend."

"Your cawing will not deter me," Semjaza said to the angel. How dare this wind sprite confront a chieftain of Watchers who had been victorious before the high Throne. From his ever-darkening core he spewed curses over Hadriel, but the wind angel was unphased. "You damn yourself by your own choices, yet you think to use the holy name to bring wrath on others." Hadriel laughed merrily, caught the tail of the west wind, and disappeared.

Semjaza's sight was clouded with rage. Hadriel would one day bow to him, he decided. He would cover the mouth of that lowly wind keeper and make him his slave. He paused among some high, wispy clouds, orienting himself to what he must do next. He needed to attend to things in Nod, though craving for the body of the madwoman urged him in another direction. But alarm registered in his spirit. Something was not as it should be. He looked in the direction of his grove of magic. The vibrations of the mysteries were gone; another energy had replaced them. He winged downward, aghast to see that many of the precious oaks had been severed near the roots. Smoke billowed from metal forges that had been set up where his cauldrons of wool of bat and adder's tongue had boiled that morning. The fine cushions his apprentices laid on while being indoctrinated by aerial spirits were trampled with mud.

He descended into what was left of the grove. His students were gone, except one. Azazel was leading the half-dressed girl beneath a tree, singing one of his ballads. The fire of seduction was in the angel's eyes, willingness carved into the student's drugged smile.

Semjaza wanted to erupt with rage. Azazel's audacity made Semjaza want to erupt with rage. He would destroy the powerful Watcher with the breath of his mouth. But such evil emanated from Azazel that he held back. Myriad Noddish brutes were carrying back-breaking loads of oak logs from the severed trees to the new forges that glowed with heat intense enough to melt ores of the earth into metal. Members of his own cohort, manifesting in bodies as tall as the oaks themselves goaded the men on with whips of sharp light and the hum of a strong Luciferian tremor moved the ground. He would have to find another way to reclaim his territory. He strode to the forges. From spouts in the sides of the furnaces ran streams of fiery liquid before which men held stone molds to catch the molten substance in the shapes of swords, daggers, and arrows, the regalia of war. These weapons were the defining symbols of Azazel's long-intended vocation as the founder of war on earth. Angry as Semjaza was, he felt irresistible pleasure at the sight of these accouterments of suffering.

Azazel turned from the woman he was ready to conquer. He was even more enthralling in male splendor than the last time Semjaza had seen him, swathed this time in a robe that captured every nuance of light and shadow as though that fabric held the secrets of the cosmos itself in its folds.

"Where are the amulets and raven feathers? Where are my students?" Semjaza said.

Azazel seemed amused. "You take a spontaneous journey and expect people to focus without you?" he said. He gestured to the forges. "Oak burns hottest. I will take what I need and move on when I am ready."

"You have authority over much, so why must you disturb my territory? Semjaza said.

"Sacrifices must be made to the ultimate glory of Lucifer," Azazel answered. "The magic you thought to peddle here is somewhat useful in distorting reality in the minds of men, but slow to work. The magnitude of destruction I will accomplish through war is neither slow nor subtle. Many lives can be snuffed quickly through the tearing of flesh and spilling of blood."

"But these things are mine," Semjaza insisted again.

Azazel adopted a look of mock confusion. "Since when do you, a condemned angel, set down standards of right and wrong?" he said. "Wasn't Lucifer's impulse at the rebellion raw covetousness? Our creed is always, 'What is yours must become mine.'"

Semjaza felt his own limitations strongly. He could not fight Azazel, and the horror of Tartarus was still with him.

Azazel was inspecting some of the molds spread on the ground with their lethal contents hardening to blades and spears. "Besides, you and your cohort are only here because I provided the key," he said.

Semjaza's ire rose. "It is I who petitioned the Throne directly; it is you who owe me." He must calculate like a cat yet not underestimate Azazel, the right hand of Lucifer himself.

Azazel smirked. "Your petition was nothing, and you make a fool of yourself by bragging about it." His look was sly. "Did Lucifer seek God's permission to start that war in heaven?"

Semjaza's mind whirled back to that ancient day. It had happened in the twinkle of an eye. Lucifer, light bearer, had been the high and jeweled one, his cherubic beauty dazzling the host of heaven as he stormed the Throne. It had taken an instant for Michael to send him embedded in prongs of lightening down the sky.

Azazel was laughing, mocking. "Don't sulk. Semjaza," he said. "Only the end result matters." He gestured at the forges. "War is one of Lucifer's most brilliant ideas, the best. He says that I remain and you leave." He unhinged one of the molds and a half hardened, glowing blade fell into his hand. The man stoking the forge gave a shout of warning, then stared at Azazel's unharmed hand, impervious to the heat. The stoker and other men knelt before Azazel, sweat streaming from their bodies in the heat. "Hail to Azazel, god of war!" they cried.

Azazel looked down with distaste at the groveling men. More men joined the ones at Azazel's feet, eager to be part. They did not seem to notice Semjaza.

"I do the plebians a good," Azazel said, as though he and Semjaza were alone. "Men are compelled to worship something and are miserable without it." He gestured to the numerous bronze blades cooling under the trees and the iron hilts ready to be fastened to them, each engraved with a human skull. "I will make open war on the Sethites, and you will see in those I have trained a perfection of aggression and hatred unknown on the earth until now." His expression was as though he was consuming something and insatiable for more. "We will stop the breath of all Sethite men. Sacrifice at Adam's stinking altar will cease forever and their women will be ours."

Semjaza imagined Baraqua at her fireside. That hair— "You will take all the women?" he said, as though it was of little importance to him.

Azazel leered. "Is there one among them you insist I spare?" he said. Then he seemed to crumble slightly. He cried out and scanned the sky, and an expression of terror distorted the artfully composed features. "Of a truth, Tartarus awaits us," he said in a hushed voice, as though he had seen something he could not bear.

Triumph welled in Semjaza. So, even the crafty Azazel feared the destiny. He took the moment of Azazel's weakness to disappear into the sky without another word. Let the grand seducer have the oak grove. Let him slaughter in war as he would. Azazel would have to put sons between himself and divine judgment like the rest of the Watchers. He returned at light speed to the wasteland of Dûdâêl. An idea was forming in his mind that would make Azazel timorous with envy. With one deft movement he plucked the four-sided pyramidic alabaster crystal from the seventh mountain. He formed a funnel wind, wrapped himself and the crystal within, and moved northward across the lands with the richest soil. Into the whirlwind he sucked masses of fertile loam as the funnel leveled villages and carved out canyons, drawing everything of value into its core. He guided the funnel to the center of the sea just below the mountain of the Sethites, and at the chosen place he sprang free from the screaming vortex and watched the whirlwind let fall its load in thundering avalanches of rock and earth. For hours the sea writhed with turbulence and threw up waves against the shore of the mountain. As the sun neared its setting, a land mass appeared high above the line of the water. The great mound of earth grew until its size was sixty-six stadia long.

Semjaza straddled the island and set the massive crystal at the highest point. Immediately the sides of the pyramid began to emit energy and absorb the afternoon light, and the angel felt his own energy surge.

Now the crystal began to emit unearthly music with the lilt of Lucifer in it. Whispered promises of love and everlasting life moved within breezes across the island as the shoots of young plants rose out of the ground and small trees shot up, budding before Semjaza's eyes. Flowers gave off their scents, and Semjaza noticed that the stamens of some of the exotic blossoms were as cunning as the talons of birds of prey. Human beings would never guess.

"I am equal to the High God," Semjaza thundered. "In my greatness I have wrought something out of nothing."

CHAPTER 26

What is it that always is but never comes to be,
and what is it that comes to be but never is?
PLATO'S ACCOUNT OF ATLANTIS
IN *TIMAEUS AND CRITIAS*

Baraqua and Jared went with many others down the mountain the day after the tumult in the Flood Sea in order to observe the miraculous new island that glittered far beyond the shores of the mountain. The older Sethites stayed a dignified distance from the water's edge, but younger people waded into the water to battle the enormous waves that still pounded in the aftermath of the island's coming into existence, its appearance like a glowing cloud from where they stood.

Shai came to them and handed Baraqua one of the devices tipped with curved glass that Sethite scouts used while on mission, though it was a mystery where they had obtained them. "Everything is larger seen through this," he said. He did not meet her eyes directly.

But Jared protested. "Why would we want to see more of what has its origin in evil?" he said. "Some of my brothers took boats to its shores last night at sunset and turned back. They felt the deception."

Baraqua was annoyed. Something in her wanted to defend the subtle thrill that hummed in her heart regarding the island. "How can your brothers speak so since they did not explore the island?" she said, taking the magnifying device.

She felt Jared studying her. Did he suspect anything beyond the possibility that she might be pleased by Shai's presence? She could never let him know her struggle with attraction to the shining man.

"Cities in the sea do not appear overnight, Baraqua," Jared said. "There is nothing good there." But she raised the device to her eye anyway, and what she saw took her breath. Before her was the city she had dived to beneath the lake of Elda so many years before. Dwellings of white stone were built on the sides of gradual slopes ascending to the top of the island. At the apex, a pyramidic crystal radiated light from within. Around the island, trees heavy with ripe fruit grew, and hanging vines adorned city walls between lavishly tiled fountains. The elder Enosh had created a fountain of forced water once, an amazing invention that sent sparkling drops high into the air in arcs to splash again into a clear pool. She had been fascinated by it. But these fountains were far more advanced and looked to be made of the sublime rock called marble. She could have stood all day watching the water of those fountains rise and fall, the shining people on the curved pathways, and the strangely fertile look of the land.

"Eden must have been like this," she whispered. She had never felt so conflicted. The man on the lake had promised her this place as her inheritance, her right. How could something so beautiful have an evil source?

Something caught her eye. "By the stones of the altar, I see Yammah, daughter of Yusuf."

Jared snatched the magnifying device from her and trained it into the sea. "She is great with child and walks beside one of the shining ones," he said. "I wonder where Yarih is."

But there was no more chance to look at the island, for a commotion was starting further up the beach. "In one day, the gods give rebirth to Eden," sang a group of young men who were playing in the waves as though they were children. One plied a lyre, though he seemed to know nothing of the instrument. "The gods will share their women and we will give them our hearts in exchange," the men sang. Other men were hauling a small boat across the sand and arguing over who was to take it into the water first.

Two of them began to fight, and Jared ran to them and pulled them apart. "What nonsense is this?" he shouted. "You would seek women among devils instead of through the council of the dream angel?"

Baraqua skirted around the group to better hear. She saw the sulk in the men's eyes at Jared's disruption.

"Ah, the son of Mahal, who never deserved Dinah." It was Tarshish, son of Enosh, who stood within the group. "Since Adam is not here to reprimand our every word and gesture, this false elder seeks to rule over us." Tarshish looked around the group, his eyes darting. He laughed nervously at the blank looks of the men, and Baraqua thought he had never looked more like his father.

"Do you know that this imposter's wife is still a virgin?" Tarshish said, and appraised Baraqua's body with his eyes. A few of the young people laughed nervously, though others hung their heads out of respect.

"You know nothing of it, Tarshish," one of Jared's cousins said, and moved nearer to Jared.

"I know a virgin when I see one," Tarshish answered, his eyes narrowing. "And I know Jared is ignorant of the proper way to woo a woman."

A few people walked away. Naom had been standing with Azure and some of her daughters and approached Tarshish. "Son of my body, do not bring a mother grief with such disrespect," she cried.

Tarshish laughed. "Ah, the woman my father left in order to pursue better things threatens me with tears. Will you rent your garment again before the people to show your false piety?"

Naom paled. She looked small and vulnerable. Baraqua went to her and led her away.

"My son, my son," Naom wailed into Baraqua's shoulder as Baraqua guided her into the trail that went up the mountain. Baraqua could think of nothing to say, so neither spoke again as they climbed, each one subdued under Tarshish's humiliating words. In the camp Baraqua took Naom to her tent and brought her orange water. Then she went to her own shelter. The people would know soon enough what Tarshish had said and she did not want to answer questions. She changed into a sleeping garment, though it was early in the day. She would sleep awhile and things would look different. She sat very still before the incense burner where she usually prayed, but the prayers seemed to fall to the ground before they left the tent. The way the morning light filtered through the ceiling depressed her. She knew she could not let the words of a fool disturb her, yet it was a terrifying thought that her life was so transparent that a person like Tarshish somehow knew about her. No doubt he had ridiculed Jared for his virginity as well after she left. To bruise others was easy for one who did not value virtue or duty, who lived life by rules others did not dare embrace.

"We reap from the seed we sow," she muttered. She had thought herself secretive, clever, but knew now that she was as obvious as a child. Dinah had known something all along and even calloused Tarshish had intuition.

Jared came into the tent and sat down across from her. Her sleeping garment was cut low and after a while she saw in his eyes a longing for her. But they stayed in their usual places, both desire and resistance between them as always.

"Adam sent the son of Enosh to the tent of chastisement for a week, but I wager he will leave the mountain before sunset," Jared said. He did not speak of what Tarshish had done and Baraqua did not blame him. The words had cut deep into the things they both feared most. He sat eating fruit from a bowl and she wished she wanted him. He was fine of form in the manner of the best-looking men. She would not tell him how drawn she was to the island and tried to push down the sense of her own right to follow the carved walkway past the orchard and up to that mysterious crystal. She despised herself for wanting it.

In the morning ten bodies were found washed up on the southern shore. Against many warnings some had tried to swim the sea's erratic current out to the island. Seven women had left in two boats. They sent a message to Adam that they would take up life with the elder Enosh, the new viceroy for beings no human men could ever compete with.

CHAPTER 27

And the sons of men in those days took from the cattle
of the earth, the beasts of the field, and the fowls of the
air, and taught the mixture of animals of one species
with the other, in order therewith to provoke the Lord—
BOOK OF JASHER 4:18

The giants turned against them and devoured mankind. And
they began to sin against birds, and beasts, and reptiles, and
fish…Then the earth laid accusation against the lawless ones—
I ENOCH 7:4-6

Baraqua stood in the easternmost orchard of the mountain, the place where mysterious trees grew that each bore three varieties of fragrant fruit. Legend spoke of seeds that had blown out of Eden and sprung up in that fertile location to remind the people that in paradise, as soon as fruit was plucked, a new piece blossomed and ripened within a day.

She had come to the orchard with Bathshae and a few other women. But some had babies to suckle or a meal to prepare, and Obed was fretting on the blanket where Bathshae had set him to play while she worked.

"Return to the camp without me," Baraqua had said to Bathshae as her sister loaded the wagon with baskets of the Edenic fruit. "I'll follow you soon with Eli." She wanted to finish filling her basket. Their mother had been low of spirit and she would bring her some of the succulent red fruit, for it was reputed to treat melancholy. But the sky was darkening more quickly than she had considered. Jared's brother Eli dozed under a tree. She would not tell Jared that his young brother was more a nuisance than a guard. She pulled gently on an overly ripe persimmon and it fell into her hand. Had the forbidden fruit Eve plucked that dreadful day in Eden come away this easily from the tree of the Knowledge of Good and Evil?

She thought about the miracle of the island four days before. It was all the Sethites spoke of now and seemed to dispel some of the gloom that had settled over the camp since the incursion over the western mountains, for the island looked truly beautiful.

But Adam was distraught at the people's interest. "For shame, to speak of this island as though it is paradise itself. Have you dug beneath the surface of what looks like soil or eaten fruit from its alleged trees? Nothing good will come of a place that casts such an eerie light."

Baraqua had said nothing. She abhorred her own curiosity about the island, but the desire to see it would not leave her.

"Please, help me." An unfamiliar female voice came from the trees beyond the orchard. Could one of the fruit pickers still be there, perhaps with a twisted ankle?

She walked toward the place where the voice had come from and pushed some vines aside. Before her, deep in shadow, was the head and shoulders of a woman about her age, lying beneath a tule tree. The girl's face was not familiar or comely. It was streaked with dirt and her short hair was matted.

"Send me where I won't suffer anymore," the girl moaned. Baraqua took a step toward her and stifled a scream. What lay beneath the tule tree was not a girl at all, but what appeared to be a mixture of a human woman and a snake of substantial girth. It possessed the head and shoulders of a woman, but where arms, torso, and legs should have been, the body of a spotted serpent coiled, meshing seamlessly with the human shoulders—two beings in one. Baraqua's hands tingled with shock. She could barely control her breath. She turned to run, stumbled on a root, and fell.

"I won't hurt you if you will help me." The voice was clearly human, yet somehow animal in its tenor. Baraqua forced herself to face the creature. Even in the dimming light, Baraqua could see that the eyes looked serpentine, with narrow, elongated pupils.

"What is it you suffer from?" Baraqua said, forcing what she hoped was courage into her voice.

"You mock me with such a question," the creature said in its peculiar tone. "Don't you see the horror of my existence? One of the gods implanted the seed of a snake within my mother and I am the result."

The gods. Yes, the shining ones. Was there anything they would not taint? But Baraqua shook her head. "Snakes breed according to their kind, as do human beings, birds, and sheep. These kinds are fixed from the Creator's hand and cannot mix." She said the words by rote. Everyone knew the law of kinds.

"And yet this impossible mix is before you," the creature said. "My mother died giving birth to a humanlike creature with the teeth of a lion that sought to make a meal of me. I escaped to this mountain, for someone told me there was decency here."

"You expect me to believe something I know is impossible?" Baraqua said. Her mind whirled. She must have gone to sleep under the fruit trees and dreaming. She would soon awaken. The moon would be in the west and then morning would come to the sky.

"Then don't believe it. But I beg you to take my life since I am unable to." The creature nodded toward a nearby stone the size of a large round of bread. "Bring that stone down on my head or I will be at the mercy of those who would breed me with yet another creature and produce something even more hideous."

"How is it you appear to be a young woman when the gods have not been on the earth long enough for you to be more than a child?" Baraqua said.

"The lifespan of the serpent whose spell-cast seed entered my mother lives but a few years, so my human traits developed quickly," the creature answered. It writhed, clearly miserable. "Kill me now, I beg you."

"My people do not kill what has the breath of life in it, either human or animal. We eat only plants and certain sea creatures without the blood of life in them."

"The laws of what is permissible or impermissible are changing. Things will no longer be what they were," the creature said.

"Whatever your body may look like, you still speak and reason, a human trait," Baraqua said. Her mind was in turmoil. That she was talking like this could not be real.

A slender, divided tongue slipped from the human mouth and retracted. The eyes filmed and the creature's face looked less like a young woman than the moment before. Or was it the fading light that made it seem so? "I have brain to think and tongue to speak with, but not a soul. I know well that I am a twilight being with no rightful place in the order of the cosmos," it said.

"How can you have such depth of thought?" Baraqua said. It was as though it had prophetic powers.

"I do not know," the creature said. "Perhaps as a warning." But suddenly it began to deteriorate. "Truth is… brutal," it articulated, clearly finding it difficult to form words as it had. "…witness… deeds… spawn of evil ones… if good and evil there be." The tongue darted and retracted, and the serpentine coils undulated. Baraqua backed away.

"You will… regret—" The human mouth stretched wide, snake-like, wrapping the face, lipless. The human neck was vanishing, leaving a long, protruding serpent's head with eyes on either side of the face.

Baraqua eyed the stone. God's prohibition was holy. But Adam had never taught the people to account for the thing that sprawled before her.

Something heavy slid along her back. The creature's coils had reached her in an instant and were wrapping her middle. She felt contractions against her ribs, the coils circling her, imprisoning one arm. The pressure forced the air from Baraqua's lungs and she gasped, trying to draw another breath.

"One of us... die," the creature said, the words barely discernable. What was left of the human shoulders began to move rhythmically with the powerful serpentine muscles. Baraqua's vision narrowed, darkness seeped into the rims of her eyes. She groped for the stone with her free hand, felt its weight. Was it heavy enough to kill? She raised the stone and heard it strike something hard. She gasped as the coils relaxed, drawing in the breath that would save her.

When she had freed herself from the coils she sat weeping until the halfmoon rose, shaking too hard to stand. She would not look at the face of the being that lay silent, dead. She finally rose and found the tree where Eli had been, but he was not there. She forgot the basket of fruit and made her way to the tent where Jared sat staring into a low fire with a half-eaten bowl of potage in his hands. "Where were you?" He sounded both angry and frightened. "Eli looked everywhere." She fell into his arms and he carried her to her sleeping mat. She told him what she could, her voice shaking, the horror of the changing face of the creature rearing in her mind with every word she spoke.

He brought her tea to make her drowsy, then rummaged at the back of the tent for a shovel. "Eli will be punished for leaving you," he said. I am sending your father to watch over you until I return."

"No one must know of this thing," she said.

"The people have a right to know," he answered. "The snake woman was right; everything is changing." He went into the darkness, the tip of his torch pushing back the night.

Rasujal and Bathshae came, built up the fire, and Bathshae made her eat of the day-old potage, heated until it steamed.

"I heard what the son of Enosh said about you and Jared," Rasujal said. "Remember, daughter, the dream angel is never wrong."

She said nothing to that, for the less said, the better. The hot soup was relaxing her insides.

"It was not human after all, that thing in the trees," Bathshae said. Baraqua wondered whether her sister was only trying to convince herself.

"It sounded human," Baraqua replied. Something had changed in her the moment she brought the stone down on the creature's head. Something was breaking apart. She was not like the others, for she had murdered what had the breath of life in its nostrils. She would have to confess it to Adam.

She went back into the tent and her father kept the fire high outside, burning back the night of her horror. She woke to see Jared sitting beside her, the moon low. Jared looked like he was going to be sick.

"I set a makeshift headstone over its grave," he said. "May God not oppose me for marking the memory of a monster." He said nothing more for a long time. She wanted to take his hand but did not. To touch anyone might cause her to go mad. She would keep as still as she could until the sun showed its cleansing face again.

"There was nothing in my vision or my father's about serpents with human faces, or about an island born in one night, or shining, inhuman men women find irresistible." He looked at her with sincere appeal, as though seeking her thoughts. "This enemy is a shadow, a ghoul. Even if we had the Cainite weapons legend says Tubal-Cain forged at the doorway to hell, would they make a difference against such powers?"

Baraqua remembered a hymn the women sometimes sang while beating out flax. "The Lord is my strength, a high tower of safety."

He took her hand. She saw then who he was; a good man visited by a dire revelation, with a longing to do what was right.

"Please find the rind of a lemon to cleanse my hands," he said. "I may never be rid of the odor of what I buried beneath those vines."

Baraqua woke toward dawn, her heart strangely peaceful. She had dreamed of the city in the sea in its ethereal radiance. But Jared was right; nothing that quickly cultivated could be good or truly real. The same ones who had formed that island were the authors of the misery of the creature she had killed. They were a race of deceivers with power to cause great suffering. She pulled at the thread around her neck on which Shai's pearl hung. It snapped and the jewel slid into her hand. Her neck felt bare without the cherished emblem, yet clean. To gain one thing, another must be set aside, for a divided heart would never be free. She pushed the pearl beneath her sleeping mat. She would toss it into the river so it would be impossible to retrieve.

She wept then. It was for the loss of the pearl, but more for the blindness of her own heart. It was time to relinquish fantasy and value life with Jared in their humble Sethite tent.

Jared stirred on his mat. "Do you weep because you believe you murdered?"

"Is it an aberration to believe she possessed a soul?" she said.

"*She* told you she had no soul," Jared said quietly. "Yet I too struggle to know, for something against reason compelled me to place that grave marker."

"I weep also because that creature symbolizes me," Baraqua said, relieved that it was not too hard to be honest with Jared. "It is as though I had to kill one part of me to save the rest." She moved closer to him. He smelled of lemon rind and of the sweat he had shed to bury something neither of them could comprehend. She thought about kissing him. She realized she had never wondered until that moment what the feel of his mouth on hers would be like.

CHAPTER 28

And the women became pregnant and they bare large
giants, whose height was three thousand ells.
I ENOCH 6:3

Semjaza studied the woman's enormous child belly, sagging to the side like an entity in itself as she slept under the influence of the potion he had given her. The birth of his child could not be long in coming, for with his angelic sight he could see a restless outline within the hugely distended womb. Unlike the women who were bearing the children of Armaros, Azazel, and others, this child would be too large for this girl to deliver, and live. The pallor of her skin and the receding eye sockets told him that she was dying already. The skin of her midsection had become a mass of bloody fissures to accommodate the creature within. Semjaza turned away. The madwoman's death did not matter. It was a necessary sacrifice in the establishment of the earth's new order and the dissipation of the race of Adam.

He moved his hands over that nest of his offspring. A low growl came from the womb as he pressed at the top and sides of that container of power. This was no whimper of a tiny infant, but the sounding of a being with promise for something much more. He knew the female body well enough. Maybe he should press the child out or conjure it forth. He would decide later.

He went to the mouth of the cave and cursed the night, the lowly dwelling, and the woman who had become a burden to him. He thought of Azazel's five women from out of the southern deserts— regal and black-skinned, their long necks ringed in circlets of gold. The faces of Armaros's women were serene beneath jeweled tiaras, quick to learn spellcasting and enchantments, skilled in seduction and admired by all. Each of those women had already borne a boy-child, toothy and well-formed, growing already to great size. Shrines were being erected to the young princes by the peoples of the land.

But delivering half-angelic children through the bodies of normal women had still not been easy. Semjaza was pleased that Azazel had been forced to humble himself before Lucifer when his wives came into distress, donning the skin of a common wolf and hopping through fire in order to see his sons born alive.

The girl stirred in her sleep and murmured Semjaza's name. Her lips twitched and she ran her hands unconsciously over her belly. He tore the front of the blood-stained garment from her body and saw that the skin fissures were opening still wider. He would never debase himself in the fire dance for this girl. But he would make sure the child was born, by whatever means were necessary. He did not know if a child fathered by an angel could die within the womb as sometimes happened with human beings.

Something flashed in Semjaza's mind. He saw the man Jared somewhere with Baraqua. Thick golden cords of love aligned them, which had not been there before. How could this have happened so quickly? With a roar he streaked from the cave. In an instant he was outside Jared's tent. Nothing would deter him from taking Baraqua as a virgin.

Baraqua was finding Jared's kisses unbearably sweet. Who was this man she had balked to touch? Here in the tent, he was her entire world. There was no hurry to consummate, now that they understood who they were to each other. The delicate song of a nightingale came from the trees. He kissed her again, then whispered words in Edenese.

"You mock me because I don't know the language like you do," Baraqua said, pretending annoyance.

"It's a measure of verse I composed when I was young." He said it almost shyly.

"Is it titled, 'Poem to an Unknown Girl?'"

"Almost. But I believe my heart wrote it for you."

Baraqua did not tease again. She had used words to keep Jared at a distance too long. To submit to love was better.

Something butted against the side of the tent and one of the poles that supported the structure snapped with the force. Jared was on his feet in an instant, grabbing up his chert knife. Baraqua pulled her gown around her. It could not be a renegade wind. Air currents were never this strong on the mountain.

The sound of a snarl and ragged breath came from beyond the tent.

"A lion stalks," Baraqua whispered. But lions and saber cats lived in the crags in the western cliffs. They did not bother Adam's kin. The warm glow from Jared's kiss turned to stark fear.

"Something wilier than a lion is here," Jared said. Claws slashed at one of the tent walls, shredding it in an instant. "This intends to destroy us," Jared said. "Put on foot coverings and prepare to run."

With shaking hands Baraqua laced her slippers tightly. But who could outrun a lion?

Jared transferred the primitive dagger from hand to hand, following the growling of the beast with his eyes as it circled the tent.

"Get to the back where the wall is thicker," Jared ordered. But it was too late. Something neither could see had entered and Baraqua felt herself lifted out and above the trees. The arms that encircled her looked human, though the head was obscured from her sight. But she knew: the sire of Awan's son had come for her.

CHAPTER 29

...they defiled... they begot giants and monsters—
BOOK OF THE GIANTS

Sunrise the hue of ripe melons was tinting the sky when Michael stepped into a cave on the east side of the holy mountain. Baraqua, the Seed Bearer's bride, was chained at the ankle in a far corner, Semjaza's work. It grieved him that the metallic-looking band that secured her foot to the rock wall was not of a material of the earth, effective to constrain her only because her human eye and mind believed she was constrained. Such were the ways of the fallen ones, forging chains of deception out of everything.

Baraqua was straining to move closer to the girl Awan, who lay on a haphazard mound of dry grass on the cave's filthy floor. She was barely able to reach Awan's arm, and weeping with frustration. The archangel settled near the women, who for this encounter would not be able to see him. He could protect and defend to some extent, though he did not have authority to take them from the cave or alter their own choices. He seethed with righteous anger at the size of Awan's belly. Semjaza and his cohort were crueler than he could ever have imagined to the women who were bearing their otherworldly children. How splendid Semjaza had been in the former epoch, that glorious era lost forever—

211

"The womb waters are poured out on the ground now, dearest," Baraqua was saying to Awan. "Try to roll closer to me so I can deliver your child." She turned her eyes to the top of the cave. "We are nothing on the earth, God of Adam. Yet have mercy on us now," she whispered, then strained again against the shackle, clutching Awan's arm.

Awan opened her eyes and Michael saw the glaze of the root drug there. Asraelel, one of the gentle angels whose vocation was to succor the dying, appeared at the girl's head, anguish in his countenance, and set his hand on the girl's brow.

A birth pain seized Awan and her features contorted. "All this pain to give birth to a god?" she whispered to Baraqua. "I am privileged above all women."

Baraqua bit her lip. "Call upon God Most High, cousin. He may yet spare your life and your child's."

The dried froth of an advanced thirst wreathed Awan's cracked lips. "I serve no god but Semjaza," she whispered, then shrieked as another pang gripped her. When the contraction lessened, she spoke again. "See, I give birth to my young prince in a room adorned in silks. My lord has provided it."

Michael sensed Semjaza's gloom and the Watcher entered the cave again to stand with spread legs at Awan's feet. "Spare her," Michael said, repulsed at the Luciferian gleam that now animated Semjaza's eyes completely. To be dead to repentance toward God was a fearsome thing.

"I have my own authority here, archangel," Semjaza sneered. "The madwoman has given her will over to me."

It was true. Though sick of mind, Awan had chosen her way. Semjaza smirked, the humanized face a fairly accurate representation of the vine dresser Baraqua loved. He bent to touch Baraqua, but Michael thrust his sword between them. "You will not touch her," he said.

"I will have my way in the end, despite you," Semjaza growled. He put his hands over Awan's engorgement and Baraqua seemed suddenly aware of him.

"Oh, Shai, you have come in answer to my prayers," Baraqua said, her face brightening. Apparently she could see Semjaza. "Go quickly and bring two midwives and some strong men, for Awan will die without help. Bring balms and hot water and clean cloths."

Michael's spirit was charged with holy indignation, for Semjaza's powers of deception were remarkable. Baraqua had taken off Shai's pearl but she was not yet fully delivered from her delusion. The leader of the archangels raised his eyes to a realm far above the reeking cave. He must not dwell on the evils of earth but on the glory of God. Human suffering was the tool God still used to bring glory to himself. After eons, that law of the cosmos still mystified Michael.

But Semjaza did not move. Baraqua voice quivered. "Why aren't you doing as I ask, Shai? Awan may die." Yet a girlish lovelight came and went in her eyes as she pleaded. Michael cringed as she reflexively felt for the pearl that was no longer in the hollow of her throat.

Semjaza knelt before Baraqua, ignoring Awan. "Trust my wisdom, Baraqua," he said in a remarkable mimicry of Shai. "We will deliver her child and take him with us to the ship I have crafted, where a room looking out over the sea waits for us. We will sail to the foundations of the earth like we once dreamed of. There you will see that I always keep my promises."

Baraqua's lips parted and she leaned toward the angel as though she longed for his kiss. Then she drew back sharply, disgust in her face. "Who are you? Shai would never speak like this while someone lay suffering." She shook her shackled ankle. "Release me and I will go myself for the things we need."

"Remember when I promised you the city in the sea," Semjaza said, and Michael raged inwardly at the changed tactic.

See him for what he is. He willed the thought toward Baraqua. Did you bring this woman into being to see her destroyed? he pleaded with God.

"A tower of white stone awaits us as our bedchamber. You will rule with me," Semjaza was saying. The voice was no longer Shai's, the borders of the Watcher's disguise disintegrating.

See with right sight! Michael willed, longing to do more to influence her choices.

Baraqua's forehead creased and she sat back on her heels, hurt and bewilderment in her face. "Shai never talked to me of white towers. What are such things while someone dies?"

"Leave them," Michael said to Semjaza. "I will deliver the child and bring him to you, only let the madwoman survive."

"The Throne consented to this," Semjaza retorted with a sneer, his eyes absorbing Baraqua with her tangled hair and ankle in its cuff.

"The Throne weeps over it," Michael replied.

"Who are you talking to?" Baraqua said, her eyes darting around the cave. Michael saw that her strength of will was waning.

Awan opened her eyes and inhaled quickly as she saw Semjaza. "You come at last, my lord."

With a cry Baraqua threw her body across Awan in a gesture of protection. "You are no human man, but one of the Shining Ones," she said to Semjaza. "You lap your tongue at me while the mother of your child perishes."

The Watcher pushed Baraqua aside. He unsheathed a jeweled dagger at his waist. "Yes, my cow, it is your lord," he said as he lowered the dagger into Awan's belly. He reached inside and pulled out a large male infant with the features and proportions of a human being, but whose arms and legs were as thick in brawn as a grown man's. Something unearthly glimmered around the child's eyes, the false, deceptive light passed from its unearthly father, and Michael grieved. What horrors would come upon the earth through such creatures. The baby released an inhuman roar as Semjaza dropped it onto a mound of bat droppings and watched it squirm as it struggled out of the birth sack.

Baraqua stared, her mouth moving as though she wanted to speak but could not. Awan's body convulsed and was still. The succoring angel gathered her spirit as the body released it, then rose out of the cave with the spirit in his arms. Michael bowed his head. Awan would rest in the shadows of the underworld that day. Her soul was no longer in bondage to a sickened mind.

Baraqua was whimpering, muttering, peering into the bloody cavity as though she searched for something. Michael breathed a healing word close to her ear and placed one of his wings in a protective position, and Baraqua withdrew her hands and sat staring at the body. The infant crawled to its mother's body. It sniffed at the remains of the child-belly where it had nested a moment before.

"Leave her alone!" Baraqua screamed, trying to drive the creature away. But it snarled and   pushed Baraqua hard against the cave wall, then splayed its sturdy body across Awan's motionless chest and began to suckle from one of her breasts. Semjaza snatched the suckling from its source of sustenance. "Her milk will make you as mad as she was," the angel growled. The creature howled, striking its father with large hands. Semjaza stuffed it into a sack and reached for Baraqua. "You are my bride now," he said.

But Michael's sword was so menacing that Semjaza recoiled. "The one who chose to cleave to you is gone," he said. "This other will never submit, and her rebellion would taint the strength of your offspring." He was not sure if what he said was true, but he would believe it out of faith in the dream angel. Duma had never been wrong.

Semjaza's eyes were bright with a hellish fire, and Michael remembered the day when the ardor in Lucifer's eyes had been only in holy service to God. "I will offer this one something she will have no choice but to accept," Semjaza said, nodding toward Baraqua. He tucked the sack under one arm and released the restraint at Baraqua's ankle with a gesture.

Baraqua lunged and scratched at his face with her bloodied hands. "May God in his heaven punish you for this deed," she screamed. Then she stared. Her fingernails had made no mark on the man's skin. "You are as cold as the dead," she whispered.

In the Watcher's expression Michael saw that he searched within for some shred of virtue to render him attractive to the woman he had given up so much to obtain. But the anti-virtues were too entrenched. Beneath his exterior was a vacuous space and the putrefaction of the damned. "You will never conceive by Jared," Semjaza said. "One way or another, you will bear my children."

Riding on the first piercing beams of morning light, bats poured through the cave opening after their night of feeding, gorged with the blood of beasts and the bodies of insects. They attached themselves to the walls and ceiling and folded their webbed wings into position for repose. The Watcher disappeared, and Michael began his vigil beside the weeping Seed Bearer's bride.

CHAPTER 30

Though she sat all day beside Awan's body, Baraqua could not remember a single prayer for the dead. Her tears would have to suffice as mourning for the girl who had forfeited her life for living too long under the charm of lies.

The day was waning beyond the entrance to the cave. Thirst clawed at her throat as bats began to stir in preparation for another nocturnal flight. She must make an effort before darkness fell to get Awan's body out of the cave. Rojj and the elders must be told and a proper ceremony for the dead arranged. Adam and Seth would preach, the women of the prayer caves would chant, and Awan's family would scatter the petals of black roses over the corpse of their kin.

Yet all day a presence she could not define had been with her, a disk of moving light she could see only with inner eyes, cleansing and illuminating. The presence had sustained her reason, her grief, and her sense of reality. *Under the shadow of your wings, I sing for joy.* The familiar words from the Sabbath liturgy rolled through her. Except for the horror of Awan's motionless, mangled body, she felt she could stay in the cave forever. So much seemed clear that had not been before and she saw her great weakness starkly: even after the kindling of love with Jared in the tent the night before; even though she had taken off the pearl, something in her had still responded, if only for a moment, to the being who looked so much like Shai. Something in her craved what wasn't real, lacked the ability to discern. She was only different from Awan, Yammah, and Yarih by degrees.

She forced herself to stand and take off her own outer garment, then laid it on the floor of the cave. She rolled Awan's body onto the gown and with strips of cloth from what remained of Awan's clothing she secured the makeshift shroud at the five stations for the Sethite burial—the ankles, knees, hips, heart, and forehead. She grasped the feet of the corpse and dragged it outside the cave. The evening air was sweet with ripening fruit and the tang of a nearby spring. A donkey she recognized from her own father's droves was foraging nearby. She herself had named the buff-colored male Jubilee, a mischievous animal who often wandered from the others.

"A rogue has become my salvation," she muttered with a sad laugh. She touched a place on Jubilee's hip and the donkey knelt obligingly while she loaded the body across its back. "There now, you'll bear Rojj's dead to him," she said. The donkey looked solemnly over his shoulder. She did not doubt that he understood.

Rojj was among his goats in the meadow high above the cave, a place he rarely came. He stared at the donkey.

"You graze late today," Baraqua said. She could not bear for the first words from her mouth to be about Awan. She looked down at her blood-stained undergown and arms and began to weep. "I could not save her."

Rojj walked to her, took off his cloak, and draped it around her shoulders. The warmth of his body was in it, and the smell of an honest man. He went to the donkey and put a shaking hand on the shrouded body. The look in his face was of someone who believes suddenly that he has lived too long.

"Don't remove the shroud to wash her body," Baraqua said. "Bury her as she is."

He seemed not to have heard. "Do you think it's possible she loved me, even for a day?" he said.

"She spoke your name before she died," Baraqua lied.

The bright fire before her mother's tent was warming the aches in Baraqua's body. She had washed and dressed in fresh garments and been made to sit quietly and drink a tea brewed to steady the heart. Bathshae had not left her side since she and Rojj had trudged into the camp with their gruesome burden. Adam had sent scouts to bring back Jared and his men, who had left to search for Baraqua after she had disappeared the night before.

"You are safe now," Dinah said for the third time since the sun had set. It was what Dinah must say. But the words made Baraqua's stomach turn. Awan's butchered torso reared in her mind and she lifted her head reluctantly to look at her mother-in-law. "Had you seen what I did, mother of Jared, you would not believe any of us will ever be safe again." How frail flesh and blood were, and how finite the human mind against the cunning forces that had come out of the sky. Why had the people who were said to be God's chosen been offered only vague prophetic visions as a warning?

"You should not have had to endure it," Baraqua's sister Eha said firmly from across the fire. She moved clumsily in her nervousness and handed Baraqua another bowl of leek potage, which sloshed over the rim as Baraqua took it. Baraqua stared into the steaming soup. She wondered if she would ever be hungry again. Though surrounded by people who loved her, she ached with loneliness. For to sit with the dead makes one so.

Eha chattered on. "If it hadn't been for Awan's waywardness… the girl did not have the sense to comb her own hair—" Several women laughed nervously.

"Sense!" Baraqua interrupted, but she was too tired to be angry. "How can you speak so of that poor wretch neither the skill of the herbalists nor the prayers of Adam could cure?" She let out her breath heavily. She was sorry to embarrass her sister but she blurted on. "Were Yammah and Yarih wayward?" Eha dropped her eyes. A spot of spilled soup was on her gown.

Seth and Adam stood soberly at the back of the group that had gathered to hear the story of Awan's demise. "Let this sorrowful day be a reminder that none of us is beyond deception," Adam said.

Baraqua's voice rose. They must be made to understand. "These beings who crouch in the shadows now will soon manifest as beautiful beings beyond comprehension. They will deceive many and humble our people, perhaps to the death." Her voice sounded old. "I know that only the God of the altar can save us, if even he."

"We must remember the promise to Eve," Adam said steadily. "No power can eradicate divine will."

Havah heaved her large body onto the seat beside Baraqua. "Tamara disappeared from the lower gardens last night," she said gravely to Baraqua. "Her betrothed could not fight off the man whose face shone like the moon."

Tamara. The one Jared should have married. She imagined the disk of light that had been with her in the cave. It was not something she could talk about. "They have taken Tamara's body, but she will never give her heart," she said with full conviction.

"How is that possible, daughter?" Gayile sputtered. "Once a man possesses a woman's body, he has her soul."

"Not true, good Gayile," Seth said. "God created humanity in his image, with a free will. The body may be in bondage while the heart remains free."

Jared and his men came through the trees and Jared took Baraqua in his arms without a word. Naom and Dinah led them to a new tent because the lion-like creature had made shreds of the other one. Baraqua lay down in the darkness. The scent of herbs was strong, for the tent had belonged to a widowed midwife who now lived with her son's family. It would be theirs until a more suitable one could be made. If only the midwife had been at Awan's side with her skill. If only— How she hated Awan's murderer.

"What happened is a mercy," she murmured to Jared as he snuffed the lamp.

"What do you mean?"

"To die is not the worst thing. Awan's fragile mind could not have borne the sight of her son."

But was this true? Obed had deformities of body and mind according to what people call normal. Yet Bathshae's love for him was no less than that of any other mother. In her deranged state, would Awan have seen beauty in the creature lodged in her womb?

Jared's arms were around her. How warm he was after the dank cave. She imagined herself in a meadow of lilies, lulled to sleep under the healing sun.

"The weight of my vision grows heavier with each horror that occurs," Jared said. "Trusting divine guidance is a struggle each hour."

"God will help us," Baraqua said. It was a common enough saying. But now she must live by it. She thought of the newly formed island. It should not be there, that place spun of magic and illusion, luring young people in hopes of an easier way. Yet God had allowed it to rise, haunting the sea. She wished she had never seen it.

A thought occurred to her. "Did you go out to the island in your search for me?"

"We tried," Jared said. "But unusual waves rose as we approached the shore, pushing us back."

She woke twice from a dream about bats that suckled from a dead woman's breasts. She woke a third time to see Jared watching her in the dim light of the oil lamp. He brought her hand to his lips.

"Every hour I searched for you with Shai and the others I seemed to be searching for myself," he said.

"Shai was with you?"

"He confessed he had once unbound your hair and begged my forgiveness for it."

Baraqua closed her eyes. The pearl had probably been trampled in the dirt when the women cleared away the remains of the old tent.

How foolish she had been, how blind to what mattered. "Did you forgive him?" she said.

He laughed softly. "I told him no normal man could resist hair like yours." He ran a finger along her jawline. "You are my soul. If I had been free to decide, I would have chosen you."

She could not think how to say what she imagined he might want to hear. Maybe she would learn. Her heart had chosen Shai and he would always be part of her. Yet something higher than her heart had chosen Jared. Somehow, that choice was right.

"Something not of this world was with me in the cave," she said. "I would be more fit to bear what is ahead if I could feel it near me now."

"It is there even if you don't sense it," Jared said without hesitation. "You are not the same woman who was taken from me last night."

"How do you know?"

"Maybe I too have sensed such a presence."

Despite Baraqua's caution, the heartbroken Rojj looked beneath Awan's makeshift shroud and bore the consequence in his dreams. He dug a grave in a secluded place, far from the traditional burial field. "So that no one will hear me when I come to weep," he told Baraqua.

The people gathered and Awan's mother knelt without expression beside her daughter's grave. When most of the others had gone, Baraqua laid a spray of gaudy amaryllis over the shroud, Awan's favorite flower. Then Adam committed the ravaged body to the red earth from which his own body had once been formed.

CHAPTER 31

Baraqua stood in the shadow of Adam's high altar, but her eyes were not on the forebear as he slit the throat of the yearling lamb. The chant of consecration swelled around her, the ancient lyrics bringing an ache to her throat. How gracious God's promise was, that the death of an innocent animal could atone for humanity's corruption. She studied the crisp line where shadow contrasted with sunlight at the edge of the blood-stained altar. Both truth and falsehood, shadow and light, had their roles on the earth since Adam had come out of Eden. The lamb itself was both condemnation and absolution.

Something she could not see hovered suddenly beside her. *Be my wife and I will spare your people in the hour of destruction.* Her body went taut. Who was speaking, and what was this about the sparing of lives? She felt coldness at her left side and she knew the Shining One was nearby.

"Show yourself," she whispered.

You know who I am. Don't pretend that you don't still think of the vinedresser night and day, and of me. I am worth ten of him, for his eye is on every unmarried girl in the camp these days.

"You do not know what I think about," she spit out.

Do not doubt that I have power to kill everyone on this mountain, for two hundred like me do my bidding in an instant.

She eyed Jared where he served at the altar with Adam, Seth, and Kenan. He was splendid in the carefully embroidered liturgical robes, a gift from his mother. Jared held high the torch of cleansing fire while Adam read from the *Chronicles*. It was the story of how the sentient stars had sung for joy on the sixth day of creation as they observed the beauty and majesty of the cosmos God had brought forth through divine Word.

The city beneath the lake is still yours, a nuptial gift if you become my bride.

Sweat trickled down her back beneath the Sabbath gown. She slipped away from the people and went into the trees behind the clearing. "You dare much by seeking to woo me after what you did to my cousin," she whispered fiercely.

You rebuke me in this matter, yet you murdered the snake woman in the orchard. She was more human than you know. Atone for your sin by saving the lives of your people.

The accusation struck hard. She remembered the pressure on her torso, the inability to breathe. Had there been another way? Should she have sacrificed her own life in order not to be guilty of the sin of murder?

You serve yourself as we all do, the unspoken voice continued. Eve saw that the fruit of moral knowledge was good for food, so she ate. She would have justified her choice forever if she had not been turned out of paradise to grow wrinkled and bent. Obey me and you will atone for your sin and live forever in my palace.

Self-condemnation filled her. She ran further into the trees, her headscarf trailing. He was in the leaves, the light, his face constantly before her. He was Shai, with lips that longed for hers; a lion, magnificent in power; a god who could blot out a mountain with the tip of his thumb. She stumbled beneath a tree, far from the altar where the smoke from the sacrificial lamb rose into the morning sky. Her face met the earth where night crickets still beat out their rhythm in the grass. Her heart was weak as water, running into the ground.

Baraqua took up a stick and poked at the evening fire. She could not put off telling Jared. A large chunk of charred cedarwood crumbled at her prodding, scattering its glowing contents. A breeze wafted across the back of her neck and she jerked involuntarily. Was the shining one nearby, come to take her away already?

Beside her, Jared ate methodically of the potage she had carefully seasoned. He deserved a good meal after the long day on the threshing floor. How dear he was. She thought about the night she had finally received his seed and her attraction to him since. She had barely started to learn to love him, and now her victory would not matter at all. She pondered again whether it would be adultery to cohabit with a being who was spirit. Would the shining one allow her to visit Jared? She put down her own bowl of food. The sooner she told her husband, the easier it would be on them all.

"The one who murdered Awan came to me during the liturgy yesterday," she said.

Jared turned. It was as if he knew something already. "And?"

"He and the others will destroy the clan and our mountain unless I agree to be his." There. It had come out easily enough.

"And you refused, of course," Jared said, setting down his empty bowl.

She felt strangely calm. "I vowed I would go. You will choose another wife, and she will bear you Anointed One."

There were taut shock lines around his lips. "And what about the child who already lives within your womb?"

She could not allow herself to think about the child. "I have to do what he says, or he and the others will kill every Sethite. These beings have the power to destroy with little effort."

"Then perhaps you never really rebuked him in the cave that day," Jared said quietly. "Perhaps the peace-bearing presence that came to you was only a tool of your imagination." He got up and began to walk beneath a boa tree.

Some men were passing along the trail beyond their camp. All carried clubs or chert knives at the ready.

"Do you think those things will keep them away, you fools?" Jared shouted at the men. "Don't you know that the strength of these creatures is not of this world and that they are coming for us?" He laughed bitterly. "You may as well go to your tents and lie down to die."

The men looked at each other in confusion. They bowed and touched their fingers to their foreheads out of respect. When Jared said nothing more they moved on.

Baraqua went to where Jared stood. "Is it not written that it is better for one to be sacrificed than for all to die?"

Jared's eyes blazed. "Fear makes many conquests, Baraqua. If you do this thing you will be forgotten and unsung, a byword forever."

Anger sparked in her. Didn't he understand she was trying to save him and the others?

He ran a hand over his face. "And do you want to go with him?"

She felt discomposed, as though she were a piece of broken pottery. But she must say it all. "I am delivered from my attraction to him and to Shai," she said. "But Adam preaches that love offers itself for another, just as the lamb's life is offered for ours."

"God never asks that we sacrifice our souls, only our selfishness," Jared said.

"But the man swore by his god that he would not harm the people if I became his," she pleaded. She could not bear it if this one she now loved did not understand.

"His *god?*" Jared flicked his hands in frustration. "His god is Lucifer, the liar who turned Eve into the traitor of the cosmos."

She took a step back and spoke coolly. "This the best course for all involved. I love you and want you to live."

"How do you define life?" he said. He looked unbearably sad.

She said nothing. In a moment Jared spoke again. "When will you leave?"

Her own voice trembled. His words made it more real. To walk away from Jared and their tent, to step into the unknown—

"When he comes for me," she said. "He has loved me since I was a girl." She hated the pathetic justification. "Another womb will serve as well as mine to produce the next Seed Bearer."

"I am weary of hearing you say this," Jared said. "It is obvious you think nothing of yourself, me, the dream angel, or of our unborn child." He picked up his cloak. "I will have to carry the burden of my vision without you." He tossed the cloak across one shoulder. "I want to lock you away and set a guard until this horror passes," he said. "But that would be to keep you from making your own choice, which I will not do." He turned, went into the trail, and disappeared from her sight.

Somewhere nearby, Baraqua thought she heard a lion roar.

CHAPTER 32

"Time passes, and still you have not obtained your prize," Michael said. He could not resist gloating as he stood in Semjaza's throne room at the pinnacle of the glittering new city in the sea. Though the sun shone brightly on the water beyond and the crystal at the center of the island brought infinite rays of light through the wide openings in the walls, a stubborn pall hung over the room. The throne itself was of pure obsidian and rose almost to the ceiling, large enough to seat a dozen angelic beings. Yet the shining surface did not seem to catch the light, absorbing it instead.

"What do you know of prizes, archangel?" Semjaza said. "Is not my resistance to these women around me proof of my faithfulness to the only one I want?"

A dozen be-jeweled women with Semjaza's name engraved on their foreheads walked up and down the marble stairs before the throne. Each in her turn bowed low at the Watcher's side and murmured a request. When he ignored each one, they grasped his feet and pled pitifully. Their eyes were dull from the drug the angel plied them with day and night, which stimulated desire for nothing other than to lie in embrace with Semjaza.

"You control these girls unnaturally," Michael said. "Do you think Baraqua will find this seemly?"

Semjaza's face darkened. He was no longer camouflaging with the face and body of the vinedresser. His robes were now of richest purple brocade, more elaborate than any Azazel or Armaros had conjured. His face was of a classic human masculinity and his eyes were as enigmatic and clear as the lake at Elda. "What she thinks or feels no longer interests me. Yet if she tries to defy me by refusing to come to my bed, the Sethites will feel the sting of the scorpion."

"And what does that accomplish?" Michael said. He was desperate to convince the Watcher to allow the Sethites to live. The Luciferian vibration was powerful on the island and Michael was prepared to call on backup from the heavenly host if necessary, for Semjaza had firmly established himself on the earth through the founding of the island and his authority was supported by the very soul of Lucifer now.

He tried another tactic. "Are not the daughters of Adam's clan among the fairest in the earth and of the strongest stock, excellent for breeding with the members of your cohort?" The thought of the women of the clan who had gone over to some of Semjaza's cohort repulsed him.

Semjaza's eyes narrowed. "The cohort is nothing; there is no loyalty left among them. I care only that the girl loves me, though to love her no longer interests me," The claws of a lion protruded from Semjaza's long fingers and then retracted.

"If one is not strong in love himself, how can he expect to be loved by another?" Michael said, wanting desperately to be far from Semjaza. The evil in the room was almost paralyzing and he gripped the hilt of his sword tightly. Things were changing in the spiritual atmosphere across the earth. Azazel's warring men were feverish with the desire to fight and Semjaza's chiefs-of-twenty were restless for blood. "Remember Tartarus," he pled with the Watcher. "Don't add to your punishment by harming God's chosen people."

"Tartarus is nothing," Semjaza said, and the air of the room dimmed further. He beckoned one of the women ascending the steps to come to him. Her small frame was dwarfed as she sat upon his knee and reached up to kiss him. Semjaza bit her cheek and pushed her down the stairs. The woman lay stunned, her forehead bleeding, yet the others walked around her as though she was not there.

Uriel materialized beside Michael and glared at Semjaza. "Tartarus demanded that I serve you up today, you worm of the abyss. But I put it off for the future, when your deeds will have grown to fruition. What do you think of the stench of brimstone on me? It will one day be your odor."

"I smell nothing," Semjaza said, but for an instant he looked smaller on his enormous throne.

Uriel's eyes flashed. "The pit eagerly awaits those who have defiled themselves with women."

"I found Tartarus spacious and inviting when I visited," Semjaza said with a sniff, as another woman came up the stairs. This time he did not reject the girl but drew her close and began to caress her. He turned to Michael. "Make no mistake, nursling of the cherubim; I will do as I wish with the Sethites and with that Seed Bearer's bride."

CHAPTER 33

Baraqua shivered in the evening chill. She and Bathshae had returned to her tent after bathing at the river. "It is usually not this cold in the season when the constellation of Bethuleh lies lowest in the sky," Bathshae said as she drew Obed out of the big carrying sling and set him on a mossy spot beneath a fir tree. She rubbed her shoulders and stretched, then looked intently at Baraqua. "You have much in your mind," she said, then eased herself onto one of the wooden benches and spread her wet hair toward the embers to dry.

"Obed is too heavy for you now and it hurts your back," Baraqua said crossly to distract from her sister's comment. She was more sickened every day with the decision she had made about agreeing to marry the shining one. She did not want to tell Bathshae anything. Who aligns with a devil and hopes to keep anyone's respect?

"Obadiah is building a cart to pull Obed in from now on," Bathshae said, simple happiness in her eyes. Baraqua held her own hair near the heat and lowered her eyes. How innocent Bathshae was. The difference between herself and this sister had never felt starker.

"The strength I felt in you after Awan's death feels diminished," Bathshae persisted. "It's as though you have forfeited that rare quality you found in the cave for something else." There was no judgement in her sister's voice, only concern.

"It is you who were given rare qualities, and that from birth," Baraqua said. "Whatever I might have received of such things burned away long ago." She would not pollute the air by explaining her wretchedness. How could she tell gentle Bathshae that she had agreed to go the way of Yusuf's daughters?

Bathshae knelt before Baraqua and took her hands. "Whatever it is that pulls at your heart, choose the higher way," she said.

Baraqua shook off Bathshae's hands and stood up. "This is no time for noble sayings," she said. She imagined the shining ones invading the camp and Obed torn screaming from Bathshae's arms.

But Bathshae showed no offence. "It is a law of the cosmos that we never face more than we can endure," she said.

Baraqua could not bear her sister's wisdom, nor her innocence. "Please go," she said. Bathshae studied her a moment, then picked up Obed and heaved him back into the sling. With a deft movement she arranged that burden of love across her back and cinched the belt at her waist. Obed's crooked legs jostled her sister's hips as she walked away. Baraqua wanted to run after that small, departing figure and tell sweet Bathshae that she would never forget her, never stop admiring her.

But Shai was coming toward her out of the trail. She was relieved that no ardent emotion came to her, despite her loneliness and confusion. She made herself smile. To smile in a friendly, artless way felt something like what Bathshae must mean when she spoke of yielding or of the higher way.

Shai stood before her, his skin browned by the sun. He wore thick, mud-caked breeches below his tunic and the cloak of a scout, for he had been going out on mission with some of the more experienced scouts. There was much information to be gleaned as the shining ones expanded their influence on the earth and their sons began to grow at an alarming rate.

"It suits you, this garb," Baraqua said. "I think you prefer these journeys to working in the vineyard."

Shai shrugged. "My brothers can cultivate the fruit of the vine well enough without me," he said. A new clarity and determination was in his face since she had seen him last. She tried not to think about that same face imposed on the incorporeal body of Awan's killer, nor about his rejection of her after his ardent promises. The time for expectations was past.

"I can no longer do that work when there is so much danger around us," Shai continued. "On nights that I stand guard, I hear the hoofbeats of the mutant creatures who are half horse and half man stampeding on the east flank of the mountain. In the Flood Sea, fishermen out of the old Cushite lands have seen maidens with the tails of fish instead of legs. The shining ones continue to woo women across the earth and some of the *gibborim*—that stinking offspring of theirs—are already five hundred ells tall. Mahal says his vision alluded to even taller beings. What will become of humankind?"

She said nothing. There was too much fear, too much strangeness and loss. Would God Most High put a stop to any of it? Would he stop her from what she had decided to do?

Eli came into the clearing. Baraqua did not ask him where he had gone instead of accompanying the women from the river. "A tall man with the head of a live bull lives in a cave beyond the northern outskirts of Eden," Eli said to Shai, jerking his head into the trees. "He has cursed me many times already, but I will conquer him when my brother gives me leave from watching over Baraqua." He scowled. Eli had been increasingly verbal about the unmanliness of such work when there were monsters to be stalked, even after Jared's rebuke over the night Baraqua encountered the snake woman.

"Only a fool complains about protecting the woman who might give birth to Anointed One," Shai said calmly. "And be careful not to provoke that bull. These cross-breeds are conceived by heinous practices and there is spell-power in their breath." He gestured toward the camp. "Go then to your friends; I will watch over Baraqua a while."

When Eli had gone Baraqua made her voice cheerful. "They say you leave soon on another mission."

"Yes, tonight. Adam believes this mountain is no longer safe, that the shining ones may try to chase us from our homeland. We must find a place that is still uncorrupted where the invaders or their offspring will not bother us."

Baraqua considered telling Shai about her vow to the shining one. But Bathshae had just offered council and she could barely understand how her sister thought. Nothing was easy. She only hoped the holy mountain and the Sethite camp would still exist when Shai returned from his mission

"The northern mountains are already engorged with the sons of the shining ones," Shai said. "No one is safe from the hybrid creatures that are appearing everywhere." He squinted through the trees into the east, as though he could see that far. "Things are better here than in Nod or south of the sea, where people have given themselves over to dark practices for centuries already. But we must not dishonor our God by being foolish. It is time to scout out the land and move."

Baraqua looked at Shai's worn sandals. One of the cross straps was frayed. It would not last a week on their rugged journey. The vinedresser had been to places she would never see. He had put his feet into giants' footsteps that spanned the length of two human arms, smelled their enormous scat, and seen the ruin of villages where the creatures had left their mark in terror.

"And will you travel as far as the foundations of the earth this time?" she said. Shai smiled at the mention of the old dream of the two of them sailing into the taut blue horizon to find the ends of the earth.

"We will go where God leads," Shai said.

"How can we just leave this mountain?" she said. "We are the guardians of Eden."

Shai sounded tired. "Eden fades more with every passing day, Baraqua. Only Anointed One can revive it, and in his time."

She put her palm against her low belly and was struck by her own hypocrisy: she worried about Eden and fretted that the snake woman might have been human. Yet here she was, willing to expose her own child's life to the one who had destroyed Awan with frigid calm.

"Will you eat with Jared and me this last night?" she said. Sadness descended on her with the moody dusk. Shai was leaving, and with him went the last remnant of her old dream.

Shai gestured his refusal. "It would tempt me to want to turn back time. The past and the future are mere shadows; only the present matters."

She kept her face composed. Without knowing it he had given her the answer to her question the night before she married Jared: he still cared.

"But the past can be a tutor to the present moment," she said.

"It is so," Shai agreed. "Yet our present choices are the most important. We mortals glorify a moment, a word, or the glance of a beloved one as the tilt of the sun catches in the branches of a trembling tree. We immortalize what we felt in that moment as somehow sacred and set it up as a standard for the course of our life. It has been so with me regarding you, and it was a delusion."

What he said was true. They had both been guilty of such thinking. She did not feel the stirring of her old longing for him, but a fierce protectiveness welled in her for Shai and for all the others. No one but Jared knew that the life and death of many might hang on the decision of a Seed Bearer's bride. And Jared had ceased trying to convince her.

"I assume you know Enosh and Tarshish have established themselves on the island of the great crystal, along with some of the young people," Shai said.

"Yes, Naom now wears the head covering of a widow," Baraqua said. "A Noddite girl Tarshish has gotten with child lives in her tent."

Shai looked grim. "May God restore Enosh and his son to our people," he said. But he did not look convinced. He glanced behind him. "I must go now and meet the others. We leave immediately."

They faced each other as they had so many times among the old trees when the night mists were starting to rise out of the grass. Evening doves were cooing in the acacia bushes and somewhere in the camp a child called out to a playmate, "Just one more time!"

"Don't forget me," Shai said, and walked into the trail where three other scouts waited, one leading a donkey loaded with provisions. They disappeared into the dusk, their way lit by one torch.

"Thank you for all you taught me, Shai of the vineyards," she whispered.

CHAPTER 34

And there appeared a great wonder in heaven; a
woman clothed with the sun, and the moon under her
feet, and upon her head a crown of twelve stars—
REVELATION 12:1

Michael descended along the bright swath of uncreated
light that extended away from the Throne. With him
were Uriel, Gabriel, and Raphael, and Michael had never
been more comforted by the presence of his formidable friends. The
four had received their instructions to oversee a great conflict on the
mountain of God; already the heavenlies spaces shook with the force
of their wings as they sped downward to perform the divine will.
Down through the meadows of the fourth heaven they streamed,
then moved through the crystalline dome of the earth where the
constellations and wandering stars moved in their courses through
the pathway of the sun.

"We will seek Bethulah's blessing before we descend further,"
Michael said as they settled into the constellation of the Virgin.

Bethuleh cast her radiance over the archangels. "I am mere
substance, created as a sign to herald the salvation of all people,"
she said. "May Anointed One, symbolized in the shafts of wheat and
corn I hold in my hands, soon grace the earth with his presence. And

may God Most High strengthen you, his holy servants, for the battle you will soon wage with those who have left the way of love."

The nearby constellations of the lion called Arieh, and of Coma, the woman with a child in her arms, bowed in reverence to Bethuleh and to the angels. But Dahrach, the star serpent that coiled at the apex of the sky, spoke in a mocking tone. "You say your stars proclaim God's splendor, Bethulah. Yet what of Lucifer's growing power? I symbolize that great cherub, who has gained much power on the earth since the descent of the Watchers."

Michael's voice was like the sound of waves on a rocky shore. "You must no longer call Lucifer a cherub, that class of celestials far above all the others. For that rebel has fallen from his great and unique position into abject darkness. It is to your shame that you allowed those renegade spirits to seek refuge within you the night Jared the Seed Bearer was born. If you had resisted, perhaps none of this would have happened."

"I had no say in that," Dahrach retorted. "Do I have authority over angels?"

"You have authority over your own territory, as we all do," Uriel said soberly.

Bethulah glowed brighter. "The prophecies stand, no matter what the choices of men and angels may be," she said. "On the day of Anointed One, I will be clothed with the sun while the moon lies at my feet. A crown of twelve luminaries will adorn my head, and a pair of king stars will align within Arieh the Lion to welcome the world's savior according to the promise made to Eve. It will be a day like no other."

Dahrach made a dismissive sound. "Those predictions were set in motion before Lucifer's servants impregnated the daughters of men."

Arieh roared. "Have you forgotten, Dragon, that though you inhabit the heights, your very name means 'trodden on?' Is this not enough to humble you?" He crouched beside Bethuleh, his demeanor of authority a contrast to the Virgin's meekness.

"Lucifer's power endures only a little while as God counts such things." He extended his claws. "My name means 'seeking prey.' I symbolize the culmination of victory over Lucifer in the future day."

"But things have changed—" Dahrach interrupted.

"God Most High does not change," Arieh roared again. "Already my paw presses against the neck of the star serpent Hydra, who gloats over the sufferings of men. And consider the constellation of Corvus, the prey bird who pecks at Hydra's flesh. His nine stars are the number of God's judgment— a judgment that has already begun."

"The Watchers wax strong in the land," Dahrach said. "The height of their sons will be three thousand ells."

"So it may be, but prayers rise higher than three thousand ells," Arieh replied. "The intensity of the cosmic struggle is never proof of Lucifer's superiority."

A band of the angelic harps and glories moved through the constellation of Dahrach with the hint of harmless mischief on their instruments. "The Lord reigns; he wears the garment of majesty," they harmonized, swirling through the Dragon's tail and ascending with their song.

At the chorus of high praise, something seemed to alter in the spirit of Dahrach. He sighed. "It is true that I have become proud, thinking that to align with Lucifer would bring me regard," he said. "I did not understand the devastation that would come from harboring the renegades that night."

"Then let this epiphany be to your increase in humility," Arieh said more gently, and all the stars were still. The archangels lingered, basking in the moment of peace before the hard fight ahead. Bethuleh's stars proclaimed the old promise, Arieh kept his foot on Hydra, and the woman Coma held her child close. They would not change their positions in the sky until Anointed One took up his final kingship and God remade the heavens and the earth and united them forever.

Michael felt a sweet elation. How blessed he was to serve a God who had no beginning or end, a God eternal. He laughed, and the sound of it lit up the constellations anew. "One day, my friends, all things will be made new."

CHAPTER 35

She looked hungry, the young woman dressed in the matted black fur of an animal. She stood on the riverbank across from the bend where Baraqua and other women washed clothes under the guard of five men.

"I seek the scout called Shai," the girl called over the water.

Baraqua stopped scrubbing Jared's field tunic and stared at the girl, who spoke the universal language with a foreign inflection. Eha's face was drawn with fear and Gayile gripped the hilt of a small dagger. A few women dropped the wet garments they held and walked away without a word, taking two of the guards with them. Baraqua could not blame them; every newcomer on the mountain was suspect, and they had never seen a person clothed in the skin of an animal. But there was no unearthly shine on the woman's skin, no animal appendages or marks on her body, and her eyes witnessed to the indwelling of a human soul.

Baraqua cinched her skirt high and waded into the river. Here the bottom was soft and sandy, not heavily strewn with sharp jewels as it was just outside Eden. Once on the bank, she stood at a distance from the girl. The foreigner must be tested. "Who is this man you call Shai?" she said.

The girl pushed thick hair from her face. The hair was lighter than that of most Sethites and the eyes were not the familiar almond shape. "After the strong ones invaded our land, north across the sea from here, the man Shai helped the few of our people who still lived," she said. "He told me his people dwell on this mountain, the origin of all earthly things. He said you worship a god of infinite power who once walked with human beings in a garden, as though they were his friends." She sat down on the bank and began to weep. "Why do you all stare? Does my ugliness shock you?"

Baraqua sat next to the girl. "Forgive us," she said. "We have been troubled with invaders here. Some of our young people have gone over to them."

"Have the forceful ones from the sky come here too?" the girl said, raising her face.

"Yes," Baraqua said. "We call them shining ones."

"Shai says they travel to the far corners of the earth and breed with wicked women to produce giants," the girl said. Her face was strained. So people of other lands knew the same fear the Sethites did. The girl's thinness and drawn features showed that she had obviously endured much.

Gayile crossed the river, for to comfort a young person was irresistible to her. She took off her shawl and put it around the girl's shoulders. "Tell us your story," she said. She took a round of bread from the pocket of her gown and handed it to the girl, who devoured it in three mouthfuls.

"Beings we had never seen before came out of the heavens one night and made me a widow," the girl said. "I had seen the men in my dreams that day, their feet flames of fire. They burned our great green mountain, destroyed our village with the breath of their mouths, killed most, and took away our virgin girls. I escaped to a cave beneath the mountain with my mother-in-law."

"What is your name?" Bathshae said. Despite her hungry leanness, the girl was very beautiful.

"I am Magda," she said. "When my husband's mother died of grief, I made a pyre and burned the body upon it to release her spirit, according to the traditions of our people." She ran her hand over her face, her distress growing. "There was no food and even my kneading trough was destroyed by the invaders. I had no boat to cross the sea, so walked over the northern mountains to this place. I encountered heavenly men and creatures taller than one can imagine, but I prayed to Shai's deity for protection, once hiding inside a hollow tree all night while they were about." She looked into Gayile's face. "Shai said his people are kind."

Baraqua suppressed her anger in order not to disturb Magda more. How cruel the shining ones were. "I am Baraqua, wife of an elder of our people," she said. "You must come into the camp and take food. A runner arrived this morning to tell us Shai's scouting party should reach us before the sun sets. You may speak with him then." Her heart did not feel tight at the words, but generous. Perhaps Shai loved this woman.

The women brought Magda to Jared's fireside and Baraqua had her sit on the best carved bench. Baraqua's sisters brought cold leeks, millet, and spiced honey cakes left from a recent nuptial feast, which Magda consumed as though she had not eaten in a month. Then Baraqua dressed the girl in her own Sabbath robe, for all her other garments were wet from the wash board. She massaged salve into the soles of Magda's feet, roughened by her journey through the mountains, and anointed her face until it shone. Once Magda's hair was combed, her beauty was even more obvious.

Jared and some men came from the fields and the elders and others of the clan began to gather at the fire with their own evening meals to listen to the foreign woman. Women brought gifts of scented oil, a carved wooden comb, and a length of good linen to make Magda a cloth garment. The worn animal skin was taken away to be burned.

When Magda had told her story several times and someone had placed a widow's veil on her head, Adam spoke. "You are of a good heart and must stay among us."

Magda looked at Adam for a long time. She fingered the veil over her pale hair. "I want to know about Shai's deity, who sits above the sky and makes the earth his footstool. Shai told me this deity is sustained by the praises of angels."

"You know much about our God already," Eve said from where she stood beside Adam. "The Creator of heaven and earth receives all people who turn toward him."

Magda began to weep again. "This is all well, yet surely hell is unleashed on the earth in this time, for men with the heads of bulls now lurk in the gorges of my land." She looked around the gathering with her quick, lovely eyes. "I swear by the sun and moon that I'm not lying," she said.

Adam drew Magda to her feet. "There is no need to swear by the ornaments of the sky. We believe you, for such things happen everywhere now."

Magda seemed confused. "But how can people believe a thing if something greater than themselves is not sworn by to prove the truth of the words?"

"Let your yes mean yes, not only with your voice but in your heart," Adam said. "Let your no simply mean no, with no wavering."

"I understand little of such things," Magda said. "Among you, I see how ignorant my people were."

"It is the Creator who enlightens minds," Adam said.

"My mind is dark," Magda said quietly. "My life is a nightmare from which I never awaken."

"We too wish to awaken," Baraqua said. "But we will fight against this encroaching evil until we cannot avoid it." She caught her breath. It was as though she were listening to someone else speak. She realized she had just committed to staying with her people despite her promise to the shining one. How could she cower now, when Magda believed so simply in their good God? If she and her people died because she had turned from her vow, they would at least die honorably. Almost palpably her heart felt lighter, and she sensed a new strength she had not expected.

"Magda." The voice was Shai's, standing with the other scouts at the edge of the gathering. The people gathered around the men, taking their weapons and clearing a place for them to sit. Shai was thin and deeply sunburned. The men's clothing was torn and their strained expressions spoke wordlessly of things they had seen that they might not be able to tell. Baraqua's eyes met Shai's and she smiled. How proud she was of this one she had loved.

Women scurried to pour wine and offer the men bread smeared with goat cheese and herbs, and someone ladled potage into bowls. But Shai pushed aside the food, for Magda was kneeling before him with her forehead to the ground. "I offer reverence," she said. "In gratitude for sending me here, I will be a servant to you all the days of my life." The fresh sob in Magda's throat brought one to Baraqua's. "I won't make trouble for your people," the girl said. "I will worship your god, keep your water pots full, and wash your wife's clothes."

Shai drew Magda to her feet. The light of love was in his eyes and Baraqua forced down a pang of envy, remembering that those eyes had once shone on her. She would choose to be sincerely happy for the woman who now received Shai's gaze.

Shai took Magda's face in his hands. "A servant?" he said. He turned to Adam and Seth. "Let it be known that tomorrow at dusk this woman will come with me under the nuptial canopy and become my wife."

CHAPTER 36

The sound of Jared muttering in his sleep woke Baraqua for the fourth time that night. She crawled to the pallet where her husband had lain in the throes of a high fever for three days. Her shoulders ached with the constant interruption of her sleep, a torture like no other she was finding. She felt Jared's wrists—Jared, this husband, this father of the child she now carried. How much longer could he survive in the feverish state the healers had told her they had never seen the like of?

The mysterious heat had come the night Jared, Mahal, and Kenan returned from their impulsive excursion out to the island in the Flood Sea. They had promised Yusuf they would try to retrieve Yammah and Yarih, for the girl's mother was ill with grief over the disappearance of her daughters.

"The shining ones are more dangerous than you know," Baraqua had said as Jared strapped on his chert dagger. Jared had not encountered the shining ones in the same way she had. And she was grieved that some perversion of mind made her curious to see the island that was the likeness of the one from beneath the lake.

"As keeper of the vision I must act as it moves me to," he had said. He was quickly gone and she had missed him. The three men returned after two days, exhausted and shaken. Yammah and Yarih were not with them. "Do not be deceived by this city that glitters like a jewel, for it is nothing like it appears from afar," Jared said when the people gathered to hear the men speak of what had happened. Yet he described the palatial homes, the women huge with child who peered from doorways, and the eerie brilliance of the central crystal. "It emits something more than light," he said gravely. "Do not desire it."

"Did you see Enosh or Tarshish?" Naom's voice came quietly from the back.

"Enosh, yes," Jared answered, but it was plain that he did not want to say more.

"Was he well?" Naom said.

"He walked among some other human men in the streets as they mingled with the shining ones. We called his name, but he turned away," Mahal said. He turned to Yusuf. "A man of the ancient Cushites told us that Yarih took her own life not long after she left here. Yammah came down to the boat as we were leaving and called Jared a devil."

"Why?" someone had asked in an anguished voice. There were always too many questions now. Finding answers was like trying to weave a rug in darkness.

"She screamed that I had defrauded her in our youth," Jared said. "She tossed something like an orb of mist and hurled a curse like nothing I have ever heard."

Within an hour of his return Jared could not rise from his bed.

Baraqua stared at the sunken eyes and slick, waxy skin. She did not doubt that Yammah's curse was real, for the shining ones could transform to whatever and whomever they wished, she was sure. She wondered if she would also take the fever because she was sleeping so near Jared night after night. The healers had cautioned her, but she would not leave him. What did her life matter if she deserted him now? She imagined her spirit parting from her body like leaves from a tree. She pictured she and the child who drew its life from her womb walking together into the underworld. Jared would be there to meet them.

She drew back the light covering Jared lay beneath. He had lost flesh and his tunic was soaked in sweat. At the foot of the bed Bathshae waved smoking clusters of gray-green sage to cleanse the air. The flame in the oil lamp quivered and Bathshae's shadow danced up the side of the tent. Her eyes met Baraqua's through the smoke, but Baraqua could not read her sister's mood. No doubt she was still believed in being yielded. Bathshae would, no matter what befell her and Baraqua wondered how such tenacity of heart was possible. From outside the tent came the murmur of a dozen women of the prayer caves as they lifted petitions to heaven. Baraqua's own prayers felt too heavy to rise halfway up the trees. "Mercy, Lord have mercy," prayed the women. Always mercy, that word that pled for the healing of the wounds that had diseased the human soul after Eve ate of forbidden food in Eden. Always the reminder that though God had left his throne in Eden for a heavenly one, he was said to be full of compassion for those left on earth.

Gayile woke and sat up on her pallet at the back of the tent. "Daughter, does he grow better?" she said.

"No," Baraqua said dully. She wished her mother would leave. There would be too many questions, tinged with vague, unintended accusation: if something bad was happening, someone must be at fault.

Obadiah pushed the door flap aside and came in with Obed in his arms. "He wants you," he said to Bathshae, and brought the child to her. Bathshae's husband looked sadly at Baraqua and went out. Baraqua dipped a cloth in the basin of cool water and replaced the warm one lying across Jared's forehead.

Gayile felt of his flushed cheek, then left the tent. "He cannot burn much longer," Baraqua heard her say to one of the women. "Doom is in the camp."

It was not what a scribe's wife should say, Baraqua thought angrily. She heard her father mumble a gentle reproof to Gayile.

"Someone must speak things as they are, and preparing his burial shroud cannot be put off," Gayile said tersely to Rasujal. "They should never have gone near that island."

Jared opened his eyes. They were too bright, focused on nothing in the tent. "I did not seek to deceive you, daughter of Yusuf," he cried out. He swiped at the air, staring into the scene of his nightmare. Then he turned on his side and was quiet again. The fresh cloth slipped from his forehead and Baraqua replaced it. The heat of his body terrified her.

"Do you believe in the curse of Yammah?" Bathshae whispered as Obed settled into her lap.

Baraqua was surprised, for Bathshae rarely expressed ambivalence about spiritual realities. "How can you doubt it?" she said, more sharply than she intended. Bathshae bowed her head at the rebuke and ran her fingers through Obed's matted hair.

Danel the herbalist entered the tent, the scent of sweet and bitter herbs on him. Baraqua noticed gray in his beard. Fear had taken its toll on many since the descent of the shining ones. Danel set down his bag of remedies and put two fingers to Jared's neck where the heart's energies pulsed. He poured a few sips of a strong-smelling tincture down the dry throat. A drop seeped from Jared's mouth and Baraqua caught it with her finger and sucked it into her own mouth, a bitter droplet against the curse that might come to her own body any minute.

Danel motioned for Baraqua to come with him to the other side of the tent. "This is beyond my skill now," he said. She pressed a gauze bag of frankincense resin into Danel's hand as payment, and the healer went out. She fought down hatred for Yammah.

Jared opened his eyes and groped for Baraqua's hand. "Dawn of my day," he whispered, and tried to smile. His breath was sour and his lips cracked. She smeared comfrey salve over his mouth and held up a cup of water, but he turned away.

"You must drink while you are awake," she said. His refusal frightened her. "You must get well for the birth of our baby."

"I will never see him," Jared whispered. The hollow places in his face were deeper now. He gripped her hand with surprising strength, his fingers shaking. "My life evaporates like mist under the morning sun," he said with great effort. "I wanted to make a difference, to raise my children to do good upon the earth and I wanted to fulfill my mission as an elder." A tear slipped from his eye. "But evil will have its way with me instead. My flesh will soon be food for worms and my soul will take up lodging in the caverns of the dead." He placed a hot hand over Baraqua's belly, and she forced herself not to recoil from that sick flesh so near the child. "Take care of our son," he said.

Baraqua put her hand to her throat. The sacred bride dream had been for nothing and the stars of prophecy were no more than sparks in the darkness. Everything she had given up her will for was disappearing. What did it matter that she was learning to struggle toward virtue? And wasn't the God who had created all things powerful enough to neutralize the spell of a twisted girl?

Bathshae was praying now, bent over a prayer rope while Obed slept on her lap. Prayers for the living, prayers for the dead. Did it matter?

On an impulse Baraqua stood up. Jared's hand slid from her belly. He half opened his eyes and she saw his desperate sadness. Then he closed them and his mouth went slack in sleep.

"I must get air, only for a moment," she whispered to Bathshae. "I will walk to the altar and back. Send Eli if anything changes. She picked up a light shawl and went out before her sister could say anything. Jared would not die before she returned; Danel would have told her if death was imminent.

Her sister Havah looked up from the fire. There was pity in her eyes, but the pity was only a pretense. Havah's eyes gleamed strangely, that stalker of the innocent. Her teeth were as long as a saber cat's as she chewed something she was scooping from a bowl. Baraqua saw the shadow of a tail twitch beneath her sister's robe. When she looked at her mother, Gayile's eyes were like the snake woman's, pupils vertical, inhuman and stealthy. Eha licked her lips and stared at Baraqua's belly.

"Take food," Havah said, gesturing to a basket of half burnt bread rounds.

"I will not, for you have poisoned it," Baraqua said, tightening the shawl across her chest. The women stared and tears sprang to Gayile's eyes. "Daughter, you... speak strangely," she stammered. She pulled the hood of her cloak low over her brow in the way of a mourning woman.

"Do not prepare the burial shroud, for he isn't dead yet," Baraqua snapped at Gayile. She ran into the path that bordered the elders' clearing, disturbed that her mind was now conjuring things that weren't real.

"They lurk everywhere now," Gayile called after her. "You mustn't go alone."

Baraqua turned and faced the women. They looked far away, inaccessible. "Let them do what they will with me," she shouted. She ran past the elders' clearing. The scents of sacred onycha and galbanum wafted from Eve's tent and lamplight filtered through the weave, lighting the forebear's way as she trod the paths of prayer toward that One who had formed her from a bone of her husband's side. She knew Eve would keep vigil all night. She wondered if that first woman of the earth ever doubted.

The stars were low and vivid. She walked quickly, refusing to think about soulless distortions of the created order she might encounter beyond the protection of the camp. She reached the altar, standing where its height blocked the moon. Adam had built this second altar after his estranged sons and daughters rejected him so they could descend the mountain into Havilah and amass its gold. They had increased their wickedness when they dismantled the altar and ground its stones to dust, mixing it with their wine in the belief that the dust contained power. They had not understood that the altar's purpose was to hold the animal whose blood atoned for their sin.

The loneliness of the normally bustling glade was unbearable. There was no one to stand with her now, no one to advise. The hard earth met her knees and she grasped the rough stones of the altar. Blood from the recent offering was still wet on the surface. The altar smelled of that blood, and of the passing of time and the offal of sheep. She thought of the elder Enosh, third from Adam. Was he finding the company of devils what he had hoped? Could he invent anything among them to match what the shining ones produced effortlessly because of their superior minds? She whispered a prayer for the elder's return. It was not hard to pray for one who had been as faithless as she believed she was.

She fell prone against the damp earth, breathing in the scent of night mist and of things decaying beneath the soil. Her belly cramped. The pains had been coming since Jared's return from the island. Was this part of Yammah's curse, to also harm her child?

She mumbled the prayer of repentance she had memorized as a child. "Because of my sin I stand at the gates of death. As the man Adam grew dark through disobedience at the Tree, my soul is also cloaked in darkness."

But the prayer was no comfort and evil seemed to be pressing in from everywhere. Jared was dying; celestial beings strutted across the land in godlike finery and did what they pleased through cunning and deception; girls who had been the pride of their parents were gone from the mountain, their wombs bulging with the spawn of the heavens. Of what use were the prophesies of Mahal and Jared if the people had no recourse against what was happening? Even Adam did not know what to do. She wept silently into the grass. Brokenness was all she had left to offer.

In the glow of a blue moon Michael gazed on the woman Baraqua, prostrate before Adam's altar. "What do you say of her character now?" he said to Uriel, who had just arrived from his post at the gates of the underworld. "Nothing is more beautiful than a woman who finds her way back to the Eden within her heart."

"Her contrition seems real; perhaps Duma chose wisely after all," Uriel said carefully. "We will soon know."

"Agreed," Michael said. "We will attend her closely this night, for evil crouches near with gloating in its loins." He had already detected Semjaza's presence beyond the altar and could hear the screeching of some of his cohort in the distance. They had taken the forms of large scorpions and in cruel glee were stinging the feet of Sethite night sentries. That the sounds made by the tormenters was beyond human capacity to hear was a mercy; the guards were aware of nothing but their own agony and wondered how scorpions had come to the holy mountain.

"Semjaza knows his chance may be over, for the heart of the woman inclines increasingly toward the light," Raphael observed, and dispersed a healing scent over the mountain. The three archangels moved down the sky and came to rest beside Baraqua.

"Soon her struggle will be resolved," Michael said. "She does not realize that every drop of sweat and every prayer this night will become a potent weapon in the battle we will all soon wage."

CHAPTER 37

That the woman stayed so long before Adam's despicable altar was making Semjaza uneasy, and the smell of atoning blood that lingered on the stones sickened him. Since his turning away to Lucifer, he could not bear the look of that shrine of devotion that set the mountain of God apart from all others on the earth. A power was there that he could not deny. There was always power in blood. He shuddered at the sound of prayers rising from the camp of the Sethites at that moment, a vigil plea for the life of Jared. There was no discounting the prayers and fasting of Adam's kin, for Semjaza was finding that his movements were less precise than they had been the day before and doubts about certain strategies swirled in his ever-decaying angelic mind. Yet the woman had agreed to go with him, though in recent days he had not seen the craven submission in her eyes that had been there the day beneath the trees when she finally vowed to be his.

He inhaled like a human man about to make an important decision and imagined how it would be to cleave at last to the woman of his longing. He was desperate to know her in the way of a human man, though he did not feel toward her as he once had. The relentless coarsening of his essence since the descent had cheapened that original infatuation. She was beautiful, yes. But knowing he had the power to rule the earth was his greater focus now, and Baraqua a mere asset to raise his estimation again in the eyes of his cohort. And unlike the girl who had borne his son, Baraqua was not mad.

He had not anticipated this would happen. More than the others, he had believed in the ideal of human love, and that belief had driven him since the night he had first seen Baraqua. He prided himself in knowing he would be a more skilled lover to the girl than any human man could be, for supernatural cunning had its advantage. But his spirit was now cold, and he accepted that this death of love was the price he must pay for power. Anything to show his hatred for God.

"She is not like Dinah or Naom, with the strength to refuse me directly," Semjaza muttered, gazing at the altar. "Let her grovel one last time before that symbol of imaginary devotion." Under the influence of his angelic immortality, the length of Baraqua's days might be two thousand years, twice what humanity had been allotted since coming out of Eden. He would spirit her to the island and bathe her body in the blood of a vulture to eliminate the stench of Adam's altar. He would implant his seed in her at the foot of his obsidian throne while spell casters circled them and drew down the magic. Then he would leave her abruptly and go out to destroy the Sethites, no matter how pitifully she begged for mercy for her people. Though the mountain was Michael's territory and many among the heavenly host would join the archangel to protect it, to devastate Eden's borderlands was still within Semjaza's rights if all went according to plan. What a fool God had been to grant free will to men and angels. With few exceptions, most used that gift against their own Creator.

As to Jared, that insipid man would die despite the vigil prayers and agonized fasting. The woman Yammah had cast her spell accurately, and already a death angel from out of the fifth heaven stood waiting in the trees beyond the sick man's tent. Semjaza wanted to laugh, but it might shake the Powers on such a spiritually porous night. He must remain hidden a little longer.

Baraqua heard something stir in the trees beyond the altar. She got to her feet as another pain shot through her belly. Was the baby safe? She was spent of tears and of what prayer she had in her, and it was time to return to Jared. Whatever happened now was beyond her control. The moon seemed paler and the air in the altar clearing thicker than it should be. Night mists had crept high into the trees instead of staying at the height of a woman's knee to water the earth every night. She groped to some raspberry bushes along the edge of the clearing. She and her sisters had eaten of the berries during Sabbath worship when they were young. She pulled off a few leaves and chewed them, remembering that raspberry leaves strengthened the womb. Perhaps their properties would still the pains.

A wind sprang into the clearing and she pulled her shawl tighter. "Eli?" she called out. But no young man in the tunic of a night guard stepped forward with a sturdy club lashed to his waist. Instead, a spare, gaunt-faced man in a close-fitting white garment appeared. She took a step back. Something in his eyes was not right. The mouth, with its almost nonexistent lips, made her think of someone who would choose to have no appearance at all if it were not necessary. He might have been young or ancient, and though taller than Adam, he must be human because his skin did not shine. In long fingers the unfamiliar man held a slender silver tool with a hook at one end. The way he caressed the tool made her cold. Though insignificant in size, it looked like a weapon he intended to use.

"Are you one of the scribes who keeps to the caves beyond the camp?" she said, forcing bravery to her voice. A few of the older copyists lived an ascetic life near the caverns where the *Chronicles of Adam* and other writings were stored. They led a severe life and rejected the comforts of marriage.

"I am Kasdeja, a healer of the woes of the womb," the man said. His voice was strangely soft in contrast to the skull-like set of the face, and the flaccid underbelly of a rat came to Baraqua's mind. Snakes of mist coiled at the bottom of the man's garment, but her eye kept returning to the tool in the man's hand.

"I need no midwife yet," Baraqua said carefully. She looked past him to the trail that led back to the camp. She willed Eli or one of Jared's other brothers to appear.

"I am no midwife," the man said. He made a ghastly attempt at something like a compassionate expression. But the effect was like cracks opening in hard earth. "I know your husband is dying and that your unborn child is malformed and witless. I can do nothing about the husband, but I can relieve you of the burden of a worthless child." He shook his head like a man on the verge of mourning. "A young widow, especially a privileged woman like yourself, should not have to bear double shame and hardship."

Baraqua's breath caught. A malformed and witless child... worthless? She willed her voice to be strong. "How would you know these things? I have not seen you among the vigil-keepers, and no scout was sent out with news of Jared's illness to surrounding lands. As to the child, the midwives assure me he is healthy." She felt another belly spasm. Why was she justifying herself to this stranger? Fear crawled up her back. She wished desperately to be somewhere else.

"Midwives know nothing in these cases," the man said. He waved one of the pale hands dismissively. "They do not know that when one woman in a family produces a malformed child, her younger sister always gives birth to the same." He held up the silver blade as though to make sure all was well with it. He spoke casually, as though calling her attention to the stages of the moon. "The pangs are the sign that your son shall be just as your nephew Obed is."

She forced herself to breathe evenly as another cramp bit into her side. She thought of Obed's wide, grinning mouth with the trail of saliva running on his chin; the strange smiles; the vague reek of feces on his body. But the man had an authority about him she could not deny. Had God sent him in answer to her prayers before the altar? She pictured herself a widow, alone in a musty tent with a helpless, silent child beside her, begging someone to build a carrying cart so she could haul him with her when she went to mourn over Jared's grave.

"Give me your wrist and this problem will soon be resolved," the man said as he raised the hand that held the hooked tool. A small viper slid from his sleeve and wrapped itself around the tool. The serpent's head probed the air, fixing Baraqua's gaze out of unflinching reptilian eyes. "One prick of my pet's fang and you will fall into sweet sleep," Kasdeja said. "You will not even know when I move to expel the monster from your womb."

How easy it sounded and how tired she was. Kasdeja could spare her the woe of an imperfect child who could never be Anointed One anyway.

She stretched out her arm through the soft, obscure air, barely able to see the tips of her fingers in the mist. It was better this way, not to see when the viper pricked. What a relief to have someone care in her moment of crisis. But she felt no sensation of the snake's bite. Instead, Kasdeja's mouth was suddenly moving over her neck and arms as though seeking something, his breath quick with arousal. Yet she felt no actual breath and his lips were icy. What *was* this creature trying to invade her?

"Life, death; it will all be the same when we come together this night," Kasdeja was saying, his words slurred with desire. The voice was no longer deferential, but dangerous as a rockslide. His body felt cold as death.

She pushed him away and turned to the altar, running her hands over the stones still wet with the sacred liquid that atoned for humanity's ancient treachery against God. She thrust her bloodied palms near Kasdeja's face. "You are no healer of the womb's miseries, and my child is not worthless," she shouted.

Kasdeja stared at her out of unholy orbs of sight and recoiled at the blood on her hands. And then they were not alone. A handsome man with a face as diaphanous as water appeared out of the trees.

He wore a robe of deepest purple that seemed to contain many hues, dimensions of reality, and mysteries hidden in its folds. His expression pricked something in Baraqua that brought up old longings that she repelled immediately. She did not recognize him, yet she knew who he was.

The man spoke to Kasdeja with a growl in his voice. "I sent you to remove the worm, yet you have tried to invade her womb with your own seed," he said. "You, who said you despised the female body—"

"But her beauty—" Kasdeja said. He looked confused, and he seemed to have lost the strict control over himself that had been there before, as though his limbs would separate from his body any moment. The tiny scimitar fell from his fingers and from within him erupted something like the wailing of infants.

"Her beauty is mine," the robed man growled. "You will spend eternity in Oblivion for this. Go there this moment." Kasdeja seemed to diminish within the fog, but did not leave.

The man turned to Baraqua. "I have come to hold you to your promise," he said.

"I don't know you," Baraqua said, "and I never promised you anything."

"I manifest in a different form this night, the better to woo you," the man said. "I am still he to whom you promised body and eternal soul."

"I could never be happy with one who trades one man's face for another, as though a face was something to be discarded." she said. She felt nauseous in the presence of the two.

"Your happiness is nothing compared to what must come for the betterment of the earth," he replied. "My will must be done."

His will—She knew she did not have intelligence enough to best this creature. But she remembered that Adam had told Magda to let her yes be yes and her no be simply that. This was the way of integrity.

"I will not go with you, for a vow made to evil is null when one repents," she said simply. "I will walk the straight path, with or without my husband and son." She held out her bloodied palms again, and the man in purple winced.

"Women of the straight path do not break vows," he said.

"What would you know of the straight path?" she countered. But he had known, once. It had been this one's choice to depart from God, for God himself had not created evil. She tried to remember what it was about him that had made her want him all those years ago on the lake, this bloodless caricature who was neither human nor privileged angel because he had desired to be both on his own terms.

"You will lose everything for this choice," the man said, his voice like the sidling of a desert serpent. "Your child is already a legless stump and its sire will die this night. Your people will be carrion for the hawks before the day is over."

"God will decide what is best," she forced from her mouth. The words were agony to say, to choose. God's will, her submission. What he said about Jared was probably true. She would miss her kind husband when the fever finally burned away his last breath. She remembered the night of the child's conception and the unexpected joy of closeness to the man as together they fulfilled the will of stars and angels— the will of their God.

The handsome creature's arms were suddenly around her, and it was as though the snake woman was upon her again. This time she would have gladly killed. She raked her fingers down that face, if it could be called one, cringing at the sensation of something that was not really skin. The angel released her and backed away, for some of the blood was on him. He went to his knees as though weakened.

"You forsake me, cruel spawn of Eve," he said, swiping at the blood.

"I count the day happy when one like you calls me such," Baraqua replied. There was nothing more to say or do. Dawn was seeping between the trees to the east. With her heart pounding, she walked between the entities she wished were not real. No pain pulled at her belly. The infant voices within Kasdeja wailed louder. "Mercy, mercy," they cried pitifully. But she would not go back. Their cries and God's pity must suffice.

People were in the trail, Bathshae with a warm shawl in her hands and Obadiah with Obed in his arms. Bathshae did not ask why her sister's hands were stained in blood, only grasped them in hers. "Jared revives," she said breathlessly. "Minutes ago, he sat up and begged for water. His skin was cool and he asked for you."

"God Most High has looked kindly on his people's petitions," Obadiah said. "Yammah's spell is broken."

Baraqua reached for Obed, something she had never done willingly before. The child held out his little arms and settled into hers, studying her out of the wide, watery eyes that gave no clue of anything except love.

"This night more than one spell has been broken," Baraqua said.

CHAPTER 38

And over the righteous and holy he will appoint guardians from
among the holy angels, to guard them as the apple of his eye.
1 ENOCH 100:5

Michael had not expected the attack from the Watchers at midday. Why wouldn't the corrupt ones wish to hide their murderous strategies beneath the cowl of darkness? But though the hour surprised the archangel, he was not unprepared when he saw Semjaza and his cohort manifesting in their earthly guises above the holy mountain; star priests and warmongers, wizards and keepers of the cauldron; stalkers of innocent children; disrupters of marriage and of the beauties of creation swarmed the clear sky. Semjaza was attempting to organize his cohort for the assault to come, but Michael noticed with slight amusement that many even among his chiefs-of-tens-and-twenties were not attentive, instead lurching crazily away from the ranks with their eyes fixed on tents and shelters on the earth below, in hopes of spying undressed women at their bathing troughs.

Below, in the Flood Sea, two of the Watchers' already extraordinarily tall sons curled their lips in brutish pleasure as they swam the breadth of the sea, their eyes fixed on the lush mountain they were appointed to destroy. One was the son of Awan. Even

Michael was astonished at the rate the giants had grown in such a short time.

The other archangels flanked Michael in the sky and watched Azazel strut on the steppe of Nod among his armored warriors, flaunting weapons of war wrought from the metals of the earth, as Azazel looked on with a sadistic glint in his countenance.

Uriel's righteous anger flared. "How slow Tartarus has been to claim Semjaza and Azazel. They have deserved its torments from the first hour of their descent, yet instead, they have so far been shown great mercy."

"They will not share a shred of that mercy with the Sethites today," Gabriel added ruefully.

"Baraqua's refusal to bend the knee to Semjaza will make him doubly cruel," Raphael agreed.

Michael looked long at each of his friends. The four had strategized all they could, based on God's counsel. Their task was to protect the Sethites and prevent as much bloodshed as possible. The outcome they could not yet know, for the free will of men and angels was an unpredictable factor. Michael signaled for Gabriel to sound his trumpet. Before the crystalline blast had died away, the heavens lit up as leagues of bodiless powers from the principalities, keepers of heights, and every angelic hierarchy with a vocation for battle filled the sky. With valor and elation in their faces and clad in brilliant armor, the great ones swept down the firmament to do Michael's righteous bidding. Finally, a semblance of vengeance against the traitors of heaven was in their grasp. The Watchers swarming in the lower atmosphere cursed into the multitude above, and the sound of their ravings was like the thunder of many skies.

Semjaza was before Michael in an instant, his armor an imitation of Azazel's, his huge form imposed against the clear blue sky, blocking the sun. "Who gave you leave to interfere?" he said to Michael in a voice so malevolent the archangel had to will his own composure. "Will you try to take Baraqua for yourself?" Semjaza added with a leer. "It's said she desires men in white."

"If it were in my power, I would send you to the lower tier of hell this day," Michael retorted, disgusted. He gave a cry of command, and the heavenly multitude dove through the swarm of Watchers and filled the air above the mountain with tier upon tier of their majestic presence, every breastplate and shield emblazoned with the holy name of God as they began to do battle with members of the cohort, wielding blindingly bright swords and crying, "Holy! Holy! Holy! Lord God of Sabaoth reigns!" Behind the warrior angels, the hierarchies of harps and glories chorused the praises of God. The Watchers cringed at the sound, struggling to descend lower in order to take up positions against God's people, and concealed within the folds of their garments Michael saw balls of sulfured fire.

"We will burn the mountain to a blackened wasteland, just as we did Ermon," Semjaza said to Michael with a final sneer, and dove into the mix.

Uriel, Raphael, and Gabriel descended into the Sethite camp, taking up positions in the elders' clearing, while Michael stayed above the fray to assess the situation. The two young giants were crawling out of the sea, masses of sea grass wrapping their ankles. They were only half grown, and Michael shuddered at what their power would be once they reached three thousand ells in height. They started up the southern flank of the mountain, muscles flexing as they uprooted trees in their path. Azazel and his three hundred were now marching out of Nod, clutching the barbed spears and double-edged swords Azazel had taught them to cherish above all else. Michael shuddered at the thought of the death that lay in those weapons. There would barely be time to prepare the Sethites before the swarm of self-important brutes ascended the eastern slope of the mountain, intent on killing the people who kept to the ways of the true God.

He was in the elders' clearing in an instant and spoke to Gabriel. "Worse than the iron weapons they carry is that Azazel has taught them to truly crave murder," he said. "We must supply the Sethites with armaments, for there will never again in the lifetime of Adam be a day like this one, or more at stake for the people of God."

Adam emerged from his tent with a cry, bewildered, rubbing sleep from his eyes. "Something is not right," he cried, peering in his disorientation into the treetops. "I have seen in a dream that evil has returned, despite our vigil."

Azure was passing by with a basket of grain on her shoulder. "But nothing is amiss in the camp, my father," she said. "Jared still rests in his tent and the people have broken the fast to return to the fields. All seems well."

"All is not well," Adam said, looking intently at Azure. "Something foul infects the wind."

Azure began to weep. "Will they strike again with the fever and infect more of us this time?" she said.

Eve came out of Adam's tent and spoke to Azure, cinching her robe as though for work. "It is as Adam says. Go and tell all you meet to gird for battle as best they can." Azure dropped the basket and ran, kernels of wheat spilling over the ground. Other people were gathering, and Eve spoke louder. "Be strong and courageous, for there is work ahead." On the forebear's head was the fragile tiara of the substance no one knew the origin of, signifying an important event.

Naom came to Eve with three of her grown daughters. "We will fight with you," she said. "The girls have not yet broken the fast today, so are still strong in spirit." Michael saw a new radiance in Naom's face, the fruit of her endurance of the suffering she had borne over Enosh.

Adam shed his outer garment and tied back his hair, and Michael was relieved that he and the other elders understood the seriousness of what they faced. "I see shadows like tattered cloth blowing," Adam said, his eyes peering beyond the trees again. "Above us move streams of mighty ones who come in force, both good and evil." He looked at the people who waited for his instruction. "Fight by whatever means and with faith, no matter how things seem, for victory is not always to those with brawn." Adam clenched his hands. "O that I could see more clearly into the realm that lies beyond human sight, as I once did. I used to walk with cherubim and chorus with the heavenly ones, in that time when God made his abode in Eden." He seemed appalled to have to compare that time with the present. "That was the time of bliss, before Lucifer mocked me with the promise of hidden knowledge. The stench of that snake has not left my nostrils since, and I smell it on the wind now."

Mahal and Kenan ran in from the fields with more men, some clutching clubs or flint weapons, a few awkwardly carrying heavy leather shields they had brought back from excursions to southern lands where men made use of such things. Dogs barked and growled, circling trees and whimpering as they looked into the sky. Small children were crying, and Michael wished he could shelter their eyes from the otherwise invisible forms of supernatural creatures that their innocence sometimes allowed such little ones to see.

"Women and children must go at once to the prayer caves, for wicked Noddites climb the mountain as we speak," Mahal said breathlessly, and began to guide a group toward a hidden trail that went down the western side of the mountain between the cliffs. "Go to Akliah," he told them. "Pray with her that God saves the Sethites this day."

Rojj pushed through the crowd. "I have alerted the keepers of sheep," he said. "A crack on the head with a shepherd's crook may do more damage than people expect." The goatherd had been despondent since Awan's death, but now there was fresh color in his thinned face.

Michael was relieved to see Baraqua and Jared enter the clearing. Today would be their reckoning. Had Baraqua prayed enough before the altar to be prepared? Determination was in Jared's face, though he did not look strong of body. "I have been as cowardly as a calf in this time of crisis, when as a prophet I should have led." Jared said to the people. "Forgive me, all."

"No one could have been more faithful," said Adam. "You endured the consequence of trying to save Yusuf's daughters. Lead now with courage."

But Seth looked troubled. "We will soon be at war with immortal beings we cannot kill." He struggled for the right words and turned to Adam imploringly. "What of the human men coming up to fight? You have always forbidden the taking of life with breath in it, both of men and animals."

"Though we will still not kill for food, that law forbidding defending our own lives was for another time," Adam said without hesitation. He continued to glance around the clearing and into the sky, where his eyes were often drawn. "A time before angels gave up their splendor to take wives after the manner of men; before the mountains and valleys were emptied of peace and the dignity of the soulish animals I named in the ancient day was mocked through hideous cross-mixtures." He walked among the people with gravity in his face. "Whatever celestial beings have done or will do, we are men of flesh and blood whose duty is still to guard the precious Seed that will one bring us Anointed One. We must protect that Seed at all cost." He turned to Baraqua. "You must go to the caves."

"I respect what you say, but I won't go," Baraqua said without a pause, and Michael was gratified. "My penance for far too many things will be to fight this day. If I had kept my vow to the shining one, none of you would be in this danger. If I die, I die."

Jared ran his hand over his face. "Do not speak foolishly, Baraqua," he said with undisguised irritation. "These invaders would have tried to destroy us no matter what vow you made."

But Adam gestured his agreement with Baraqua's words. "Sometimes to trust God with what is most precious is the only way."

At Michael's sign, the four archangels then moved swiftly to put into the hand of every elder a sword of light whose polished hilt was the color of the heavens, and into the hands of every elder's wife a longbow of silver and a quiver of ruby-tipped arrows. When

Michael approached Adam with the gleaming weapon, the forebear cried out and went to his knees, for Michael opened Adam's eyes to see him. "You are the one who helped me build the first altar," Adam said in a shaking voice. He leaned on the sword of light that no one but the other Seed Bearers could see, then spoke to the people. "Bow, one and all, before the captain of the Lord's army, who shows great mercy to sinful Adam this day." The people went to their knees and the dogs stopped growling.

"Your prayers of penitence over the centuries have been heard," Michael said to Adam. "Do not fear, for God Most High is with you, though there will be woe today." Then he opened Baraqua and Jared's eyes to see him as well. "All heaven rejoices over this woman who mocks death," Michael said to Baraqua.

Baraqua stared at Michael, her face drained of color. "Yes, holy one. I choose to mock death for the greater good. You are the one I saw standing in Eden so long ago." She paused. "Will we conquer today?"

"Victory and defeat are in the hands of the Lord," Michael said. "Fight with all your strength, and do not lose heart."

Jared took Baraqua's hand. "No matter what happens, remember that I have never loved you more than I do now."

The elders were testing the movements of the swords of light. Baraqua and Jared's feet were suddenly shod in golden sandals latched to the knees. Baraqua sprang forward reflexively, her movements as quick as a leopard's. Naom tore off her widow's veil and threw it aside as she looked into the east. Michael had opened her eyes to see Azazel at the head of the Noddite warriors who were coming through the trees, the men's heads shorn and eagerness in their faces as they strode behind their leader.

Men scurried into position as they waited for Adam's orders. They were untrained for conflict, but many prayers came from their lips. Naom drew an arrow from her quiver and notched it, her eyes on the thick stand of birch trees beyond the elders' clearing. Enosh was striding out of the trees beside Azazel, his garment of an elegant, flowing style and his beard cut in the manner of a Noddish conjurer. Naom cried out but did not lower her bow.

Enosh gestured into the clearing and spoke to Azazel. "Behold, the traitors who must be swept from the earth for the new order to advance," he said. Naom aimed the arrow at Azazel and Enosh quickly stood in front of the massive angel, as though to protect him.

"Stand back, husband, for I will do this," Naom said, and Michael saw Enosh's eyes flicker with fear.

"You have no power to hurt me," Enosh said to Naom. Some of the people gasped at such a saying from the mouth of their estranged elder to his wedded wife.

Naom pulled the bowstring tighter. "I dedicate this arrow to my husband, a better man than he knows himself to be," she said. She released the arrow with a precision that astonished even Michael. Enosh ducked and the arrow found its mark in Azazel's chest. The angel winced as the other-worldly dart went through his incorporeal body without leaving a mark and pierced the bronze breastplate of the man behind him, as though the breastplate were made of parchment. The wounded man fell to the ground, astonishment in his eyes. "It was not to be this way," he whispered from where he lay. He looked up beseechingly at Azazel, who towered over him with an amused look, as though the man's suffering was a cool drink on a hot day. "A parting word for me, Master," the man whispered. But Azazel ground his boot into the man's face and he and the others moved forward, trampling the fallen warrior.

Enosh backed against a tree, horror in his eyes as he stared at Naom. Naom ran toward him, but he cried out and disappeared from the clearing. The Noddites surged and Sethite men shouted warnings to each other as they clamored against the enemy. The bright heavenly host were descending like a wind into the clearing, tangling with members of Semjaza's cohort or taking up sentry to protect the Sethite men.

Michael stood before Baraqua. "I will shield your womb during the battle," he said, and Baraqua nodded. Michael sadly scanned the summit of the mountain with its healing springs, stands of fragrant, towering cedars, and fields of exquisite flowering plants that were more beautiful than those in any other part of the earth. Would the mountain of God be intact when this was over? He had authority that day to help the people but not protect the land itself. The Watchers had their own authority, and Michael did not know yet what they would be permitted to do. And he could not predict whether they would unleash the balls of fire they held within their robes.

Baraqua sprang backward in her golden shoes as one of Azazel's men ran toward her. She put out her foot at light speed and tripped the man, whose unprotected head struck a rock. In the girl's eyes, Michael saw the gleam of a victor.

Though many Sethites fell at the hands of Azazel's horde and the cruel cunning of the Watchers who strengthened them, the war angel had not expected fierceness in young boys or wiliness from goatherds and scribes, who captured many with hastily made traps of birch saplings that slung the armored men high into the trees or uttered such powerful prayers that some fainted with fear. The elders' swords of light found their marks as well, and their wives were remarkably skilled with the silver bows, outwitting those who expected feebleness in women.

Baraqua and Jared worked together as though they were one person. Baraqua would jump onto the back of one of Azazel's men, covering his eyes as he sliced the air blindly with his heavy sword, until he stared in death at the touch of Jared's heavenly weapon.

Baraqua lured ten hulking men after her into a cave of hungry saber cats, then cleared the entrance while the cats' massive paws brought the men down.

"You will never again doubt this woman," Michael called to Uriel, who was sending one of Semjaza's chiefs-of-ten sprawling into the sky.

"Blessed be God, who has accomplished this great deed," Uriel answered with joy.

Then Michael saw the giant. Not far from the cave, Baraqua was staring up into its face where it stood looking down from between two massive redwood trees. Evil was strong in the creature's alluring, magnificent features and Baraqua's hand went to her mouth. "Awan, despite it all he has your eyes," she whispered.

Jared appeared, sweat streaming from his face. "Come away from this fiend," he said to Baraqua, panic in his voice.

Baraqua looked hard at Jared. "You and I will avenge my cousin today."

"But what of our child's safety, and yours?" Jared shouted. But Baraqua had already leapt onto one of the giant's feet through the power of the gaiters. Jared launched himself after her, scrambling up the giant's other leg, the sword shimmering between his teeth.

"It is too much," Jared called in a muffled voice. "God does not expect this of you."

"*I* expect it," she shouted back.

Take the creature's life or it will take yours, Michael whispered to Jared, not caring whether Jared believed that the thought came from an angel or from his own mind.

Baraqua climbed higher, shimmying up the giant's forearm. Intrigued, the monster held up its arm to see her better.

"Do not look into its eyes," Jared shouted. "Adam dreamt this day that the abyss of Sheol lies within them."

"It is between those eyes that you must aim your sword," she called. "That is the vulnerable place." And Michael wondered how she knew.

Semjaza appeared suddenly behind the head of the giant, almost as large as his son. He wore the garb of an archangel and radiated a beatific light, the ultimate disguise of his shadowed nature.

"So, a discarded chit comes to toy with my spawn?" Semjaza said.

"Your disguise does not confuse me," Baraqua said. "I come shod in the shoes of war and the husband of my heart will take down this son of yours this day."

"You will do nothing, woman rejected of God," Semjaza sneered, the garishness of his countenance dimming.

"Look well, Semjaza, for the fire of God is in that woman today," Michael called out.

"May you rot in Tartarus, archangel," Semjaza growled back.

"Now!" Baraqua screamed as the giant began to swing its arm to dislodge her. Michael kept his place beside her, tense with hope. He had the power to slay the giant with one stroke of his sword, but not the authority to do so— not this time. This was Jared's test. He watched as a glance of deep meaning passed between Baraqua and Jared. The chords of marital love that bound them became thick ropes of gold. His heart ascended in thanks as Jared launched the sword. The blue-hot blade seared the air and pierced the giant's head directly between its eyes. There was an explosion of light, the giant's eyes emptied, and Baraqua and Jared jumped away. The giant's body crashed backward through the trees and the earth split at the impact, opening a deep crevice.

Michael wrapped himself around Baraqua the moment before she hit the ground. Jared scrambled to her and took her in his arms, his voice rough with feeling. "My wife, my child," he murmured. He kissed her mouth and cheeks and hair, his tears mingling with hers.

Around them the battle ceased, for the crevice had split to three more. Michael scanned the area. Semjaza and the Watchers no longer smudged the air with their elusive forms and the Noddites were disappearing through the trees. Sethites were bending over their wounded, trying to drag them out of the way of the opening earth. Women who had not fled to the caves were renting their robes before the motionless bodies of husbands and sons, as though oblivious to the danger. Many of the heavenly host remained to succor the wounded and bereaved.

Jared picked up Baraqua and carried her toward their tent, out of the way of the crevices. People bowed in reverence as they passed, and even Azazel's wounded men, groaning on the ground in pain and bewilderment, dragged themselves out of the way of the man with the astonishing glow in his face, who carried a woman with flowing hair out of the field of blood.

"Did it happen the way my mind tells me?" Baraqua said as Jared laid her on her sleeping mat. She was suddenly too exhausted to keep her eyes open.

"Yes," Jared said. "But how is a mystery beyond this world."

Chapter 39

*And to the north of the garden there is a sea of water, clear
and pure to the taste, like unto nothing else; so that, through
the clearness thereof, one may look into the depths of the earth.*
THE FIRST BOOK OF ADAM AND EVE 1:2

Trusses of sand grass taller than men bent with the wind beside a crystal-clear sea at dawn. Hidden within the grass a cluster of people in worn and faded clothes were gathered around a dugout shelter carved into the dunes. The roof of the shelter was a tangle of beach weeds, planted there as camouflage. Other shelters huddled on either side, their roofs forming one long, sun-bleached concealment against the eyes of the enemy, the canny Nephilim.

The uneven rupture of a newborn's first cry filtered from the dugout and the people stifled outbursts of joy. Jared's child was born, the new Seed Bearer! But they must be quiet, for the Nephilim had sensitive hearing. Despite their tattered robes and the sparse feast they could provide for the new parents, for a few moments it would be to them as though they still lived in honor on the earth's highest mountain, in the centuries before everything changed.

Dawnlight squeezed through the uncovered window where Baraqua lay on a birthing mat in the dugout. All night she had labored to bring her son into the world. Now Bathshae held up the tiny infant for Baraqua and Jared to see. The child blinked against the light and released another cry. "He breathes well," Bathshae said.

"Not like me at birth," Jared said, and stroked the baby's face. "Praise be to God that there was no entity to battle this time."

Baraqua heard the cautious celebration outside. The women had ground dried tubers into flour and made a type of honey cake for the occasion. She was hungry for one. She imagined the sunrise bleeding over that sea, their sea, an hour's distance from the charred remains of the holy mountain they had once called home. She was safe, sheltered, loved. The sea air was pure and good. And though she was now a vagabond among other vagabonds, her child was safely born.

Gayile pushed aside the limp cloak of her dead husband Rasujal, which served as the door to Jared and Baraqua's shelter. "The firstborn son of Jared has the aspect of Anointed One in his eyes," she called out to the people as quietly as she was able. The women did not dare take out their tambourines to dance and the men did not beat drums. But Baraqua knew they smiled.

Baraqua thought of her father, who had died trying to pull his daughter Havah from beneath a felled tree during the fire that had lost the people their mountain six months before. Havah and Rasujal had both died, along with too many others to mourn properly. Yet God had spared all the Seed Bearers and their wives, and many of their children. She imagined Adam and Eve standing by faithfully in the grass, with Seth and Azura, Mahal and Dinah, and Kenan with his prophetess daughter, Zyla. She knew Naom would be standing apart from the others. Her encounter with Enosh on the mountain had drained the eldress of her remaining vitality.

"Suckle the child now," Bathshae said, showing Baraqua how to hold the baby as he fed.

Tears were on Jared's face. "What right do we have to love this much?" he whispered, and Baraqua had no reply. The baby's face was too beautiful to bear. Her love for Jared made her want to weep.

"I am unworthy," she said. Yet wasn't every gift to humankind a mercy, all of them undeserved?

"You are more than worthy, giant slayer," Jared said, and grinned.

"It was you who drained his eyes of life," Baraqua replied. Now that the birthing was over, she was suddenly sleepy.

The ground began to tremble. It happened almost every day, and the midwives attending Baraqua went calmly to their knees and Baraqua held the child closer as the familiar spirit of fear swept through the shelter. A Nephil was in the land—a *gibbor*, one of the mighty men who prowled and ravaged with incomprehensible strength wherever they chose. This one was not close enough to be a danger to the Sethites who huddled by the Crystal Sea, yet the next time it might be. The room leaned slightly and righted itself as dust sifted from the earthen ceiling with its protruding roots. The sandy plateau above was only partially strengthened with wooden slats. Baraqua wondered how long it would be before the makeshift homes collapsed.

"A Nephil stalks," Gayile said, as though no one would have discerned this without her saying it. Baraqua and Bathshae exchanged a glance. Their mother would always say the obvious thing because she found security in saying something. Her voice was more strained than it had been, and the embedded lines of her grief over Rasujal quivered around her mouth. Baraqua shifted on her pallet and cradled the child carefully. Would God Most High fulfill his promise and keep the new Seed Bearer alive despite it all? Colonies of the mighty ones now made their homes in caverns among the high mountains to the north. No one knew how many there were.

Gayile clenched her fists. "How can it be divine will that these creatures are allowed to thrive on God's good earth?" Her lip trembled. "They will smell this special child and come to devour him—cannibals without conscience, drinkers of blood."

"Be at peace, mother of my wife," Jared said. "Two nights ago, as I lay on the sand beneath the stars, I saw an angel as tall as the holy mountain itself overshadowing this cove. God will not abandon his people."

Gayile sniffed. She preferred people responding to her fears with fear in kind. "I am not privy to acts of wonder like my son-in-law is," she said. But no one would blame Gayile. Everyone imagined the worst these days.

But for a moment Baraqua did not care about gibborim. She could not take her eyes from the child— the chin and mouth so much like Jared's, eyes with the hint of herself in their shape, and a skin tone like her father's. How proud Rasujal would have been.

"We must take the child out to Adam and Seth to be blessed," Jared said.

Gayile had started to massage Baraqua's feet with oil of chamomile. "Not before he is properly washed and swaddled," she said. Then her shoulders sagged as she remembered. "There is no swaddling cloth for a thousand stadia, and we are beggars on the earth."

Bathshae held out a handful of linen strips. "People have sacrificed to provide what is needed for the son of Jared," she said with a tired smile. Cloth was precious now, for the people had not yet seeded fields for flax.

"We will not swaddle our son," Baraqua said. It was time to speak of what she and Jared had agreed on.

Gayile's response was predictable. She raised her hands and let them drop. "I lie down at night sodden in grief, yet I'm not allowed to care for my grandson."

"There are reasons you must understand," Baraqua said. She wished she could be alone with Jared and the child. But duty came first. Duty brought the greatest joy.

"Swaddling has been the custom since Adam's first children," Gayile protested. "The child's back will grow crooked without snug wrappings."

Baraqua rummaged at the side of her pallet and pulled out a square of oat colored cloth—amateurish looking, askew in shape. "For the first forty days of our son's life we will wrap him in this," she said, holding it before the women.

Gayile looked as horrified as if a Nephil was peering through the window. "Wrap Anointed One in this rag?"

Baraqua fingered the piece of cloth she had kept so long. "It symbolizes my divided heart. Our son must know from infancy that doing the noble thing brings out the truest self."

Gayile stared. But Bathshae put her hand on Baraqua's arm. "This is fitting," she said, and set the swaddling strips down.

"Let me at least wash the rag first," Gayile said. "The Nephilim have noses as sensitive as foxes."

Jared stood and cinched his belt. "Let the monsters slaver, Gayile. Nothing will hinder God's direction for our child. He has been born for a great purpose."

The faces of the midwives were solemn as they took in Jared's words. His esteem in all the people's eyes was great since the slaying of the giant on the day the mountain burned. But Baraqua wanted her mother to understand more. "This cloth bears the scent of time, the time it took for one like me to put away rebellion," she said. "It is a holy scent and will repel all evil." She set the baby on the square of cloth. Its limbs were perfect, its dark eyes luminous. She felt a stab of shame, remembering how she had almost succumbed to the wiles of Kasdeja in her moment of desperation. How dark the human heart could be.

Jared helped Baraqua stand with the infant in her arms. He put his hand on the baby's head. "May he know from infancy that earthly refuges do not exist. May he abide always beneath the wings of the Almighty."

Baraqua drew the edges of the cloth around the tiny body and they all went through the low door and into the grass where the people waited. The sea glowed under the sunrise as the people crowded around the new parents and the precious infant—this might be Anointed One! Anyone observing the scene on the beach encircled on three sides by high white cliffs would not guess that these people had barely survived the destruction of their lands or guessed that devils terrorized them even now.

Adam and Eve came near the baby. They had both been wounded during the battle on the mountain and Eve's burned hand would never be the same. Adam had received a gash on his neck, now healed to a thick scar. Eve touched the child's forehead. "Blessed be God Most High, who has not forgotten the promise he made to me after I sinned in paradise. May this child be formidable and lead us back to Eden."

Adam took the baby from Baraqua. "What is the name of the child?" he said.

"He is Enoch, meaning 'dedicated one,'" Jared said.

Adam looked intently into the child's face. "This Enoch will be a great teacher; many will draw near to hear his words," he said. "But I see a life unlike any who has ever lived, and a lonely path through unknown places."

The people were quiet, taking the new name into their mouths, whispering their thoughts to each other. The name's meaning was from their own language, not Edenese like Jared's name, with its destructive prophecy. But there was uneasiness in their faces as well. What did Adam mean by unknown places?

"If he will journey along the paths of heaven, then surely he is the very savior of the world," Shai said excitedly. The scout stood beside his wife Magda, whose belly was mounded gently with child.

"I have no vision or instinct that Enoch is Anointed One," Jared said firmly. "His mission is something else, and a prelude to the coming of Anointed One." His eyes pled: *I know you need hope, but I cannot give you false hope.*

Shai swallowed, looking almost ill with disappointment. Baraqua remembered his exhortation that she marry Jared and bear the savior of the world. He and the other scouts had labored hard to find the sheltered cove where Anointed One might grow up in safety. But he gestured his agreement with what Jared had said. No one would doubt Jared or Mahal in anything now. Shai offered Jared and Baraqua cups of wine fermented from the fruit of transplanted vines he had found still living on the holy mountain after the fire. The people spoke in low tones as they drank their wine and ate the honey cakes made of the strange root they must endure until wheat could be planted. They were happy to have anything extra. Want of so many things had changed what seemed important.

"It is too high a thing for me to understand," Gayile said sadly, and Baraqua had never seen her look so fatigued. But her mother lifted her head and brought a makeshift cushion from the dugout and made Baraqua sit down on it, then pressed a handful of the honey cakes into her hand. And when Baraqua looked up from her wine, Mahal was standing before her. The old shame filled her; her father-in-law had not spoken directly to her since the night he called her unworthy. The faded elder's robe, his only garment since the fire, hung limply on his thinned body, and worry over the people's future plagued his face. She wished she could return to the dugout to lie down, as women ought to after giving birth. But nothing was like it should be anymore. She must be present and cheerful for the people. She must endure whatever Jared's father said to her.

Mahal sat down in the grass beside her. "Daughter, I have never been so wrong about anyone," he said abruptly.

Baraqua did not know what to say. Mahal looked as though he might lose courage if he waited to say more.

"I had no right to rebuke you that night, and my wife has never stopped reminding me of it," Mahal continued. "Imagine saying such things to a Seed Bearer's bride while the people looked on. It was beneath me."

"But you spoke rightly," Baraqua said, surprised that the words weren't hard to say. What did she have to hide, now that she had wrapped her child in a blanket that symbolized her own inadequacies? "I understand only now how much you suffered to present your son to God as a pure offering," she said. "Of all the women in the camp, I was least acceptable as a wife."

Mahal dared a slight smile. "The dream angel knew who was acceptable," he said. "You are a woman of grace, and your feats in the battle are the crown of your character."

"It was Jared," Baraqua said. She could not bear to bask in the full glory of that day. She could not remember when the golden shoes had left her feet.

"My own harshness humbled me, for I have always prided myself on my gentleness compared to many men," Mahal said. "I see now that I was still seeking their approval that night." He shrugged. "That night... I was overwhelmed when my vision became reality. I wanted to control something, anything. So I attacked you, and I am deeply ashamed."

"I believed myself clever then, yet I never stopped considering your words," Baraqua said.

"Well then, let us put it all aside," Mahal said, standing up. "I must offer a blessing to my newest grandchild."

Baraqua looked after him. Losing the mountain had taught them all much.

"May God Most High be exalted this day, for I have finally reentered the land of the living." The familiar male voice resonated from the curve of the sheltering cliffs. Supported by a crude crutch, a strongly built man was limping across the sand toward the people. His torn and soiled robe was trimmed in emeralds at the neck and his face was hidden by an unkempt beard that was completely white. Baraqua got up and moved through the people to see. The man had stopped walking in order to rest. When a gust of wind blew at his robe, she saw that one of his legs was cut off at the knee.

Naom ran up the sand. She dropped to her knees before the man and embraced his good leg. "My Enosh, my Enosh," she said, and began to weep.

Yes, it was Enosh. He had aged much from the day he had come to the battle in his fine attire. The people murmured and exchanged looks full of meaning. Why was the traitor here? How could Naom forgive him after the suffering he had caused?

Enosh dropped the crutch and knelt awkwardly, balanced on his one knee, and buried his face in Naom's long hair, for her head covering had been destroyed in the fire. "Forgive me, good wife," he murmured seven times, and the two wept together under the rising sun.

Enosh finally lifted his face and spoke. "People of God, forgive the unworthy son of Seth. I have disgraced my standing and sinned against heaven and earth. I return with no expectations, though I have nowhere else on the earth besides here to rest my head or my heart."

Something broke among the people at Enosh's words. Some began to wail while others turned their faces away, struggling with their anger and losses. Life had become a troubling dream from which they never woke, and Enosh was a harsh reminder. Jared came to Baraqua and put his arm across her shoulders. "He is truly repentant," he said quietly.

"His sorrow is evident," Baraqua agreed. "The shining ones must have brutalized him, for he looks older than Adam."

"Our Enosh was lost and now is found," Naom said from where she knelt, her wet face joyful, the wind blowing her hair. She beckoned to her daughters, who came and embraced their father. They helped Enosh to his feet and the four walked toward the people. Some nodded their welcome or embraced the elder shyly while the faces of others revealed nothing. They had little energy to give to welcoming a traitor.

"He is a spy," Gayile said, loud enough for Naom to hear, and Baraqua cringed. "He will lead the shining ones here and they will make an end of us for good." There was no Rasujal to rebuke her abruptness.

Kenan spoke. "My father was ready to die from his own wife's arrow in order to protect—" He broke off, agony in his face. "He shamed her. How can I receive him as though he has done nothing?"

"I have no excuse, my son," Enosh said. He leaned heavily on the crutch, as though his remorse took all his strength. His eyes were on Adam. "I was enamored by their advancements, envious that everything their minds conceived became reality. The beauty of their cities, their cunning devices—" He broke off. "They devised a sleek, circular wagon that transports people through the air with the ease of a bird." His eyes strayed into the sky, as though imagining what he spoke of, then returned his focus to the people. "It may always be my weakness, this desire to be superior to the other peoples of the earth. But I see now that things are not always as they appear. By the mercy of God, I will be content with a humble life as I await the coming of Anointed One." His eyes fell on the baby in Adam's arms, and he glanced at Baraqua. Then he lowered his eyes as though he dared not speak another word.

"Who among us has not betrayed another person, even if it appears a small thing?" Adam said. "Our loss of the mountain has taught us not to rely on ourselves but on the fortitude of God Most High." He went to Enosh and embraced his grandson as though Enosh had not directed Azazel's men to the camp; as though Enosh was as honorable as other men.

Enosh looked away as Adam embraced him. "Do not be so lavish, for I have sinned greatly."

Seth came to Enosh and embraced him as well, holding him as though he would never let him go. Then he put his son at arm's length. "Only sin, my son?" Seth said. "Repentance is far more interesting than sin."

Naom looked at Enosh almost timidly. "And Tarshish?" Her voice broke at the center of the name that meant, *to shatter.*

Enosh sighed. He looked weary enough to sleep for a week. He held Naom's hand to his cheek. "They made an end of our son in a sacrifice to Lucifer two moons ago," he said in a tone raw with grief. "It cost me my leg trying save him, but my effort counted for nothing."

The people brought Enosh into the grassy enclave and set food and wine before him. But the elder did not touch the food. "They promise much," he said, and his eyes darted frequently, as though he saw things others could not. Baraqua thought of the encounter with the snake woman near the orchard. Enosh must have encountered much worse.

The people were parting to let someone through, and Akliah and Hekat the Cainite entered the circle of the people. Akliah carried some sort of garment. She stood before Baraqua, unfolded the garment, laid it around Baraqua's shoulders and fastened it at the neck. It was the undyed mantle of an initiate of the prayer caves, and this time the weave was fine and without flaw.

Akliah spoke so that all could hear, despite any giant that might be on the steppe. "We of the caves have never honored anyone beyond our community in this way. But today we recognize Baraqua as one of our own number and offer her the mantle of our community."

The cloak was warm around Baraqua's legs, and the sleeping child comforted her arms. Surrounding her were those with whom she had suffered greatly in a shadowy camaraderie of loss. Jared was beside her. She lacked nothing.

She made her voice strong. "Let it be written this day that God Most High suffered long with a girl who was ignorant of everything but herself." She held back the tears that would come later. "Henceforth, let this girl be called Hannah, *favored one*, for she has drunk deeply of the heady wine of God."

THE END

Thank you for reading *The Seed Bearer's Bride*. Reviews are the life blood of an author's world, and we love knowing what readers think. If you liked this book, please consider posting a quick review now—just a couple of sentences from your heart. This will help other readers get in touch with earthy biblical fiction, plus make me very happy. Review right here Thank you! For those reading the paperback, it's this: shorturl.at/gzRT3

And feel free to contact me directly: www.jeanhoefling.com

As a bonus, here's the first chapter from the next book in this series, another story based on the Bible, populated with real people figuring out life just like the rest of us. This time it's Enoch, Jared's son, who "walked with God" and disappeared from the earth without dying, "for God took him" (Genesis 5:21-24). What great fodder for fiction, yes?

Enoch: The Giant Slayer
Who Walked into Heaven

And in the twelfth jubilee, in the seventh week thereof, he
[Enoch] took to himself a wife, and her name was Edna,
the daughter of Danel, the daughter of his father's brother.
BOOK OF JUBILEES 4:20

And the women have borne giants, and the whole earth
has thereby been filled with blood and unrighteousness.
1 ENOCH 9:9

The giant lumbering out of the misty northern mountains was moving fast. It was larger and stronger than other Nephilim Enoch had encountered, judging from the heaviness of its footfall, and causing the earth many stadia south of the mountains to tremble. The youngest elder of the Sethites smiled wryly; the hybrid creature—the spawn of a dark angel who had mated with a human woman— must have been eating well. But then they all ate well, those thieving, blood-lapping ravagers of the earth.

Enoch continued to stride through a forest of delicate golden larch trees that was parallel to a high cliff, striated in gray and white marble. His spear was carefully shafted along his back and a short dagger was jabbed in his belt, for the one the people called Giant Slayer was always prepared. He would kill this approaching giant as he had the others, and size did not matter. Success was a matter of his own cunning pitted against the giant's; of thinking like the monster thought and respecting its supernatural powers. At least, this is what Enoch always told himself. The fact was, anything could go wrong. Self-confident as he was, it was no small thing to confront one of the powerful sons of the Shining Ones, the fallen angels. The angelic prowess inherited from their celestial fathers made them incomprehensibly evil, and not to be flirted with. Even to look directly into a Nephil's face had resulted in the death of good men, for the giants' cunning in spellcasting and their accomplishment in the art of the evil eye was the stuff of young men's ballads.

Enoch set his legs wider to steady himself as the forest floor trembled again. The creature was still high in the blue mountains the people called Devil's Nest, full of deep canyons and fir-covered peaks where a man might go mad from the density of the trees. But in a few minutes more the monster would reach the grassy steppe, searching for food or indulging in the mere caprice of causing misery. For where there was demonic evil, there must be misery. The human population was denser on the grassland than in the mountains, and many flocks of sheep and goats grazed there. Unchallenged, the giant could devour domesticated animals by the hundreds in a sitting. This particular brute might be many ells taller than the six Nephilim Enoch had so far killed. But when even the smallest one's chin already brushed the tops of the tallest trees, what did a dozen cubits here or there matter?

Even more disturbing was that the Nephilim—"fallen ones," or Gibborim, "mighty men—" were increasingly fond of human blood. The forebear Adam, the earth's first man, had discerned that this growing bloodlust was connected to the giants' diabolical rituals in the company of their angelic fathers, and no community was safe anymore from the fruits of their consort with Lucifer, the high enemy of God. Though a towering angel had long protected the enclave of the Sethites, Enoch's people, wise men among them knew that protection might not last forever. The spiritually discerning knew that the Shining Ones had sent their sons out over the earth to weaken the minds and bodies of all humanity. The goal of the Shining Ones—called this because of the angelic illumination on their skin—was to kill or dominate every human being and eradicate all knowledge on the earth of God Most High, the Creator.

But Enoch refused to shrink from the presence of the Nephilim as most men did. He refused to call them mighty. Risk and danger were food and drink to him; his bravery was a gift from God, he grudgingly admitted. He would rather live with the death angel breathing behind his ear than seek the physical safety most people required. Even among the Sethite elders—the most spiritually astute men on earth—Enoch was unique in his physical strength. He would take this Nephil by employing the usual strategies; that is, if the girl Eeda arrived in time. Success depended not just on Enoch's skill with a spear, but on the musical craft of that beautiful girl, the middle daughter of Danel the potter.

The larch trees shivered. Small animals were scurrying into dens and wind began to moan high in the stately cedars to the north. God's good creation understood the approach of one whose existence was out of the natural order, an unholy union between a celestial being and a human female foolish enough to have offered her womb for the prestige of notice by a Shining One. Enoch disciplined his mind not to think about those unimaginable, forbidden trysts carried out beneath both full and new moons. He tried not to dwell on his limited knowledge of the giants' blood-drinking rituals on the mount of Ermon, the height where the Shining Ones had first descended to earth on the night of Enoch's parents' marriage a generation ago. But it was impossible to avoid almost constant thought of the monsters. The Nephilim crowded into people's nightmares and were the subject of countless songs, from the western lands of Cush to the sea-bordering settlements of U'ez and beyond, eastward, into the enigmatic land of Nod. But when people woke from their troubled sleep the nightmares did not turn to vapor but came out of the mountains again to torment them with murder and magic. If the giants were not curtailed and continued to grow in number, the earth and its people would eventually be destroyed.

Another ground shudder shot through the forest floor. Enoch lost his footing and was thrown against a tree. He lay on the mossy earth with the air chased from his lungs. He knew he should be terrified, but he grinned. Let the beast come. He hoped it had only one eye in the manner of the repulsive cyclops he had seen several of. "One less eye not to look into," he said, his voice hard with irony.

There was a sound of something splitting. Beside where he lay, a wide fissure was opening in the forest floor, etching its random path eastward beyond his sight. He rolled away from the crack as larches, date palms, dragon trees, and even enormous cedars and thick-trunked angel oaks split and leaned into the depths of the crevice. The earthy scent of decay and unseen subterranean life rose out of the fissure, and tree roots protruded from the sides like the rungs of a ladder. He got up and looked deep into the crevice. If he descended far enough on those roots, would he reach Sheol, the territory of the dead? He did not fear the underworld; when he found himself there one day he would make of its shadowy depths as much an adventure as he did the present life.

He laughed into the sky. His blood ran warm at the thought of felling the monster this day. He pictured the smooth, well-worn shaft of his spear in his hand, its tip ready to find its lethal mark. At the young age of sixty-five among the long-living Sethites, Enoch was still young and at the height of his powers. He jumped across a narrow place in the crevice. He must quickly get to the top of the cliff in order to see how far the giant had travelled. Surely Eeda had felt the earth quaking and would join him quickly. They knew each other's habits of movement over the land so well that she would have no trouble finding him, for footsteps told every tale.

He cinched his tunic tighter in preparation for his climb, imagining the impressions left by the monster's enormous feet as it came into the vast, loamy steppe that stretched southward to the Flood Sea. The six-toed indentations of the feet of many Nephilim covered the land.

They were large enough for ten men to stretch out inside. When ground water rose inside the impressions, they filled to become foot-shaped ponds the people called Devil's Water. It was said that gray spirits hovered near the ponds at the rising of the half moon, and no one would lead their cattle to drink from those places.

"I drink that water all the time," Enoch could not resist shouting as he approached the cool, smooth cliff. "And I can frighten away a gray spirit with a laugh." The giants' hearing was acute, but Enoch did not care if this arrogant brute heard. Bile rose as he thought of the suffering and destruction to the earth these creatures wrought daily. Then he smiled. In their way, the giants respected him, for he had done to them what others dared not try. He had even come across a depiction of himself on the walls of one of the enormous caverns that dotted the northern mountains, large enough for smaller Nephilim to enter. The vast wall mural had been a remarkably accurate representation of himself in vivid azure and saffron paint, the figure's spear poised, his lips thrust in concentration, his long hair flying.

"He who pierces" was written beneath the image on the cave wall, not in the universal language of the earth, but in the jumbled tongue of the Nephilim which Enoch had learned snatches of through painstaking observation. Since that day in the cave Enoch had dyed his tunics golden ochre and his gaiters bright azure from crushed minerals found in the east, as another sign of his defiance toward the giants. If the pious of his clan thought him extravagant in wearing such bright colors, he did not care. After all, did any of them risk their lives to eradicate the sons of the Shining Ones?

At the base of the cliff he paused, straining to hear anything the Nephil might be saying. Though unable to change appearance or travel on the wind like their angelic fathers, spells from a Nephil's mouth could paralyze a man, render a young woman barren, or drive a child to a fetal state with tormenting visions. Like their human mothers, the hybrid beings breathed, ate, and drank in the mortal way. Their bodies could be injured, could bleed and die. Where their spirits went after death, even the forebear Adam did not know.

"Today is your doom, mortal sack of flesh," Enoch muttered, and the chuckle of mockery and disdain came easy. He kicked off his hemp sandals and tossed aside the thick, colorful gaiters that wrapped his shins. He pressed his bare toes and the tips of his fingers into tiny nubs on the cool rock face and began to climb. A surge of energy pulsed through him as he made his way swiftly up the stone. On rock he felt completely alive, connected most with life in the intense, physical way he instinctively functioned. Scaling a sheer cliff was as easy as walking. He had conquered this one as a child and knew it like his own thoughts. It did not bother him that one false move would send him to a certain death below. What was death but a passage from a familiar world to one that was not familiar, yet? He had stopped wondering long ago where his extraordinary confidence came from. Like all Sethites, he possessed innate respect for the Creator and the power of spiritual beings, both wicked and righteous. He never doubted that God was with him in some way, yet secretly wished it was not necessary. Who was God Most High, after all? Adam often told of how the Creator, the omnipotent one with no beginning or end, nor any need nor lack, had once been visible to Eve and himself in Eden. Since the couple's exile from that bower of light and grace, the mysterious divinity made his throne above the brassy blue sky in *shamayim,* the high heavens.

Sweat poured off Enoch's face. The physical exertion was especially pleasant after three days of inactivity in the dugout of his father Jared—the monthly tutelage in study, writing, and discourse with other elders to prepare him for the fulness of his own eldership. There had been lessons by Adam's son Seth on the meaning of the star constellations that foretold the coming of Anointed One, the Savior of the earth. With finely tipped quill and new sheets of painstakingly prepared palm leaves, the precious *lontar,* he had dutifully practiced the simple script cybers of the earth's language. Into the *Chronicles of Adam*, his clan's written history of the earth, he had added a detailed account of his last giant slaying, with emphasis on the exact placement of his lethal spear tip in the creature's forehead. It had been a great day, the sun as high as his spirits as he decapitated the creature. Some brave, future giant killer might need that explanatory precision and would want to savor his account.

He had not yet possessed the body of a grown man when he had first gone out into the steppe to confront a hulking Nephil who was glutting itself on a pile of cattle whose necks the giant had broken like a child snaps twigs before devouring him. A rage he had never felt had risen at the sight: was it not the duty of at least some of Adam's descendants to defy the evil that had infiltrated the land and to bring the earth back under human rule? That day of the first killing, people from nearby villages had run to marvel at the sight of the tangle haired Sethite boy severing the Nephil's massive head, whose forehead he had pierced with an ordinary spear. He had not understood then, nor did he now, how he had found the strength for it. It was always as though an unseen hand guided his own. The people had stood by that day as vultures picked at the staring, inhuman eyes and then died after eating of the giant's strange flesh. Enoch had been the subject of countless ballads from that day forward.

On the last day of the tutelage there had been hours spent with the forebear Adam, who had further instructed him in the lost language of Eden, a lyrical tongue of few words with no written form that only the Sethite elders knew, and that only because Adam was determined the language not be completely lost. He and Eve had spoken little in that time before sin, before expulsion from Eden, Adam liked to explain. For in that bower of innocent delights, communication had most often flowed naturally between their two minds, with God, and with the members of the Divine Council, angelic rulers whose thrones had stood in Eden in that day. Enoch had been willing to do his duty once again on the three days of instruction, yet he vastly preferred the thing he applied himself to now.

"I am no scholar like the others," he admitted as he pulled himself over the top of the final overhang and stood looking out over the land. "Perhaps I am mad, but I prefer the company of these diabolical fiends than to sit quietly and form the sounds of obsolete words." Why was

Adam so obsessed with that time in Eden? Certainly, he and Eve had eaten of forbidden food and lost both innocence and glory. Their stories of those days could make a man weep. Sin had not only changed their bodies and hearts but made God more distant to them and caused thorns and thistles to grow where once all plant life grew unblemished.

Yet all that was in the past, Enoch thought. It could never be retrieved. The present moment was all that mattered, for it was the only thing one had control of. And the present moment for the son of Jared on this day held the anticipation of another dead giant.

The breeze was cool and fresh on his sweating body as Enoch scanned the land around him—grassland, mountains, and seas. He took out the curious, glass-ended tube he had thieved years before from one of the Shining Ones who had left a waist pouch unguarded while he seduced a half-dressed girl on the beach of the Flood Sea, and Enoch had dared to relieve the angel of his possession. Too many women had succumbed to the angels' exaggerated masculinity and charismatic words in exchange for the favor of their wombs. Few survived the act of giving birth to the enormous Nephilic fetuses. And even fewer received the promised rewards of magical powers or marble houses in one of the angels' luxurious cities scattered across the earth. The Shining Ones were masters of the lie.

Enoch rotated the tube to bring the misty northern mountains into focus. Why a Shining One would need a device to magnify sight was a puzzle. Adam had sighed as he turned the curiosity over in his hands. "They forfeited many things on the day they broke faith with God Most High. Perfect, supernatural sight was the least of them."

He quickly located the giant through the glass, striding naked through thick stands of fir with the carcass of a deer in one hand. The Nephil was streaked with blood and dust as it leveled swaths of magnificent trees in its wake and scanned the countryside. Enoch chuckled. This one indeed had only one eye, though its face bore strongly the human traces of a clearly beautiful mother. The skin looked human, stretched over powerful musculature. Yet Enoch had seen the giants up close and knew how scaly—almost reptilian—their skin really was.

As though it sensed Enoch's presence, the Nephil's eyes suddenly focused in his direction and its sensual mouth curled cruelly. Maybe it had heard his taunts or even recognized "one who pierces." It paused for a moment, as though assessing the number of strides required to reach the cliff. It thrust its chest forward and resumed its lumbering walk with what Enoch imagined was new determination.

Enoch shivered. His father, the pious elder who had once downed a Nephil himself, would have knelt then and prayed. He would have sought God in this, as in everything. But Enoch did not pray beyond his elder's duties at the ancient stone altar where the Sethites offered the blood of a spotless lamb every Sabbath. The holiness of God Most High required it, and Enoch respected that requirement. But in everything else he was practical: he would do his part with the skill God had given him and God would supply the rest if he so willed. So far, the deity had always willed in Enoch's favor.

The young man slid his well-crafted spear out of the holder across his back and gripped the smooth shaft firmly. He began to focus on the perfect timing needed; the precise aim; the courage not to falter for an instant. A moment of hesitation, any show of vulnerability or doubt, would mean death. He remembered the legendary story of his mother and father who, before the Shining Ones had burned the holy mountain, had brought down one of the early-born giants using a sword forged of pure light, given to them by God. Men were worthier in that time, Enoch knew. His father surely was. He himself had no such heavenly weapon, for that mysterious sword had disappeared after the battle. He was surprised how alone he suddenly felt. The smooth, charismatic evil emanating from the giant, long advanced in the steppe now, was unusually powerful. Enoch did not know how he would manage this if Eeda did not come. Eeda! The thought of her made his heart move strangely.

"Enoch, son of Jared!" The familiar female voice came from further down the cliff and Enoch ran across the rocky plateau and looked over the side. Climbing the rock face as rapidly as he had was Eeda, as graceful on the rock as a swan on a glassy lake. Love for the girl caught in his throat. Never would he find another like her, more courageous than many men and, to his eyes, the loveliest among the unmarried women of the clan. In recent months his attraction to her had become unbearable.

"Are you saving the brute for yourself, selfish man?" Eeda called out. "Must you have the full measure of glory this time?" She looked up at Enoch and laughed. Her arms were muscled and brown, and the new bow and sheaf of arrows Enoch had given her on the day of the commemoration of her birth were fastened across her back. Her pouch was about her waist. He let out his breath with relief. The miraculous flute would be in that pouch.

Enoch made his voice dramatic to hide his emotion. "Can't you climb any faster? I am faint with waiting for you." He teased, yet it was the truth. He did not know what he would do without Eeda. She pulled herself over the lip, lithe in the blue woman's garment that brushed the middle of her calves. Like Enoch, she had discarded her foot coverings for the climb, and her one ornament was the tooth of one of the giants they had felled together, which hung from her neck on a strand of spun silver. He forgot the approaching monster for a moment and impulsively pulled the girl to him, though such a thing was not allowed unless a Sethite couple was officially betrothed. Eeda's waist-long hair, the color of low embers, was plaited down her back, loose strands of it curling around her cheeks, and her wide-set gray eyes brimmed as usual with an expectation he could never quite understand and that fascinated him. She loved him, that he knew. She had since their infancy, growing up along with him on the shores of the Crystal Sea, their daily lives entwined. Today she smelled of sea grass and lavender flower, and of the sweet child's scent of the two little nephews she looked after when her sister was at work at the potter's wheel.

He forced a casual tone to his voice, unwilling to admit even to himself how much her presence unnerved him. "You must stop meeting me in such places," he said with a grin. "The old women will whisper that it is unseemly for a girl to hunt the spawn of devils at the side of Jared's rebellious son."

Eeda laughed again. Like Enoch, she lived for the moment and cared little about what others thought of her. "Be safe at all costs," she answered, imitating the lisping voice of one of her worrisome aunts. "For after all, we human beings are completely helpless against the blood-thirsty offspring of Lucifer."

He had never known another like her, though he had travelled the earth. He wanted to kiss her, there on the heights with the fragrant wind bringing up the sea air that was mingled with sun-melted spruce sap and freshened by the moist, grassy scent of the wide steppe. It was as though she had bewitched him in this moment when death breathed close. He must be careful or he would forget that not far away strode an appalling manifestation of wickedness, and that he had vowed to destroy it.

But Eeda was not as distracted by Enoch as he was by her. Her eyes leveled into the north, and she pulled away from his embrace. Anger replaced the carefree expression, furrowing the skin above her gray eyes. She took the glass tube from Enoch and focused it on the giant. "It has much blood to its account, don't you think?" she said gravely. Though the Nephilim were male, she and Enoch never referred to them as anything but "it." The creatures might possess spirits, being partly human, but they behaved like animals.

"Despite its powers—and I see the lips moving in what must be an incantation— I do not sense there is cunning enough to resist us," she continued. She handed the magnifier back to Enoch and from her waist pouch drew a small, well-oiled wooden flute carved with ivy and river roses. Near the mouth hole was a detailed engraving of the tree called Life that had once flourished at the heart of Eden. A flush came to her cheeks as she put the flute to her lips. There was no time to speak his heart about her loveliness, about his need for her. He must face the responsibility he had chosen.

His struggle seemed to be reflected in her face. "Let us slay our enemy then, son of Jared," she said calmly. It was what she always said, but there was something deeper in her meaning today, he sensed. Enoch forced himself to turn again in the direction of the giant and put the magnifying tube to his eye again. It was as though he was doing it for the first time. What absurdity was this, to think he could kill a being fifty times his height? The deer's blood was caked around the giant's mouth.

A haunting melody began to flow from that narrow length of carved wood at Eeda's lips—mysterious and insistent, winding its way as though seeking prey. Enoch let out his breath in relief. Eeda would once again work her magic. Surely God was with her in a way he did not understand. And from the little she had ever said, neither did she. He transferred the spear from hand to hand, weighing, thinking, waiting for readiness or the courage that seemed so lacking this time. The music would do it all; it must! By some strange, divine inspiration coupled with Eeda's instincts, the sounds she made through that flute had power to meddle in the mental powers of the mighty Nephilim. By the mercies of God, the sound weakened the brutes. It must happen this time as it had every time before. It must!

He walked to the very edge of the cliff, waiting in agony as the giant shambled closer, the sun now reflecting off the scale-like skin of its muscular forearms. He saw himself as he never had before—a strong, supple man with skill and courage, yet nothing in the sight of the giant, and susceptible to death. Death—to never see Eeda again? Would the ogre think to hoist itself onto the plateau, or would the music impair its thinking on that point and cause it to simply stand there, giving him the chance to hurl his spear into the vulnerable space between its eyes? The creature's expression was grim, the mouth wide and sensual, a heavy, bony brow half covering the enormous eye Enoch must not look into, whatever else. The music continued, stirring the air, flowing ever northward, doubling back within itself to weave variations on the melody which rose in pitch and increased in tempo. Would it have its effect?

The Nephil's expression softened. The expression of grim blood-lust turned to something like confusion. It cocked its head, dropped the remains of the deer, and covered its ears with the massive, bloodied hands. Enoch's courage flowed through him again as Eeda played on. Her concentration was, this time and every time, on this one thing she must do. Enoch knew she would not allow fear to rule her. She would think of nothing except the next note her breath and lips must write on the wind. Enoch imagined the music swirling around the giant, ordering it to cease from its indecencies. The sounds trilled high, full of desperate conviction about the power of hope and of the sanctity of human and animal life, as though the girl herself raised a hand to forbid it work further evil. Above all, the music reminded the giant that one day the prophesied Anointed One would stand upon the earth and lead all people back to the paradise called Eden. Nephilim could not bear to be reminded of Anointed One. Enoch knew with a nameless instinct that the music had never been more authoritative on this point.

But now the giant's one eye was fixed on Eeda and malevolence filled its rheumy depths. An unexpected thrill of fear shot through Enoch and he whirled to look at Eeda. It had never occurred to him to consider that something might happen to her, though they both knew the dangers of what they did were real. A vision of life without her flashed before him, like a grave yawning. He could not remember a moment when he had not loved the daughter of Danel. Nothing could happen to her this day.

Eeda lowered the flute, panic in her eyes. "Son of Jared, pay attention! He is upon us!" she screamed.

Enoch swiveled, his eyes suddenly level with the monster's, this wanton mutineer of God's order. The aura of otherworldliness around the filthy head was more visible than with some and Enoch marveled that despite their revolting strangeness, the giants embodied a certain allure that was unexplainable and had been the demise of some who had given in to it. If only he had his father Jared's sword of light. If only he had his father's strong reliance on God Most High.

The Nephil's jaw sagged, revealing the characteristic two rows of long teeth with pieces of flesh caught between them and exuding a breath so putrid Enoch wondered if the exhalations were poisonous. He thought of the wanton murders, the destruction of life, the false miracles that captured the gullible. How dare the Shining Ones deceive and produce such foul children. He hated them with a perfect hatred. He carefully drew back the spear, this weapon of one chance only. The spear traced the contour of his arm, left his hand, arced, struck. But it did not sink into the forehead he had aimed for but pierced the lone eye. Black blood spurted from the shattered orb and a look of incomprehension came to the giant's face. It clutched at the cliff and shuddered, disbelief in its face. Then it fell backwards, as though pushed, into the trees at the bottom of the cliff.

The cliff shuddered with the impact of the fall. Eeda lost her balance and the flute flew from her hands as she began to roll in the direction of the pitching rock. Enoch sprinted to her, threw himself over her, and they rolled together toward the side of the cliff they had climbed. *God of Adam, save us*, Enoch cried out within his mind. No one but God could save him now. He felt a crack in the rock and with a contortion of movement jammed the toes of his right foot into it. By some wonder, he and Eeda jerked to a stop and pain shot through Enoch's leg as the wedged foot held them fast. He gripped Eeda more tightly and dug his foot into the crack still deeper, the agony of it taking his breath. He focused on that pain and on the girl in his arms. There was nothing else in all the world. Pain was honest, real. Eeda and the pain would save him.

Eeda was crying a little, and Enoch stroked her hair, breathing deeply, forcing himself to remain conscious. There was no familiar, giddy rush of victory. There was no joking between them about what they had accomplished in their youthful stealth, no commentary on the giant's deficiencies. Of course they would still sever the head of their quarry and drag it back to the Sethite enclave in the blood-stained cart they kept for that gruesome task, for this was part of the ritual of many years. Children would poke at the giant's empty eye and marvel at the six-toed feet and two rows of flesh-clogged teeth. The young men would add another refrain to their songs about the daring deeds of Enoch and Eeda among the Nephilim, and Enoch's parents, Jared and Hannah, would shake their heads in mock disapproval, but be secretly proud. True, their son had exposed himself to danger once again, but hadn't they once risked their own lives to do the same? And all in the clan would comment that there would be less Devil's Water on the steppe. One less earthquake, and human lives saved.

When a few days later Enoch and Eeda would return to the foot of the cliff to go over what had happened, the body of the giant would be gone. It was always this way. The father of the creature would have come to take away and bury his dead in a secret place.

The cliff stopped moving. Enoch sat up and carefully pulled his foot from the crack, the skin gone in places and several bones showing. He refused to even grimace; he had saved his beloved Eeda through excruciating pain and was grateful. Eeda cried out at the state of his foot and began to babble that they needed water and bandages and salve. But Enoch merely tore a piece from the hem of his tunic and tightly wrapped the place to staunch the blood. He would not miss the wonder of this moment with Eeda because of a bleeding foot.

He held her as the sun fell further down the sky and the bandage soaked up his blood—blood well spent. The carved flute lay broken in two a pace from where they huddled. Fading sun began to spread molten gold across the western sky and the air chilled slightly. Eeda looked up at him, wordless and calm. Something had changed between them; they would never return to the bantering friendship of only a day ago.

It was now that he must speak of his longing for her, his desire so long unexpressed. "Sixty-five years is young to marry, according to the traditions of our people," he heard himself say, and hoped he did not hear a tremble in his voice. "Though it does not matter, for my grandfather Mahal was my age when he took Dinah to wife. And my father was one hundred sixty-two years when he begat me." Why was he rattling on like a snake's tail? His heart pounded. Her face so near to his had left him floundering for even a shred of his usual bravado and composure.

Eeda's voice was low. "It is because you are afraid to say what you really want to that you recount histories of our people that I already know," she said, and put her hand to his cheek. In her eyes Enoch saw things he knew he would never understand. She thrilled and mystified him. His love for her terrified him. Yet beyond the mystery and terror was love. Love would overcome all the rest.

Enoch took her hand and kissed it, abandoning any concern that she knew him too well. She always had, after all. "The dream angel visited my sleep this morning and my father was pleased when I told him that Eeda, daughter of Danel, filled the vision," he said. He kissed her hand again. "Bless me and be my wife."

"I will love you to my last breath," Eeda said simply.

"You *are* my breath," Enoch answered in a rush. The truth of it stunned him. Should an elder, a giant slayer, say such things? The light of the setting sun gleamed on Eeda's eyelashes. She had never looked more beautiful to him as she leaned in to receive his kiss.

Sign up to receive a notice when this book about Enoch launches! www.jeanhoefling.com

Printed in Dunstable, United Kingdom

70715024R00178